The Warrior's Mission

Warriors of Ériu

Book Three

By Mia Pride

To all the women who have suffered from some form of violence, neglect, or abuse, physical or emotional. You are not all alone. May you find your inner strength. I'm always hear if you need to talk or need help escaping a bad situation. Miapride.author@gmail.com

Love, Mia

Chapter One

80 AD

Rain pelted his head as he tied up his horse to the wooden post outside his family's home. Darkness had fallen hours before and every bone in his body ached from his journey west, but he should have been used to the elements by now. These scouting missions had become more and more frequent as trouble continued to brew. At two and twenty summers, Flynn Mac Greine was more than used to living in a world full of war and he would do aught for his king, Tuathal. But on this night, when the rain felt more like boulders crashing down on his shoulders, he was more than happy to finally be home from his latest mission. He would report to his king on the morrow. For now, he was certain his mother would have leftover stew for him like she always did.

When he went to open the door to seek comfort from their hearth, his brother came up from behind him, also soaked to the bone and weary from their journey.

"Forget something, brother?" Brennain said, and shoved Flynn's satchel into his hands.

He was so tired that he had almost left his satchel out all night in the rain. Not that it mattered. The leather sack was already as wet as it could possibly be, as were its contents in most likelihood. "My thanks," he grumbled, and he slung the satchel over his tired shoulder.

"Mal has been finding more and more clever ways to hide," Brennain grunted as they walked through the door.

"Aye. And by the time we report to Tuathal that we have located his camp, he will likely have relocated yet again," Flynn whispered. "I will not stop until the man is dead."

"Mayhap, but that was not our order."

"I know this well, Brennain. 'Tis the only reason I let him live. My arrow could have ended the bastard's life in the blink of an eye and he deserves it too, for the treatment of his poor daughter."

Only a few moons ago, a lass named Elwynna had come to their village of Ráth Mór, seeking to warn King Tuathal of her father's attempts at building an army. She was the kindest of lassies, but she had been ill-used by her father, who allowed his best warriors to take turns with her. Elwynna had been injured during a battle that day, but their healer, Maggie had taken her in and nursed her back to health. Since then, Elwynna had found love and married one of their finest warriors, Àdhamh, who was also Maggie's brother. All three of them lived together in a small cottage very close to Flynn's own.

If one thing made Flynn's blood boil, it was the misuse of women. He had seen it too many times in his life and though the women in his own family were renown across the land as brave and powerful, that was not the case for many other lassies, such as Elwynna. Flynn would like nothing more than to take the life of her pathetic father, who was also the very cause of all these tiresome missions.

"You visit their home often, do you not?" Brennain whispered as they carefully dropped their sodden satchels on the hard-packed earthen floor of their home. His parents were likely asleep, and the brothers never wished to awaken them.

"Nay. I visit when I have business with Àdhamh, 'tis all." Flynn scowled at his brother. He knew where his meddlesome brother was going with his question and he had not the patience for another interrogation. Flynn was naturally a private, reserved man and, unlike his brother, he would not sleep with any lass who batted her eyes in his direction. He was a man who sought his relief as needed, but he did not tend to need it as often as his woman-loving brother.

"I believe you visited Maggie on more than one occasion," his brother prodded. Flynn wanted to box his brother's ears but they were equally matched in height and size, both being larger than average. Their father, Brocc, was not only one of the largest warriors in the land. He had been king of his own tuath for several years before joining High King Tuathal's ranks. Everyone knew well enough not to mess with the three Mac Greine men, and Flynn also knew better than to try to best his brother. It would only end up with them both rolling on the floor until they were red in the face, and then their mama would come and box both their ears.

"I sliced my cursed arm open during warrior training and she is the cursed healer of the cursed tuath. Aye, I went to see her... to get stitched up." He was much too wet and cold to deal with his brother's prodding observation at the moment.

Brennain snorted in complete disbelief, but blessedly left it alone. So what if Flynn found Maggie's shiny blonde hair mesmerizing when the sun was at its highest and shone down on it, making it gleam like the wheat in the fields on a breezy day? And so what if her bright blue eyes reminded him of just the way the ocean gleamed on the horizon? So what if her skin was as white as fresh buttermilk, her lips the same shade as the pink roses growing outside in his mother's garden, and her curves reminded him of... well, his bed, and all the things they could do in it? All right, so he found Maggie to be beyond perfect. It did not mean that he visited her far too often or decided even his smallest wounds required her skilled touch.

Unclasping his cloak, he heard it fall to the floor with a soggy thud just as he pulled his tunic over his head. His trousers clung to him like a second skin and proved much more complicated to remove as he struggled to yank them down his muscular legs. His mother would be angry if he left them in a pile on the floor, as many years of scoldings had taught him. Wringing them out over the hearth fire, he watched the flames pop and hiss as the droplets of water rained down on them.

Draping the garments over a bench, he shot his brother an exhausted look over his shoulder. "I am done. My bed is calling my name. Good night."

Just as he reached his bed and pulled a warm, dry fur over his bare torso, his brother smirked and began to strip his own clothes off. "Good night, brother. Sweet dreams of Maggie."

Flynn growled at his brother from across the room and chucked a bar of soap from the table by his bed at his brother's head.

Brennain dodged quickly and the soap landed in the hearth fire. "Arse," Flynn murmured to his brother.

"Och, Mama made that soap just for you with fine spices. She will have your head." Flynn stilled. Brennain was right. His mama made the best of soaps and she had gone out of her way to make that one just for him. He would owe her an apology on the morrow. She was the sweetest mama any child could ask for, but raising two rowdy lads had made her half-crazed at times.

"Go to bed," he huffed. How two grown men could argue like wee lads, he was not sure. They were only one summer apart in age, and both had the black hair of their father and bright green eyes of their mother. Little distinguished the two physically, but their personalities often clashed, Brennain generally being extremely loud and outspoken. Flynn preferred to stand back and observe in silence. 'Tis what made him one of the very best informants Tuathal had, and that was precisely why Flynn also preferred to keep away from others. People asked too many questions and he knew more than most in this village. It was best to keep it that way.

Turning over in his bed, Flynn closed his eyes and allowed his thoughts to drift. As usual, the swirling thoughts in his mind shifted into the form of a beautiful lass with blue eyes and golden hair.

* * * *

"Och, thank the gods you are home safely!" he heard his mother's shrill cry of delight just before her arms encircled him in a hug. Still abed, he groaned as his mother's grip tightened like a vise around his chest. "I always fear the worst," she wailed.

"Let him go, Una. He is a Mac Greine warrior. He is capable of aught and more," his father, Brocc boomed from the other side of the room. Cracking an eye open, he saw his papa leaning against the wall as he bit into an apple, almost consuming the entire piece of red fruit with one bite. Even at almost fifty years of age, his father was large, fit, and formidable.

"If I want to dote on my sons, I shall," his wee mama said indignantly, before squeezing the life out of him once more.

"I am fine, Mama. Go torture Brennain instead."

Brennain laughed from the table as he slurped down a steaming bowl of porridge. "She already did, wee brother. I also told her that you destroyed her soap."

"Awe... shite," Flynn murmured as he sat up and ran a hand through his disheveled black hair. "I did do that. My apologies, Mother."

Waving a hand in the air, she brushed his concerns away. "'Tis all right. I am only glad to see you have returned. I can make more soap, but I cannot make more sons."

"We can try," his father suggested, coming up behind her and wrapping his arms around her waist. She giggled as if they were a newly courting couple and not a married one of over twenty years.

Groaning, Flynn found his trousers and yanked them up his hips quickly, tying the string. His parents never stopped with their love play and it was enough to make a man go mad. He loved his parents, but with his father being a king and his mother being one of the legendary Sisters of Danu who helped save all Ériu two summers ago in the battle that won the High Throne for Tuathal, he and Brennain had grown up with heavy expectations of success. Sometimes all Flynn wanted was a wee wife and a home of his own, but until then, spying for the king was his life's work and he was the best at it.

Walking over to the cauldron, he grabbed a clay bowl and filled it with hot porridge. Steam rose up and the sweet smell of honey filled the air. He loved how his mother sweetened their porridge with honey. "We must eat quickly and report to the king," Flynn said around a mouthful of food.

"Aye," Brennain agreed, standing quickly from the table.

"Did you gather any new information?" their father asked; he finally loosened his grip on his wife.

"Nothing that will be of use. We found his camp, but until Tuathal is ready to gather troops and rid the world of that bastard Mac Rochride, the bastard will only continue to move about the land, gathering more allies as he goes."

"Tuathal has his reasons for waiting. He has spent his entire life fighting battles... and winning. He knows what he is doing," his father claimed.

"I know. But until then, 'tis my responsibility to keep an eye on the man and continue to report back. And every time I do, the man moves again." It was a frustrating mission, but it was essential, he knew. He only hoped his orders would change into something more fulfilling soon.

"We need to report to the king right away. Let us go now, so we make it to warrior training on time," Brocc stated, moving toward the door. His sons followed without question. Flynn was more than ready to report to Tuathal and, hopefully, be given more orders. He quite enjoyed the work of an informant. He was naturally quiet and reserved, and years of training had taught him to be stealthy, observant and cautious. He longed for more someday, but as an unmarried man, he was the best person for the task.

The village was already bustling as the people of Ráth Mór set out to do their daily tasks. The ironsmith pounded away in his shop, and the smell of freshly baked bread drifted on the cold wind. The road was still muddy from last night's downpour and Flynn dodged a fairly large puddle to his left. Though a few clouds floated overhead, the sky was as brilliant a blue as... Maggie's eyes. He winced at his foolishness. When had he become such a sorry sot? He had bedded enough bonny lassies in his lifetime and none had ever truly stuck in his mind. And yet, aside from small conversations and needing her aid with a few less than severe wounds, Flynn hardly knew the lass.

She was the sister of Àdhamh, he knew that much. They had come to Ériu from Alba after their other sister, Paulene, had been murdered by her cruel husband. Maggie had lived a sheltered life and was quite shy. She also seemed fearful of men, especially larger ones, which included him. He did not ever want to cause her fear, so he found himself torn between seeking her out one day and keeping his distance the next. There was just something about the lass that drove him wild. Unfortunately, he could do naught about it. Nor would he. He was busy serving his king and his missions were dangerous. Every new order put his life at risk and he could never drag a woman, especially one as innocent as Maggie, into his chaos.

Smoke billowed from the tops of pointed thatched roofs as their occupants burned their hearth fires. It was a familiar comfort and one he never took for granted. On any day, he could end up sleeping upon the soggy forest floor with naught but his plaid and cloak for warmth. The comforts of home must be appreciated whenever possible.

"You are quiet this morn, Flynn," his father commented when they approached the king's large home.

"He is quiet every day, Pa," Brennain chortled. "'Tis nothing new."

"Mayhap not, but I know my son well enough to know that he is stewing on something."

"Nay," Flynn shrugged. "'Tis naught. Only wondering about my next mission," he lied. He would rather be gutted with his own sword than admit he had been comparing Maggie's eyes to the cursed sky once again.

Speaking of Maggie, her brother Àdhamh was diligently guarding the entrance to the king's home with a harried expression on his face. His hazel eyes widened with warning when they approached. The sounds of a wee babe crying from within caught Flynn's ears. "Is something amiss?"

"Aye. King Tuathal and Queen Leannan are distraught. Their wee lad, Fedlimid, has a fever. My sister and wife are in there now, trying to calm the poor child... and his parents."

"Is it serious?" Brocc questioned with worry in his voice.

"I cannot possibly know," Àdhamh shrugged. "I pray not. You may enter; King Tuathal still wishes to speak to you." Àdhamh stepped aside and pushed the door open.

The hearth fire flickered from the gust of air and the sounds of the wailing child intensified as they slowly walked through the entrance.

"Truly, I believe he is only cutting teeth," he heard Maggie's sweet voice say as soon as he entered the home. His gaze immediately

11

raked over her, his heart rate picking up so fast it felt as if he had been kicked in the chest by a horse. "The lad is approaching one summer of age and I can see his wee gums are swollen. Often it can cause discomfort and a wee fever," Maggie continued while she rummaged in a basket atop the table for an item.

Her golden hair gleamed in the firelight and her purple dress fit her curves perfectly. She had not yet noticed his arrival, which Flynn preferred because it allowed him to silently observe her in her natural state. Most times when Maggie saw him, she shut down, becoming silent and evasive. Flynn believed she feared him and it made his heart ache to think such a thing, but mayhap it was best. The more she avoided him, the easier continuing his secluded life of gathering information about the enemy would remain. He had no time for complicated relationships, and he knew that if Maggie even showed him the slightest bit of favor, he would be lost to her spell.

"Here." She took a small clay jar with a wax seal out of her basket. "'Tis a tincture of chamomile and lavender. Simply rub it on his gums to help soothe the pain. Also, soaking a clean linen cloth in cold water and applying it to the gums will soothe and numb the swelling. Chewing on something such as a carrot will help the tooth break through the skin. I truly believe this will help wee Fedlimid. If his fever does worsen or you see other signs of illness, please fetch me."

Queen Leannan calmed considerably as she took the clay jar from Maggie with a shaky smile. "My thanks, Maggie. You are truly a wondrous healer. We are so blessed you and Àdhamh came all the way from Alba to join our tuath."

With a slight curtsy to her queen, Maggie smiled. "'Tis nothing at all, Queen Leannan." Flynn watched her in wonder as she spoke so assuredly, so full of knowledge. How he wished he was privy to this side of her all the time.

Just then, Maggie shifted and finally saw him standing near the door. All the color drained from her face as her eyes widened. He saw her swallow hard, the slim column of her throat bobbing from the strain, and he frowned at her reaction to him. Was he truly so frightening? No other lass had ever looked like she would flee when she looked at him.

Fortunately, Àdhamh's wife Elwynna had no such reservations and smiled widely when she saw they had all arrived. "'Tis the three handsome Mac Greine men," she said, with her hands on her hips and a friendly grin. "I have been on Maggie's heals for several moons, but I am learning so much about healing. She is wonderful, do you not think?"

Flynn, straight-faced and silent, nodded noncommittally to Elwynna's compliment of Maggie. He agreed very much with her, but it would not do to show any emotion where the lass was concerned.

"Indeed," his father fortunately responded. "'Tis a fine thing to have a skilled healer. To have two is a blessing. Ráth Mór continues to grow. We need you two lassies to keep us in fine form," he grinned.

Maggie chewed her plump bottom lip nervously and picked up her basket, wringing her hands tightly against its handle. She was clearly uncomfortable, but Flynn tried to not take it personally. His brother and father alone were intimidating, but all three of them together tended to make people stand a bit straighter. The urge to give her a small smile started to overcome his resolve to keep her at a distance. He simply could not abide her fear of him.

He was not arrogant at all, unlike his brother who could flash a grin and make lassies fall to their knees, and he knew it well. Nay, Flynn knew enough from experience that he was considered a well-made man and he had two dimples that the lassies seemed to appreciate. Still, he hardly felt the need to use them, especially when his goal was to keep his private life private. But at the moment, his goal seemed to be shifting toward making Maggie feel more comfortable around him. Her blue eyes nervously flashed at him and he gave her what he hoped was a small, inviting smile that would ease her distress, yet not invite a lengthy conversation.

So, when her cheeks turned pink, he felt he had made a minor improvement in overcoming her fear of him, but then she seemed to panic, like a doe in the woods hearing a twig snap. With no word or warning, Maggie zoomed past them and out the door, the scent of rose petals and lavender trailing behind her. Och, she even smelled good, but she had run away from him. His pride bristled.

Brennain slapped him on the back hard enough to make him take a step forward. "She likes you."

Flynn scoffed at his brother and rolled his eyes. "She likes me as much as wee Fedlimid likes cutting teeth."

Elwynna walked past him slowly with a knowing look on her bonny face. Raising one blonde brow, she leaned in to whisper, "My sister does not do well around the lads, even those with dimples."

Flynn went back to frowning, only this time in confusion. He supposed it was just as well. He would likely be on the road again by the morn. Lassies simply had no place in his life.

Once Maggie and Elwynna shut the door behind them, Tuathal Techtmar, High King of Ériu stepped forward, holding his wee son in his arms. It was quite a sight to see such a huge, powerful man gently holding a wee crying child. "Have you information on Rochride's whereabouts?" he looked at both Flynn and Brennain questioningly.

"Aye," Flynn replied. "He and his army reside in the woods to the west, for now. They move as fast as the wind, it seems. He also has more men every time I track them down."

"I see," Tuathal said with a nod. Queen Leannan, who was also Flynn and Brennain's cousin, stepped forward to listen to their reports.

"If I may, my king..." Flynn hesitated, but he needed to get his feelings out in the open. "I wish to do more on my next mission than simply locate their camp. I feel strongly that Rochride is planning something. Mayhap an attack, but not quite yet. His army grows but is still much too small to take us on. Still, my instincts tell me he is up to something,"

Putting up a hand to stop Flynn's speech, Tuathal nodded in agreement. "I am of the same mind, Flynn. I was going to ask more of you on this mission. I need to know what he is up to. You and Brennain will infiltrate his camp. He has never seen your faces and at the rate he is adding men, I do not believe he or his men will be wary of the two of you. You are a master at blending in and staying silent. Brennain is a master at casual conversation and charming information out of people. Together, I think you will succeed. It will be dangerous."

Flynn squared his shoulders and felt a rush of excitement. He was ready for this. If he was going to spend his life gathering information for his king, he could at least use a bit of adventure. Anything was better than simply using his tracking skills every time. Any man could do that; so many of his skills were being unused.

"Aye, my king. We shall do it," Flynn said, looking at Brennain, who smiled widely at the prospect. His brother always wore his emotions outwardly.

"My lads will not let you down, Tuathal," Brocc added. "They have spent a lifetime protecting Ériu."

"Aye, and I would not be where I am now if not for your family's support. I trust any member of the Sisters of Danu's family with my life. After all, I married one of them, did I not?" Tuathal looked lovingly at Leannan and she blushed gently at his compliment.

When their meeting had finished, Flynn and Brennain were anxious to return home to pack their satchels. At dawn, they would leave once more and this time, Flynn hoped to find out exactly what that bastard Rochride was up to.

Chapter Two

"*What* was that all about?"

Maggie pretended not to hear her sister by marriage as she folded another clean linen before placing it in her healing basket. Her new sister was a kind woman and Maggie loved her dearly. Knowing Elwynna had suffered so greatly at the hands of her own father made Maggie ache. It also added to her fear of men. Her true sister, Paulene, had been killed by her husband a summer ago in Alba, which was the main reason Àdhamh and Maggie had sought a new life in Ériu at Ráth Mór, serving High King Tuathal Techtmar. Maggie's mother had also been treated foully and her father eventually killed her. And now her wee sister by marriage, who was one of the kindest souls she had ever met, shared similar stories of abuse at the hands of men. Aside from her brother, Maggie had not met a man worthy of her trust.

"You can pretend not to hear me, sister, but I know you do. You cannot live your life fearing every lad."

Aye, she could. She did. It was not to say she preferred to live this way, but even the finest face could hide a beast. She had learned that early on in life. 'Twas best to live with her brother and his wife, even if she did feel like she was encroaching on their privacy since their marriage a few moons ago.

Shoving another stack of clean linens in her basket, Maggie smoothed her soft lavender wool dress over her hips and considered how to reply to Elwynna. Lying was clearly not an option. Apparently, Maggie's fear was obvious, though she did try to hide it.

"How do you do it, Elwynna?" Maggie finally whispered as she twisted her skirt in her fists. "With all you have lived through at the hands of men, how did you so easily trust my brother?"

A softness came over Elwynna's face. Was it pity? Maggie flinched and turned back around. She did not want to be a pitiful lass.

She wanted to be brave, face her fears, and truly learn to live. Her thoughts shifted to Aislin, who was Flynn's cousin and the wife of one of their warriors, Alastar. Aislin could hunt, climb, fight, and protect her tribe, and she feared no man. Yet, she was also a tender wife, mother of a wee babe, and capable of running a household. Maggie had always envied Aislin and her strength. She wished to learn to use a weapon, as well. Mayhap it would make her feel safer to be able to defend herself.

Many times, she had wished to ask her brother for help, but he was much too preoccupied with his own training and being a husband to Elwynna. Maggie was already living in their home and intruding on their married life. She could not ask her brother for more. He would do it, she knew well, but at the cost of his time with his wife. Maggie could not be a further burden to them and asking another man to help her would require a trust she simply could not fathom ever having. Nay, her life was best spent tending the ill and keeping silent. The less visible she was, the less chance a man would ever focus his attention on her. Only then could she avoid becoming a victim, like all the other women in her life.

"How do I do what, dear sister?" Elwynna's small warm fingers touched her shoulder gently, urging Maggie to turn around and engage in the conversation. Elwynna's long blonde hair was only a shade lighter than her own, but her hazel eyes were almost yellow as they looked at her imploringly.

With a sigh, Maggie licked her lips and shrugged. "You have endured so much pain in your life, caused by men. Still, you do not fear them and you found love. I have not even been violated and yet I cannot be near a man without fearing him."

"Even Flynn?" Elwynna asked carefully, clearly wanting to continue the conversation without upsetting Maggie.

Soft blue eyes widening, Maggie took a deep breath. Why would Elwynna mention Flynn, of all men? Aye, he was the brawest warrior in all the village and so handsome that her breath left her body every time he was near. It was like her heart and head stopped working every time he entered a room. Deep in her heart, she dearly wished to know him, even speak to him without stuttering like a fool. Still, he was a man, a very large man with enormous muscles who stood at least two heads taller than her. He intimidated her immensely, and though nobody could ever have a bad word to say about him and he came from a wonderful family, he was also very quiet and mysterious. She was not certain whether she should be frightened of him or in awe.

Finally, she decided to answer. "Especially, Flynn, Elwynna. And since you mention his name, I now know I am doing a terrible job of concealing my... interest," Maggie grumbled. She took her now full basket and carried it over to the door, where it would be readily available in case of an emergency.

"He is a handsome man," Elwynna interjected matter-of-factly. "I never hear of him with another lass. And he did smile at you today... until you turned white and scurried away."

Embarrassment flooded Maggie and now instead of turning white, she felt herself turning pink. She made a fool of herself. How she wished to be more confident and brave, especially around Flynn. Still, the man had shown no interest in her whatsoever. A smile meant naught. Although, she had to admit that the man spared smiles for few people. Mayhap she should feel special to have received one, especially when he had such wondrous dimples that her heart beat wildly just thinking on them.

"I admit I find Flynn attractive," she decided to share with her sister. "Still, my attraction to him cannot outweigh my fear of men, and he is quite a large one, at that. Furthermore, he is almost never within the village. He travels most frequently and he has never shown me any favor."

Elwynna scoffed from across the room and put her hands on her hips. "He smiled at you. 'Tis more than I have ever seen him do for any other lass."

Maggie felt her brow furrow. "'Tis but a smile. It means naught. Besides, I am much better off on my own. I do not think I can even stomach being touched by a man." She hesitated, chewing on her lower lip. Should she tell Elwynna her darkest secret? Mayhap she should confide in at least one person. Even her brother did not know the full truth.

Growing serious, Elwynna stepped closer and nodded, her green wool dress swishing against her legs in the otherwise silent room. The hearth fire blazed, keeping them warm and protected from the chill outside. Taking a deep breath to steady her nerves, Maggie looked her sister in the eye. "I was in the room when my mother was violated and killed."

A gasp left Elwynna's lungs as she put her hand over her heart. "Oh my, Maggie!" Elwynna tittered and stormed over to her side, wrapping Maggie tightly in her embrace. "'Tis nay wonder you are as fearful as you are. Were you a young lass?"

Maggie pulled back slightly, only so she could catch her breath after Elwynna's grip had sucked the air from her lungs. "I was not so wee. I was ten and three. Old enough to know what I was seeing but too young to do aught about it. I hid like a coward beneath the bed. But he had her on the floor and I... I saw it all. Every horrible thing he did to her before he..." her voice trailed off and she squeezed her eyes shut. It was simply too hard to speak about that awful day. The images haunted her enough, but speaking the words would feel like ripping open a festering wound.

"You never told Àdhamh of this?" Elwynna asked gently, taking Maggie by the arm to help her sit on the bench against the round wall.

Shaking her head, she tucked a stray wave behind her ear nervously, glad she had finally spoken the words. Someone in the world now knew why she feared men so gravely. "Nay. And, please, do not tell him. I fear he pities me enough. I do not need for him to think of me as weaker than I already appear."

"You are not weak, Maggie. You have seen things in this world that would cause fear in any woman. You lost your mother and sister to two violent men. But Maggie..." Elwynna put her hand on Maggie's knee and squeezed. "Most men are not so bad. You had very poor fortune to be around such a cruel man, but most men are like your brother, kind and gentle."

Maggie scoffed and shifted on the bench. "Men wage wars over cattle, land, honor, and women. My brother is a rare man. Most men will not hesitate to hurt a woman. You must know this yourself, having lived through all you have." Maggie winced after the words left her mouth. She did not wish to cause Elwynna pain.

To her surprise, Elwynna smiled. "My father is an awful man, I admit that. And the warriors he gave me to were not much better. But there were some who refused to take me against my will. In fact, more of his warriors kept me safe rather than hurt me. It was the few, however, who did hurt me, who made my life horrible. There are bad men, aye, but there are more good. I stand by that."

Maggie wanted to argue that she may be right, but telling the good from the bad was a risky business. A lass had to allow a man close enough before she could learn the truth and it was not a risk she would take.

"My thanks for speaking with me, Elwynna. I trust you shall keep my secret."

A pounding at the door had Maggie standing swiftly, rushing to the entrance. Being the healer of the village, especially one as large as Ráth Mór, meant visitors at all hours, another reason Maggie felt guilty to be staying with her brother and his wife. They were woken from their sleep too often.

"You are a brave lass already, Maggie. You save lives and bring more life into this world as a midwife. 'Tis more than most could ever do. Remember that."

With a nod, Maggie gave Elwynna a weak smile and opened the door, feeling the cold sting her skin immediately. Aislin stood at the door panting, her red waves wrapped around her face as she leaned over to catch her breath. Dread ran up Maggie's spine to see this strong, brave woman looking so harried. "Is it wee Conor?" Maggie asked carefully. "Is your son ill?" Sick babes were her greatest fear. If a child died because she could not save him, she would never forgive herself. She knew it would one day happen. Babes died every day, but still she dreaded it.

Standing up straight, Aislin breathed deeply and waved off Maggie's fears. "Nay. 'Tis my husband. A lad in training accidentally sliced his arm during practice this morn. He will be all right, but requires your stitching skills. I am afraid mine still lack, as much as I try."

Hearing Aislin doubt herself made Maggie cock her head. Aislin was always so self-assured and yet, she admitted that Maggie was more skilled than she was at something. In a way, that made Maggie feel better about herself. She knew she was skilled at stitching up wounds but, for some reason, having Aislin recognize it made her want to smile. Fortunately, she had better manners than to smile after hearing Alastar had an injury.

"Let us go to him immediately," Maggie agreed. She grabbed her cloak, clasped it around her neck, and picked up the basket by the door.

As she and Aislin walked through the village in silence, she carefully dodged the puddles, hoping not to muddy her dress. Several people milled about, trying to get their chores done before the next looming storm eventually came down on them. Angry gray clouds slowly moved in from the west and Maggie knew that once it reached them, it would rival the storm from the night before.

A drop of rain landed on her cheek and small droplets began to fall all around. Picking up their pace, she and Aislin rushed toward the outer edge of the village, where her and Alastar's roundhouse sat on the border of the woods. Their door was wide open and Aislin finally spoke. "My thanks for coming so swiftly, Maggie. Please pardon all the people. We had some family drop in to check on Alastar before their travels."

"'Tis nay trouble, Aislin," Maggie responded, then winced when she felt icy water splash up her leg. Curse it. She'd stepped in a large puddle and her purple dress was a murky brown around the hem. She probably resembled a drowned rat now, but could not truly care since she had work to do.

A hound barked wildly from inside the house and Maggie smiled, knowing it was Aislin's faithful hunting hound, Branwen. Rolling her eyes before entering her home, Aislin laughed. "Branwen gets a bit excited when we have company."

Stepping into the house, she was at first blinded as her eyes tried to adjust to the sudden dimness. It had been so bright outside with the clouds reflecting the sunlight. Walking into Aislin's home was like entering a cave. "Oomph." Maggie ran into something hard and fell onto her backside with a rather painful thump. She had no time to brace herself for the unexpected fall.

"Are you all right?" She heard a deep voice ask gently as she opened her eyes and looked up, starting to slowly adjust to the dimness. Two beaming green eyes, the color of spring leaves, were level with hers and she caught her breath. That same feeling of her stomach dropping, heart beating, and brain stopping came over her again. Flynn knelt beside her with a worried frown, his hands outstretched to her. He was incredibly handsome, and again, much too large.

Her instinct was to pull away. She could not help it. He intimidated her beyond reason. And yet, she had already made a fool of herself once this day in front of him, and he clearly meant only to help her back onto her feet. Surely a man who was cruel would leave her there or even laugh at her. His look of concern and large hand reaching for hers, were signs of comfort, not cruelty. Swallowing hard, she took a chance and put her hand into his.

When his warm calloused fingers wrapped around hers so strongly, she felt a tremor of excitement run through her. Strange. She had never had that reaction to a man before. Still, she had to remind herself that even though handsome men could harm a lass, he was surrounded by people. No man would dare hurt her in public. This did not mean he would be different in private.

That thought steadied her emotions and calmed her excitement. Wariness, so engrained that she carried it easily with her, took charge once more and she yanked her hand out of his grasp as soon as possible. "My thanks, Flynn," she mumbled with embarrassment, doing all she could not to rub her sore backside in front of him and his brother, father, and Alastar, whom she could now see clearly.

As soon as she saw the angry gash in Alastar's arm, all her embarrassment disappeared while her healing instincts took to the forefront. "Och, Alastar! That's not a wee gash!" Pushing through the wall of huge Mac Greine men, Maggie made her way to the bed Alastar sat on, placing her basket beside him.

"'Tis not the worst I have had, as you know well, Maggie," he said with a lopsided grin. He spoke true. She would never forget the sword he took through the chest last summer that almost ended his life. She had tended him for almost two moons and, at one point, was very worried he would die. Compared to that wound, this was nothing. And yet...

Leaning over to look at it more closely, she squinted and focused on the specs of dirt and grime mixed into the flesh. It would need to be cleaned. "Someone give me a candle," she commanded without taking her eyes off the wound.

Alastar visibly paled. "You... you are not going to sear me shut, now are you, lass?" he said hesitantly.

"What?" She looked up to his worried blue eyes and patted his good shoulder. "Och, nay! I only need more light so I can better see. After falling on my backside just now, you can imagine 'tis too dim in here for me."

Alastar laughed and she could not help but crack a smile. Mayhap Elwynna was correct. She knew Alastar well enough to know he was a good man. He was so gentle with his wife and child, and always made her laugh. She supposed their King Tuathal, giant beast that he was, was also quite gentle with lassies. In fact, most of the married men she knew were good husbands. The trouble was that she only knew this after they were married. How did a lass know a man would be gentle with her before committing to him, or falling for him?

She shook her head. She needed to stay focused. Flynn stepped up with a candle and held it close for her to see. Looking up to his great height, she took a deep breath and nodded her thanks to him. Once again, words escaped her in his presence. "'Twill need to be cleaned," she murmured, reaching into her basket and grabbing a clean linen cloth. "Do you have water in your cauldron, Aislin?"

"Nay. 'Tis empty. I will go collect some." Before Maggie could offer to do it herself, Aislin ran outside and slammed the door behind her. Curse it. Now Maggie was alone in a home with four huge warriors. Her head swam with fear and she could not help but take a step back, trying to keep herself calm. She really needed to overcome this stifling fear of men. But that would require a slow introduction to one man... not being trapped in a room with four.

"That lad got you good, mate," Brennain said, stepping forward to better look at the wound as Flynn continued to silently

23

hold the tallow candle. "We will make him clean all the dung out of the stalls for a fortnight for this slip," he grunted.

That seemed unfair to Maggie. The lad was simply learning. Sparring with men twice his size was likely a fearful thing. He should not be punished for simply trying to work hard and learn. Yet, she bit her lip and pretended to rummage in her basket to keep them from seeing her hands shake. Alastar would panic if he saw her hands shaking just before she stitched him up. In truth, her hand was steady as a rock when not alone with men.

"We will do nay such thing," Flynn chimed in, rebuking his brother. "He is just a learning lad. Have we all not made mistakes while in warrior training? What good does cleaning dung do us? Make him work more drills with the straw dummy. He will hone his skills and not have real flesh to wound as he does it."

Maggie's eyes widened. 'Twas the most she had ever heard Flynn speak in her life, and she was so very pleased to see how calm and reasonable he was. He had compassion for the lad and something about that made her fear him just a bit less. Granted, a man could defend a lad and still harm women, but for now, it was a comfort. She stayed quiet, waiting in turmoil, squished between the Mac Greine brothers until Aislin blessedly returned with the water.

After Aislin poured the bucket of water into the cauldron, Maggie tugged the chain suspending it above the hearth, lowering it enough to heat and boil the water.

"I must allow the water to boil before I can clean the wound."

"Whatever for?" Brennain asked, aghast.

"Well," Maggie tittered nervously. Having a large man shout at her made her anxious. He was not truly shouting at her, she knew. He was simply confused about her methods. Still, he made her want to run away. It infuriated her to have her skills questioned. Healing was the one thing she was good at and she would not allow this large warrior to question her.

"I am not certain, but linens boiled in water cause fewer infections than those that are not. I have seen horrifying infections and I have noticed that the dirtier the linen, the worse the infection.

An old healer from Alba taught me this and I believe 'tis why I have so few infections on my wounded."

"That's nonsense. 'Tis only a waste of time. His wound needs to be cleaned right away," Brennain pressed.

Like a flash of lightning, Flynn was in his brother's face. The men stood almost equally tall, but Flynn was only slightly shorter. With both having black stubble on their chins, those green eyes, and raven hair, they could almost pass as twins. "Do not question the lass. If she says the linens need to be boiled, then the linens need to be boiled."

Brennain quirked a brow at his brother and grinned, as if silently communicating some smug comment to Flynn, but he put his hands up in surrender and bowed his head to her. "I apologize, Maggie. I am certain you know best."

Maggie looked at Flynn curiously, wondering why he had so adamantly defended her, and yet, her heart beat wildly against her ribs at the ire in his eyes for his brother. He looked so formidable, yet she did not feel threatened.

"She saved my life before, Brennain. I trust her," Alastar added.

"My thanks," she murmured, and she walked over to the cauldron to check the water. It was boiling rapidly, so she dropped the linen into the water, using an iron rod to push it under fully. She stared into the bottom of the cauldron, watching the linen dance in the water as the steam moistened her face. It was a distraction from the tension in the room and she stayed silent while she listened to the men converse with Aislin in the background. She knew Flynn's father, Brocc, was Aislin's uncle, and Maggie felt envious of Aislin for having so much family. She had only a brother whom she loved dearly, but who was now married and distracted—as he should be, she supposed.

From the little she could hear of their conversation, Flynn and Brennain were leaving town once again just as soon as Alastar was patched up. By their whispers and intermittent silence, she knew they discussed something that was none of her business, so she concentrated once more on the linen, deciding it was well-boiled.

Using the iron rod, she lifted it out of the water and allowed it to drip and cool just enough to touch it.

Walking over to Alastar, she gave him a sheepish smile. "You remember this will sting, aye?" He only nodded and squared his shoulders, silently giving her permission to do what she must. As she squeezed the warm water over the wound, Maggie watched the dirt wash away. Then she gently dabbed the clean linen over the gash. He winced and gritted his teeth, but he never made a sound.

Flynn stepped close to her again with the candle, this time accidentally grazing her hip with his thigh. It was the most ridiculously innocent touch, but her face heated and she looked away to grab her clean thread and bone needle. Taking a deep breath, calm washed over her as she did what she did best. Instinctively, her needle went in and out of Alastar's flesh, creating a perfect row of stitches that she knew would heal quite nicely. He would have a scar, aye, but she had made certain it would be a straight scar. Nobody would look upon a wound she stitched and say it was flawed.

"'Tis most impressive," she heard Flynn whisper under his breath. She was almost certain he had not meant for her to hear it, so she did not acknowledge his compliment. Still, it made her bite back a smile and she was suddenly glad for the dim lighting so he could not see her flush.

"Thank you, sweet Maggie," Aislin said, and she stepped closer to observe her husband's wound. "You have a gift, for certain."

Her gifts were nothing compared to Aislin's, but she silently accepted the compliment with a nod and a smile.

"You must be off, lads," Brocc said deeply from behind Maggie, suddenly startling her from her thoughts. She had forgotten the quiet man stood near the hearth.

"Aye," Brennain said, walking past Maggie and bumping into her hard enough to throw her body against Flynn's, who was still standing next to her holding the clay bowl full of burning tallow. With his free hand, Flynn caught her around her waist, holding her tightly against him so she could regain her balance.

Panic seized her when she realized she was firmly against him. She looked up to him and saw anger in his eyes, which only frightened her further. He was angry with her and she had no idea if he would strike her for knocking into him or not. She flinched and shrugged out of his grip, feeling relief when he easily let her go, confusion in his gaze. "Are you all right?"

Swallowing hard, she nodded and turned away to gather her supplies.

"I am sorry I bumped into you, Maggie," Brennain said with a smirk. He did not look sorry at all and she was very confused by his actions. It all felt very intentional, like he wanted her to knock into Flynn, though she could not understand such an action.

Again, she only nodded and kept her back turned. The door opened, the fire flickered and she heard large booted steps leaving the home before the door shut again. She could finally breathe.

"Are you all right, Maggie? You seem shaken." Aislin asked, and placed a hand on her shoulder.

"I am fine. I need to leave. Fetch me if you need aught, or think a fever is developing." Aislin crinkled her brow at Maggie's sudden change of mood, but she just needed to get home and back to the one place she felt safe. She knew she had overreacted; a part of her quite liked the feel of Flynn's hands on her body, his body against hers. Still, the thought of being so small and helpless against a strong man had, once again, consumed her mind. Gods, she was a mess no man would ever love, and even if one could, she would likely run away.

Chapter Three

"*You* are in deep shite, Flynn."

Flynn stayed silent because if he spoke, he would likely use every foul word in their language to curse his brother for his childish behavior. Maggie was skittish by nature, he knew that much. She seemed beyond timid when around men, but the fear in her eyes when he touched her made his stomach drop. He had only been trying to keep her from falling because his arse of a brother thought he was hilarious to push her into him. But Maggie looked as if she thought he would hurt her. He did not know whether to feel disappointed, hurt, or angry. Somehow, he felt all those emotions mixed with a heavy dose of confusion and, as much as he loathed to admit it, lust. Her body was wee and bonny.

She was absolutely perfect and if his life were different, he would go out of his way to slowly woo her into trusting him. He was a large man, but he would never hurt a lass. To think she thought he would made him sick to his stomach. Still, he could do naught about it being gone all the cursed time. His life was not built around having a family and he needed to remind himself of that whenever he thought of trying to break through her wall of fear, especially now that she had been pressed against him and he had smelled her rose and lavender hair.

"I know you like her."

Flynn was going to knock his brother off his horse if he did not shut his mouth. The next storm had come on in earnest and they had been drenched from the moment they left Ráth Mór. It was nothing new to them; still it would not hurt if just once the weather would not be too wet, too cold, or so hot he felt as if he was melting into his horse. It was still daylight, but it was so dark it felt closer to dusk. They had only been traveling west for an hour and he had counted himself fortunate that his brother stayed silent. It was a rare treat. Now, it seemed his brother had grown weary of silence.

"I know she likes you, as well."

That was enough. "Brennain, you are an arse. She is clearly frightened of me. Do you know naught about lassies? She was ready to bolt the moment I touched her. What were you even thinking?" he growled. His jaw clenched and his hands tightened on his horse's reins.

"I was thinking 'twas time you and Maggie stopped looking at each other with longing and did something about it. Neither of you will, so I made it happen."

"All you accomplished was frightening the lass. I know naught about her, but she is truly afraid of men. As for me, I have nay interest in trying to know her further. I can do naught for any lass as long as I am always traveling for our king."

"Mayhap 'tis time you considered a change in your life. Find a lass. Settle down. Have wee children."

"All this, coming from my elder brother who beds any lassie he sees? Mayhap you should worry about your own life. I am content with mine."

"You are meant for a family, Flynn. Mayhap I am not. But you are."

Flynn thought about his brother's words for a moment. He remembered Brennain being unusually attached to a lass he met over a summer ago in Alba, when they had traveled across the sea to bring home a warrior Tuathal had sought out for his army. It was the same journey that had brought Maggie and Àdhamh into their lives, and while he clearly remembered the first time his eyes landed on Maggie's bonny face, he also remembered his brother having overly sweet affections for a lass named Morna. Yet, no good would come from bringing that up. Morna was a sea away and Brennain had been with many lassies since then.

"I was made to do as my king asks. That is what we are doing. Can we focus on the task now? I believe if we keep traveling west we will find Mal Mac Rochride's camp, or at least where it had been previously. Then we can track them from there. Just keep an eye out for fresh tracks." Flynn shifted the quiver full of arrows on his shoulder and then felt for the hilt of his sword before thinking of the dagger in his boot. He would not be unprepared for an attack.

Riding for hours in silence, they searched the land for any trace of a traveling army with no success. It was likely they had continued to travel west to gather more followers before confronting Tuathal again in a battle. Several smaller tribes were scattered across the land, most faithful to their high king. Several messengers had arrived at Ráth Mór over the last few months with word that Mac Rochride had approached them for an alliance against Tuathal. They were all eager to remind their king that they stood true and would fight against Mal if called upon.

However, based on the growing army Mac Rochride had gathered, Flynn knew that not all tuatha were loyal to their high king. The pattern had shown that he was predominately traveling west, but he would eventually need to go another direction to find more tribes, or attempt an attack on Ráth Mór. Yet, Mal seemed to be taking his time and Flynn wondered if it was because he knew his army was too small, or because he was biding his time while planning a grander scheme. He had no real proof, but his gut told him it was the latter. The man would need to more than double his army to even attempt an attack, which would take years to manage, if ever. But if he had a plan to cause trouble, he certainly could throw Tuathal off. This was precisely why Tuathal had bade them join Mac Rochride's army and gather information.

As the hours passed, the wind picked up its intensity until it howled like a wolf in the night and the darkness cloaked them in its void. It had not rained for over an hour, but they were soaked through and the cold wind only intensified the chill. They needed to seek shelter soon and he knew exactly where they needed to go.

"To the north!" Flynn shouted over his shoulder to his brother. He wondered if the wind had carried his words away before Brennain could hear them, especially with the sound of their thick cloaks whipping behind them. However, Brennain nodded his understanding and slightly steered his brown mare toward the north, heading for the abandoned cottage they had once discovered while on another journey to track down Mal.

Who had once lived there was a mystery, as well as what had happened to them. The house was completely intact, fully furnished with a stack of dry logs against one of its walls, and it contained two wooden bed frames complete with straw mattresses and furs. Whoever it belonged to had clearly not been there in a long while based on the dust that coated everything from the clay dishes to benches and cushions around the hearth. But, it had served as shelter on more than one occasion for Flynn and his brother, especially since it was the perfect distance from Ráth Mór to become shelter by nightfall.

Though not a single star could shine through the thick layer of clouds, the moonlight shone eerily over the land, casting a bluish hue over the towering bare trees overhead. Even if it was pitch black, Flynn had traveled this way enough to know that the abandoned shelter was less than a mile north of their location.

It did not take long for their horses, as weary as they must have been, to bring them to the entrance of the cottage. Fortunately, the rickety byre on the side of the home still stood against the storm. Dismounting swiftly from his black stallion Arawn, named after the god of war, Flynn kicked the two wooden posts that firmly held the byre roof up against the dwelling. Deciding that the shelter was more than sturdy enough to protect their precious horses for the night, Flynn grabbed Arawn's rein and pulled him beneath the roof, tying him to the post.

"'Tis a blessing to have found this cottage all those moons ago," Brennain shouted, tying up his own horse. "I would not relish sleeping in this weather, as much as I enjoy the wilderness."

"Aye," Flynn agreed. They had slept in the worst sort of weather while traveling with their fellow warriors in the past, but nobody would choose to sleep in such conditions when a dry place awaited them.

The horses secure and fed for the night, they both entered the cottage, certain it was still unoccupied for no smoke escaped from its pointy thatched roof. With the pitch dark and frigid chill that engulfed Flynn upon stepping in, he knew no person would stay within these walls without burning a fire. It was colder within than it was outside.

"I will start the fire," Brennain said. He left the door open so some natural moonlight could guide him in his task.

Flynn dropped his satchel to the ground and dropped heavily onto one of the furs around the hearth. His body ached from being wet and cold for hours. He wondered if he was catching a chill, for seldom did the elements affect him physically.

He watched as his brother struck his flint stone and a small iron rod together, creating a spark that ignited the kindling. Blowing gently to encourage the fire, Brennain tossed it onto the pile of dry logs and they both watched in silence as the sparks roared higher. Blowing on his hands, Flynn then rubbed them together to try to warm up his stiff limbs. It crossed his mind that it would be warmer sleeping outside beneath an oak tree but knew the fire would eventually heat up the room.

"On the morrow, we will be able to track down Mal if he has moved. Once we find him, we will need a cover story. Who are we and where did we come from?"

Brennain plopped down next to him by the fire, also blowing on his fingers for warmth. "We must say we are from Darini, our old tuath before we moved to Ráth Mór. I do not want him knowing we came from Tuathal's new village, or else he may try to pry information from us."

"True, but all the people of Darini relocated to Ráth Mór over a year ago. Why would we not have followed?" Flynn's brow furrowed, trying to make sure they had a plausible answer for any questions.

Brennain ran his hand through the stubble along his jaw as he thought. "Same reason most of these men defect, I suppose. Because they would rather seek their own rewards than be faithful to their king. Mal is offering these men power. Is that not what drives many men?"

"Aye, I suppose," Flynn said warily. In truth, his body ached, and his mind was too tired to plot or plan anymore. "I need sleep. Let us discuss this in the morn on our way to seek them out."

Brennain looked at him curiously. He knew Flynn was not acting like himself. He usually planned every move down to the very last detail. It was what made him good at being an informant.

Flynn truly felt wretched as another chill made his body ache. He was almost certain he had grown ill on their journey, or mayhap it was lack of rest. Either way, he would continue his mission. No illness would slow him down.

"As you say, brother," Brennain responded with a frown. "If you are not well, I can continue on without you while you rest."

His brother knew him well. "'Tis not necessary. I just need sleep."

Without another word, Flynn arose from the cushion, feeling every ache and pain in every joint of his body as he stretched and shuffled over to the bed he usually claimed as his own in this hut. Aye, just a wee bit of sleep and he would be refreshed and ready to track down Mal by the morn.

* * * *

Curse all the gods, he was more ill than he had realized. His throat felt as if he had swallowed a hive of bees and his chest felt as if a wild boar sat upon it. A deep, hacking cough forced its way out of his lungs as Flynn climbed out of bed and put his still-damp trousers back on. The hearth fire had dried most of his garments and he had endured worse than slightly damp clothing in the past. Although this morn, his skin felt so sore and sensitive that just pulling his tunic over his head made him flinch.

"You are not well enough to travel."

Flynn narrowed his eyes and stared at his brother. "I have nay choice. We must carry on. I will be well by the morrow," he lied. It cost him just to speak. His voice was raspy and another horrid cough shook his body.

Brennain scoffed and pulled his blue tunic over his head. "Whatever you say, Flynn. I can do this alone, but I know 'tis nay use to reason with you."

"Nay, 'tis not. Eat this and let us be off." Flynn tossed an apple to his brother and grabbed another for himself. However, after one bite he decided the pain of swallowing was worse than the gnawing in his stomach. He tossed the remainder of his apple back in his satchel for later.

Of all the times to become ill. He had spent his life traveling and had never been ill even once, but now that he had his most important mission yet, he was weaker than a foal.

An hour passed in silence as they traveled, aside from Flynn's inconveniently persistent cough. Mal's men would find them before he found Mal, if he could not contain his coughing. But it was a losing battle, for every few minutes, another storm of hacks attacked him, causing him to wince at the pain in his throat.

"You will get us both killed, Flynn. You need to turn around and let me handle this," Brennain growled. "Do you think I cannot do it?"

So that was his brother's issue. Brennain took Flynn's stubborn need to proceed as a lack of trust in his skills. "Brennain. I am quite positive you can do this on your own. That does not mean it is necessary. Tuathal wanted us together. 'Tis safer together."

"Not with you hacking so loud the spirits in the Otherworld can most assuredly hear you." Brennain snorted, but they kept on traveling for a few more moments before he stopped his brown mare completely, forcing Flynn to pull back on Arawn's reins.

"This is foolishness. We cannot do this with you so ill. If we get set upon, you are too weak to fight."

Flynn's pride bristled at his brother's rebuke, but he knew he was telling the truth. If they were set upon, Flynn would not be able to fight back with his usual strength. He wanted to be stronger than whatever illness consumed his body, but he was also intelligent enough to know that they must decide on a plan. Either Brennain went on alone, or they both went back to the hut until Flynn was well. It would only be a day, mayhap two, he promised himself.

"All right. What would you have me do, Brennain? I admit it. I am unwell."

Brennain snorted and rolled his eyes. "You do not say?"

"If not for this cursed cough, I would be fine to continue on. But the cold wind is only making it worse and I fear I will draw unwanted attention."

"I understand why you want to stay together," Brennain said, much to Flynn's surprise. "I think we should travel back toward the hut and allow you to rest for a day. Mayhap tomorrow you will be recovered."

Flynn grimaced. His weakened state was destroying their mission. Mayhap he should allow Brennain to go on alone, but he did not relish having his brother within Mal's camp without his aid, even if he was quite capable. "Aye, as much as I detest it, Tuathal would not want me at half my strength before stepping foot into Mal's camp."

They turned their horses south to travel back toward the cottage when the sound of an object whizzing through the air caught Flynn's attention. Before he could warn Brennain to duck, he felt a searing pain in the side of his chest and he knew before he even looked down, that he had been struck by an arrow.

Had he been in full health, he may have had the strength to grab an arrow from his own quiver, locate his attacker, and fire back. But the pain in his side felt like fire running through his veins. He roared with pain and slumped over on his horse, cursing himself for being too weak to fight and cursing his cough for alerting their enemy. He cursed his pride for not listening to his brother from the beginning. This would never have happened had he been silent and alert.

"Flynn!" Brennain roared as his horse anxiously shifted beneath him.

A large man in tattered linen garments dropped from a tree several yards ahead. The man was too far away to fully make out through Flynn's sudden dizziness, but he was likely one of Mal's scouts. Flynn felt blood trickling rather quickly from his wound and all his remaining strength went with it.

He watched in horror as the man ran the distance toward Brennain. Had Flynn not been injured or ill, he would have easily taken the man down with an arrow of his own, but with the blood flowing from his wound and the weakness overtaking his body, he was of little use to his brother. As the man came within viewing distance, Flynn saw a dagger held tightly in his grip. He reached Brennain's horse and spat on the ground. "Ye are the men who have been trailing Mal, are ye nay? If ye work for Tuathal, ye are a traitor!" the man roared.

"Watch... out..." Flynn forced the words through his weak lips as the man stepped forward again, holding the dagger, ready to strike.

Faster than Flynn had ever seen, his brother dismounted his horse and pulled his sword from its sheath at his hip. "If you are one of Mal's men, then you are the traitor!" Brennain barked.

"Tuathal killed the true High King, Elim!" the man spat. "Mal seeks his revenge for the death of his king and companion."

Brennain stepped forward and held his sword high in a defensive stance, ready for an attack. They had been taught from the youngest age to stay calm and observe their enemy. "Elim killed Tuathal's father, Fiachu, who was the true High King. That makes Elim a traitor. Tuathal has rightfully regained his throne."

With a snarl, the man flicked his wrist and flung his dagger straight toward Brennain, but with the reflexes of a feral cat, he dodged the flying weapon. Flynn watched as the weapon spun in mid-air, eventually sticking into the forest floor, surrounded by colorful fall leaves.

Effortlessly, Brennain stepped forward and ran the man through. With a gurgle, the man dropped to the ground and breathed his last breath.

Brennain wasted no time getting back to Flynn, who now felt cold and numb. "Brother, are you all right?" Brennain groaned, seeing the red soaking through Flynn's white tunic. It took much too much effort to respond when all Flynn wanted to do was sleep. His eyes grew heavy and he groaned as another coughing fit jolted the arrow still protruding from his side.

"Cursed bastard!" Brennain growled through clenched teeth, and he examined the wound. "I must leave the arrow, Flynn. I cannot risk the tip becoming lodged in your ribs or you bleeding out before I can get help."

Flynn wanted to inform his brother than he was already bleeding out, but had not the strength to argue. He would let his brother do aught to save him, but it seemed most likely he would die this day.

Soft blue eyes flashed in his mind, along with plump red lips and shiny blonde hair the color of wheat. He would never see Maggie again, never get the chance to tell her how bonny she was or to earn her trust so she would not flinch at his slightest touch. But he could close his eyes and dream of the lass during his final moments. Nobody could stop him from indulging in at least that much.

He felt his brother climb up on the back of Arawn and gently wrap an arm around his upper chest, avoiding the arrow on his lower left side. He groaned from the pain, not certain if the body aches or the arrow wound hurt him more.

"Come, Danu," Flynn heard Brennain call to his horse. If he had more strength, he would chuckle, once again, at his brother's choice to name his horse after the goddess who their mother was supposedly descended from, but the peaceful darkness was closing in on him. Flynn felt Arawn start to move with Danu's hooves pounding beside him. Brennain must have held the reins for both horses in his hands as he rode toward the hut. He was mighty skilled about that sort of thing.

"Hold on Flynn! I will get you back to the hut and then I will seek out help."

Throat burning, head pounding, and side aching from his wound, Flynn could not bring himself to care. He would prefer to be left to die, but he knew his brother would never allow it. Instead, he put his fate in the hands of Brennain and the gods, finally finding his escape in the blissful nothingness.

Chapter Four

"*Very* well done, Elwynna! 'Tis only been a few moons of training, but you have caught on quite well. Your healing skills come to you naturally."

Crinkling her nose, Elwynna looked down at the boar carcass she had been using to practice her stitching skills. The last row was about as clean and straight a stitch job as possible, still it was not as good as Maggie's work. "Are you certain? 'Tis not as well-done as your stitching," she said to Maggie as she pushed the sharp bone needle through the thick boar hide once more.

Maggie waved off her modest words and smiled. "Nonsense. Any warrior in the village would be pleased with that stitching job. And your knowledge of herbs has improved daily. The last salve you made was perfect. You must give yourself more credit, sister. Ráth Mór is a big tuath and having two healers will be a blessing."

The door to their home opened suddenly and Àdhamh sauntered in with his tunic slung casually over his bare shoulder, and even though it was cursed cold outside, his chest was covered with sweat from practicing with the other warriors. His bright hazel eyes flashed at his wife as he held a piece of dry meat in his hand, tearing off a piece of the savory pork with his teeth. When his eyes locked on his wife's stitching work, a grin spread across his face and he came closer. "Those are some fine stitches, Elwynna. You are learning quickly," he said, and he leaned in to kiss her forehead.

"See? I told you. You are truly improving, Elwynna." Maggie gripped her sister's hand in reassurance before turning to collect her healing items, packing them into a satchel. She had a few visits to make and found the satchel much easier to carry than the awkward basket she sometimes preferred.

"Well, my thanks," Elwynna responded with a sigh. "I suppose 'tis good enough. I am only glad to finally feel of use in more... appropriate ways," her voice faded off sadly.

Maggie frowned. Elwynna had not learned to do aught in the war camp with her father, aside from pleasuring the warriors against her will. Maggie knew it was still a great source of pain for her sister by marriage. She had low confidence at times and felt desperate to learn a trade, being much harder on herself than necessary.

Before Maggie could think what to say to make Elwynna feel better, Àdhamh silently strode up to his wife and wrapped her wee body in his strong arms, showing her just how valuable she was to him. Her brother was a wonderful husband, just as Maggie always knew he would be. For a large, powerful man, he was tender and kind; just what Elwynna needed.

Suddenly feeling like an interloper in her own home again, Maggie silently swept up her satchel and crept out the front door. She knew they would never mean to make her feel out of place, but Maggie had been feeling like she truly did not belong anywhere lately. She wanted to be a brave lass like Aislin, or an outspoken lass like Elwynna, who could walk into any room and make companions. Maggie cursed herself a coward. She needed adventure and she wanted love. Neither seemed within reach with her lack of survival skills and her inability to speak to men.

It was already evening and the sun was beginning its decent across the sky, streaking the earth with beautiful hues of coral, purple and pink. 'Twas such a beautiful sight that it took her breath away. She sighed, longing to see the world and do something more with her life.

A light wind grazed her ear while she walked, causing gooseflesh to rise across her skin. She was wearing a long, dark blue wool gown and a plaid cloak lined with fur, but still, she felt chilled to the bone. With little of her day left, she still had a few sick or injured villagers to check on before she had to return home for the evening meal.

The hairs on the back of her neck prickled as she heard a commotion from behind her. Men were shouting and, fearing a fight was about to break out, Maggie looked over her shoulder, wondering if she should stay to break it up or run like the coward she was. When men fought, injuries would follow. As the healer, she would prefer to prevent anyone from becoming hurt. But as a small lass, she knew if large men intended to brawl, she could do naught to stop it.

Her eyes widened when she saw the men who shouted. They were not arguing, but they did seem in a panic. Brennain was standing with his father and their king, Tuathal. Why was Brennain back so soon? He and Flynn had left only the morning before for another of their journeys, and yet, as much as she strained her neck to see better, she saw no evidence of Flynn.

Brennain was waving his arms frantically as he discussed something with the other men. A few of his words drifted to her on the wind and her heart began to beat in overtime when she heard her name jumbled within his words.

"Flynn and I... one of Mal's men... an arrow... he is hurt... alone in a hut... need Maggie!"

She gasped and clutched her chest as the pieces of his story started to make sense in her mind. As much as she hoped it was not true, it sounded as if Flynn had been injured and they needed her help. Flynn was out there somewhere, alone, and must have been gravely injured for Brennain to be so frantic.

Without further consideration, her feet began to travel toward Brennain at a run. She could not breath and her heart ached. Poor Flynn! He was such a braw warrior. To think of him injured did something to her stomach. It twisted and writhed in fear with every step closer to the men.

"Maggie!" Brennain shouted when he saw her running toward him. "Lass, Flynn needs your help. He is gravely injured!"

"Maggie," she heard the deep voice of her king from behind her and she turned quickly, almost stunned by the hesitant tone in his voice. "You must go to him. Elwynna is trained well enough to help in your absence, aye?"

Maggie's mouth was agape, her blonde hair whipping wildly about her face in the wind. All she could do was nod her head. Aye, Elwynna could manage here alone. All Maggie could think of was

Flynn and how badly he needed her. As a healer, all other thoughts or fears for herself vanished as she mentally prepared in her mind. She had her satchel still clutched in her hands. She never left home without all her salves, tinctures, clean linens, bone needles and thread for wounds. She was always prepared and at this moment, she was relieved to be ready to depart immediately.

A sudden need to command the situation came over her, just as it always did when someone was in need. "Aye. I am ready," she nodded to Brennain and shoved her satchel into his hands so he could tie it to his horse.

Then she turned to King Tuathal. "Please tell my brother I had to depart. I will return as soon as I am able. Elwynna must tend to the men I was preparing to visit this evening."

Before she could evade or duck, Flynn's father scooped her up into his strong arms and almost squeezed the air from her lungs. "My thanks, sweet Maggie. Go to him. Save my son."

Looking up into his big hazel eyes, she gulped nervously and licked her lips. Words escaped her. All she could do was nod and pray to the gods she did not let him down. She wanted to screech with repressed fear at being handled so roughly by a large man, but she had to take a deep breath when he released her and remind herself that he was simply worried for his son. He was not a threat to her.

Her father had been a large man and he would be affectionate in one moment and cruel in the next, oftentimes taking his anger out on her and her mother. Àdhamh had been safe from his rage, being the coveted son that he was, but to her father, lassies were only needed for a few reasons, and easily discarded. Though Àdhamh had never seen their father hurt her or their mama, he knew it happened and did all he could to protect them. But as a wee lad, he could not do much against the stronger man. It was a relief when he finally died, but not before he killed their mother and did irrevocable damage to Maggie. She was not certain if she could ever trust a man again. And being grabbed so abruptly by the huge Brocc Mac Greine had almost made her panic... almost. But she held herself together, remembering that Flynn needed her and the man was only frightened.

"Let us go," she said shakily, her confidence waning slightly after her jolt of fear.

"Aye," Brennain grunted as he wrapped his huge hands around her waist and hoisted her most unceremoniously onto the back of his horse.

She screeched and flailed to get free. "What are you doing?" she wailed, trying frantically to dismount.

He jumped up on the horse behind her, wrapping his hands around her waist. "You said you were ready to leave," Brennain said, incredulously.

"Not upon your horse!" she cried! Panic consumed her, and her ears began to ring. She could not, would not, tolerate being alone with Brennain for several hours, pushed so closely to his body. The very thought terrorized her.

To her surprise, he gentled his grip and leaned closer to her ear, calmly speaking to her as if she was a frightened doe. "Lass. I know you fear men. I do not know why, but I have seen it on your face. You need not fear me. I vow on my brother's life that I shall keep you safe and would never violate you. 'Tis only a few hours to get there and Flynn's life is at stake. 'Tis faster for us to ride this way. Can you please trust in me? For Flynn?"

For Flynn. Aye. Suddenly, she realized that she would face all her fears and do aught possible for Flynn. She hardly knew the man and still felt fear at the thought of being alone with either of them, but she had to take her chances to save the life of a wounded man. A man she was inexplicably drawn to, unlike any other man in her entire life. It was an odd thing to long to know a man and yet be afraid of getting too close. But right now, all that mattered was that his life was in danger and only she could save him.

"Aye," she nodded and swallowed hard, stiffening her back so she did not touch Brennain more than necessary. "For Flynn," she agreed.

With a grunt and a nod, Brennain made a sound to his horse that made the brown animal take off like the wind. It was too late to look back or change her mind. Maggie must be brave and face her fears. For Flynn.

* * * *

Brennain drove his horse so hard, Maggie felt bad for the poor beast. Normally she would speak up for the defenseless animal, but in truth, she knew they could not spare a moment. Aside from the description of their encounter and the wound, Brennain had remained focused and silent. As promised, he had kept his hands to himself, with only the necessary grip around her waist to keep her from falling to her death.

According to Brennain, a man from the enemy camp had heard Flynn coughing. The man must have been a scout, for he was up in a tree and shot Flynn in the side with an arrow. The arrow did not go all the way through and was currently still lodged inside his body. Maggie had assured him that he did the right thing leaving the arrow. Without a practiced healer, removing an arrow could be deadly. The tip, usually made of flint or bronze, was only held to the shaft by a string of gut. But when lodged in a body, the gut string softened, and the arrowhead could easily become separated from the shaft and forever lodged in the body of the victim, which usually resulted in infection and, subsequently, death. It would be most painful for Flynn, but if Maggie could widen the wound and remove the entire arrow intact, Flynn had a much better chance of survival as long as no major organs had been punctured.

To leave Flynn must have been a hard decision for Brennain, but it had been the right one. Flynn's body would not have withstood the hours of jostling on a horse. Especially if he was also ill, as his brother indicated. A shiver ran up her spine when she imagined Flynn all alone with an arrow lodged in his body and an illness weakening him. It was a bleak situation. Not many survived an arrow wound, but she would give her all to saving Flynn. At least he was inside a hut, safely hidden away in the woods. She only prayed he was still alive when they reached him.

"The hut is just through those trees," Brennain finally said after hours of silence. Her entire body ached; eventually she had given up on staying rigid. Her back and backside had gotten much too sore and she had allowed herself to sag against Brennain for support, proud of herself for even that small show of bravery. She would need to hold onto that bravery to get her through the next few days. She knew that Flynn would take several days, if not sennights, to heal well enough to travel. It scared her to think of being away from Àdhamh for so long, but she had a job to do.

Within moments, the thatched roof showed through the gaps in the trees, no smoke coming from the top. It was likely very cold in the hut, and another wave of fear and pity grabbed at her for the man hopefully still living within its walls.

As they approached the front, Maggie briefly took in the crumbling white lime-washed walls illuminated in the darkness. Based on the position of the moon hanging high above sharing its dim light with the earth below, it was likely not quite midnight and hopefully, as fast as Brennain rode, Flynn had not been alone longer than ten hours.

Brennain tied up his horse hastily, clearly in a hurry to check on his brother's wellbeing. The poor animal was exhausted and Maggie made a vow to feed the sweet creature a carrot, or any treat she could find her, in the morning. For now, no force in the world could keep her away from Flynn.

Her hands shook as she untied her satchel from the horse's saddle, saying another prayer that she did not open that door to find Flynn already gone. It was a likely possibility and she squared her shoulders, took a deep breath, and walked over to the door. One more deep breath, and she slowly opened the door, forgetting to release the breath she now held in her lungs while her eyes adjusted to the blackness within.

As morbid as it was, her first instinct was to take a tentative sniff of the air. If Flynn had perished, the smell of death may already linger. Blessedly, she smelled nothing untoward and took a few more steps into the darkness.

Aside from the thin stream of bluish moonlight casting across one section of the earthen floor, Maggie could see nothing else. Fortunately, Brennain came in behind her and maneuvered his way around her to the hearth, clearly knowing the layout of this hut.

"He is in the bed straight ahead of you, Maggie. I will light a fire," he grunted, lifting three large logs in his hands and hoisting them into the hearth. With a nod, she silently continued to step slowly forward with her hands out in front of her in case she should stumble.

When her shins gently banged into something solid, she knew she had found the bed and saw its shadowy outline in front of her, but not much else. A sudden burst of light filled the room and Maggie took a deep breath when she saw Flynn's still form, lying in the bed directly in front of her. Her heart almost came up into her throat as fear chilled her blood. He looked pale as death. His lower body was covered in furs but from the waist up, he was exposed and lying flat on his back, a strip of linen tied around the wound.

"I had to cut the shaft off so I could at least bind the wound. I hope I did all right," she heard Brennain murmur as he came up behind her to observe his brother. "With the long shaft intact, I could not attempt to stop the bleeding. I did not know what else to do."

Maggie reached out and touched Flynn's throat, praying she found a pulse. A sigh left her body and she hunched her shoulders. "He lives. His pulse is faint, but he lives. With the location of the wound..." She paused and leaned forward to unravel the now-bloodied linen from his lower side, close to the ribs, swallowing hard as her fingers skimmed over the ridges of his tight muscles. She had cared for many large-muscled men before. Muscles never impressed her much, neither had any man. And yet, even near death, Flynn was absolute perfection, with his tapered waist and rippled abdominal muscles covered in a smattering of dark hair. She had seen him without his tunic before, but it never seemed to stop taking her breath away.

Concentrate, Maggie. "Aye, you did well to try to stop the bleeding, and you left enough shaft for me to pull on when I remove it. It appears no major organs have been struck. However, we must pray the arrow is not lodged in his bone." She narrowed her eyes and ran her fingers down his ribs gently, but knew she would have to dig into the wound before she knew for certain.

"What must you do to get it out?" Brennain asked tentatively.

"I must enlarge the wound site. I cannot pull it out without the risk of losing the arrowhead within his body. That would mean almost certain death. I will have to reach in and pull the arrowhead out with the shaft. Pray he stays unconscious. This shall be excruciating."

Brennain stepped closer and knelt next to her, looking at his brother's still, pale face. "Have you done this before, lass?" His worried green eyes flickered to hers before settling back on his brother. Flynn's strong jaw was covered in a few days' worth of dark scruff and she longed to run her fingers through it, but stifled the urge.

"Aye, only once."

"Did the man survive?" Brennain asked cautiously, and held his breath as he awaited her answer.

A frown marred Maggie's face and she pushed her blonde hair behind her ear as she shook her head. "Nay. Few survive this sort of wound, Brennain. An arrow is a particularly deadly weapon because the arrowhead often gets lodged inside the body and causes a blood infection. 'Tis why I must remove it all. I cannot promise he will survive," she whispered.

"I know you will do aught you can, Maggie. We both trust you. Flynn, he... he cares for you, lass. I know he does. See that you save him so mayhap he can tell you someday."

His words made her heart pound in her chest. Brennain must be mistaken. Flynn had never shown her a single moment of interest or tenderness. He was guarded and secretive, walking this world like a silent wind, coming and going without notice to most. Only, she noticed. She knew when he was home and when he was away. And though she feared his presence at times, when he was gone, she felt his absence like an aching void.

Looking at him now, so vulnerable and in need of her aid, she knew she would never forgive herself if she lost him, even if she had no control over his fate. Slipping her satchel off her shoulder, she began to rummage through her healing supplies. She would need some ale to clean the wound, a knife, and forceps.

When she pulled the forceps out of her bag, Brennain grabbed her arm and furrowed his brow. "What will you use these for?" he asked incredulously.

Maggie felt her ire rise. Brennain had already questioned her need to boil the linens, and she was tired of defending her advanced knowledge of medicine. She had trained with the best during her fosterage from the young age of seven and healing was the only thing in her entire life she was certain of. She would reassure Brennain one last time, and then she would continue to save his brother, never accepting his questioning of her practices again.

"Brennain," she said, with an irritated puff of breath. "I am twenty summers in age. I fostered with our village healer in Alba at the age of seven. I oversaw every herbal remedy, every surgery, every stitch she did for ten and two years. She trained in her younger years on a foreign land where the medical knowledge was advanced and proven. I have skills you shall not find anywhere else in Ériu, I can assure you of that. Have you dragged me all the way to your brother's side, only to pester me and scrutinize my every move?"

Her temper threatened to flare in a way it never had before and still, she flinched, expecting him to serve her a blow for speaking so boldly to him. 'Tis what her papa would have done to her mother had she spoken to him thusly. Pulling away slightly and covering her face with her forearm was an instinct she had honed over the years. Her arm had blocked many a strike in her life. He could hit her if he wished, but she could not allow him to continue to berate her skills.

To her surprise, his face softened and a frown formed on his lips. He looked so very much like his brother, it made her heart ache and her patience wane. She needed to get started on saving Flynn, but she had to wait for him to lay his punishment upon her first.

"Lass," Brennain whispered, and gently touched her raised forearm. She flinched and jerked back from his touch. "I will not hit you. I do not know what sort of men you have grown up with, but real men do not hurt women."

"All men hurt women," she murmured, keeping her arm raised.

"Does Àdhamh hurt you? Tell me now and I will stop it."

She shook her head adamantly in refusal. "Nay, my brother has never struck me. He protects me. He is different."

He just stared at her, wide-eyed and mouth agape as he shook his head repeatedly in denial. "I do not know what horrors you have lived, Maggie, but I will not ever hurt you and neither would my brother. You are safe. As for my questioning your skills, I am sorry. I shall never do so again, I give you my vow. Now, please, save Flynn."

Realizing he was not going to strike her and wanting to truly believe his promise, she slowly put her arm down. He most likely only promised not to hurt her so she could help his brother, but for now she had to take his word.

Nodding her head slowly, she looked at Flynn one more time before pouring the ale over the wound site. "The ale shall kill any threat of infection. It cleanses the wound," she said calmly, for Brennain's sake.

Flynn awoke with a howl and began to thrash. Curse it. She knew ale stung terribly. She had used it on herself more than once and not a single man she ever used it on did not at least grit his teeth. She had hoped he was deeply unconscious enough to avoid the pain.

"Flynn," Brennain said calmly, and gripped his brother's shoulders. "'Tis only me and Maggie. She is here to help you! You must calm down, brother!"

Flynn gritted his teeth and clenched his eyes shut, but he nodded slightly in understanding.

"Maggie," he whispered, and shivers ran up her spine. He spoke her name like it was a prayer.

Brennain looked at her knowingly and raised his brow, as if affirming his statement earlier that Flynn had feelings for her. She felt herself flush, but refused to allow her emotions to overwhelm her mind. She had a job to do.

"Flynn, I can help you; it will hurt but you must be still." She shifted to her right, rummaging through her satchel once more before pulling out a tincture.

Holding it up for Brennain to look at, she mouthed, "Poppy Juice" to him, and he nodded as he took it from her. Everyone knew that the juice of poppy seeds could numb the pain of even the largest man if given in the right amounts. Many healers used it to put their injured to sleep before a major procedure, such as this.

"I am giving you poppy juice, Flynn. You must drink it," she ordered, giving him no chance to refuse. It was a foul and bitter liquid, she knew, but it was better than the pain he would feel if he refused it.

It seemed even in his pain, he knew he must do it, for he nodded his head and opened his mouth, allowing Brennain to slowly pour the liquid down his throat. When Maggie decided he had had enough, she took the small jug from Brennain with a nod and set it aside.

"Comfort him until it takes effect," she whispered in Brennain's ear. "Once he is asleep I can work."

"How are you feeling, brother?" Brennain asked awkwardly, and grimaced, knowing his question was ridiculous.

"Like I have an arrow... in my ribs..." he coughed and groaned, reaching to clutch his side in pain, but Maggie grabbed his hand and squeezed it. She had simply meant to prevent him from touching his wound, but the moment her hand held his, he calmed and opened his eyes for the first time since their arrival. His piercing green eyes bore into hers and when he looked at their clenched hands, he squeezed hers in return and forced a smile. "My thanks for coming all this way, Maggie," he croaked with a hoarseness in his voice, before coughing again and averting his gaze.

"Brennain said you are also ill. I have just the thing for that cough. We must control it or you shall only suffer further." Searching her bag, she pulled out a small clay jug, shook its contents and smiled. "'Tis a mixture of honey and *féithleann,* an herb to help with a cough." Pulling the wooden stopper from the top, she swirled the contents once more and held it up to Flynn's lips.

His eyes narrowed as he regarded her and she wondered what he must be thinking. Did he wish to question her the way his brother had? Unlike his brother, if he did have reservations, he was unwilling to speak them. Taking the small jug from her hands, his fingers brushed hers as he drank of its contents.

"There you are, Flynn. I believe it tastes much better than the poppy juice, as well. Between the two, hopefully, much of your discomfort will be eased."

Licking his lips and clearly enjoying the sweet honey flavor, he tilted his head back and yawned. The poppy juice was quickly taking effect and she sighed in relief.

"My thanks, Maggie," he sighed, and reached for her hand once more, gripping it weakly as the juice pulled him into the darkness. "It was indeed sweet, but not as sweet as you are, lass." His eyes closed and she knew she had a few hours before he awakened again.

His words touched her heart, but she did her best to disregard them. Men always complimented her in such a way after she eased their pain with poppy juice. It made their eyes heavy and their tongues loose, often resulting in quick praise for the lass who eased their pain.

Grabbing her knife, clean linens, and forceps, she looked warily at Brennain. "Let us see if he still feels that way when he awakens in a few hours," she mumbled lowly, before making her first cut into his flesh.

Chapter Five

Sky-blue eyes and golden blonde hair floated in and out of his mind like wisps of smoke. He tried to chase them, knowing they belonged to Maggie. He was in some sort of deep sleep, he knew that much for certain. A constant throbbing like a heartbeat nagged at his side, but he focused on the sweet sounds of a soft feminine voice close to his ear.

"'Tis done. The arrowhead hit nay major organs nor bones. He has lost much blood and will be weak for at least a fortnight, and he will have to be monitored constantly to ensure he does not develop an infection of the blood or wound site."

"He will survive?" Flynn heard his brother's voice and wondered why he was in his dream with Maggie, and why they spoke of blood and wounds.

"I cannot say," she sighed. Flynn felt a warm, soft hand grazing his ribs, and the touch soothed him, distracting him from his aching side.

Why were they asking if someone would survive? Who was injured? 'Twas his dream and he wished his brother would leave so he could be alone with the beauty consuming his unconscious.

"When will he awaken?"

"His eyelids have fluttered more than once. I believe he is beginning to awaken. When he does, his pain will be intense, I fear."

Just as the words were spoken, his eyes burst open in panic, pain searing through him, as if he was on fire. A loud gasp, followed by a low moan, escaped his dry, cracked lips and his throat felt hoarse.

"Flynn! 'Tis Brennain. You must be still."

Flynn felt strong hands clamp down on his shoulders to keep him still. "You will tear your stitches."

He stilled in his struggle, exhaustion and pain consuming him. "Stitches?" he repeated gravely.

"Flynn..." He heard her sweet voice again, and turned his eyes to her bonny face, wondering at his fortune. Was he still dreaming? Nay, the pain he felt was quite real. "'Tis Maggie, Flynn. You have been injured. Do you remember?"

Licking his lips, he shook his head, never breaking contact with her blue eyes, the same eyes he had chased in his dream. She felt like his only anchor in a sea of confusion and to look away would surely drown him.

"You were shot with an arrow," Brennain said from beside him, but Flynn kept his gaze on Maggie. Her blonde hair was plaited and draped over one shoulder, but small unruly wisps floated around her perfect heart-shaped face. The dark blue dress she wore made her eyes glow brighter and he could see the fire behind her silhouetting her body. He was certain a goddess stood vigil over him.

"Brennain brought you here and fetched me immediately to your side. I have removed the arrow, Flynn but you have lost too much blood. I had to increase the puncture wound to retrieve the arrow tip. You have a few stitches and you must be mindful not to rip them open."

His hand floated over to the site of his pain and he winced when his fingers touched the tender flesh. Even though his lower torso was bound tightly with linen, his wound was too raw to bear the slightest touch.

"Careful, now," Maggie's soft voice admonished, and she gripped his hand before he could do further damage. "You are still groggy from the poppy juice. Mayhap you should rest more."

He wanted to resist the urge to close his heavy eyelids. He wanted to gaze upon her bonny face some more. In the end, his mind and body won the battle, forcing him into an unwilling sleep.

* * * *

A tickle so sharp it made his eyes water tugged at the back of his throat. Even in his hazy state, he recognized the danger of coughing with the stitches. He braced his side as the rough cough came up his throat and jolted his body. Flynn grimaced and cursed the illness that still plagued him.

"I have tea. 'Twill soothe your throat."

Opening his eyes, he saw Maggie standing over him again as she had before, only this time she held a mug of hot liquid in her outstretched hands, steam rising into the air.

"How long..." He could not finish the words before another cough wracked his body and he grimaced.

With a concerned frown, Maggie gently sat beside him on the edge of the bed, bringing the mug up to his lips. "Hush now, Flynn. Drink this."

He did as she bade, feeling the warm liquid slide down his scratchy throat, the sweetness of honey on his tongue. "Were you asking how long you have been out?"

Looking up at her as he took another sip, he nodded, thankful she understood his question without him having to speak further.

"'Tis been several hours. It is now mid-day. Brennain went out to chop more wood. I also have a rabbit stew in the cauldron. Brennain caught it this morn. 'Tis a fine hideout you men have found. It has dried herbs for food and all that I need to prepare a meal. There is a wild kitchen garden just around the side. I was able to harvest some carrots. We shall eat well, at least."

She smiled as he took another sip. "My thanks," he croaked. He wanted to say something more, but he was quite weak and still trying to figure out what all of this meant for his mission. Guilt, shame, and defeat consumed him. He had failed his king. Mal and his men were close. Now that the haze of poppy juice had worn off, he could remember every detail of that day. He had been aching and coughing, which no doubt alerted a warrior hiding in the trees to their whereabouts. He and his brother had not seen him at all, nor suspected the attack. It was humbling to admit he had erred, but it still did not change the fact that they had a mission to accomplish.

A loud pounding at the door made his body tense, but then he recognized the five-knock pattern of his brother. Maggie got up swiftly to open the door and Brennain walked through with a pile of logs stacked in his muscled arms. Brennain's green eyes locked on Flynn's and a wide smile spread across his face when he saw that his brother was awake.

"How do you fare, brother?" Brennain walked over to the back of the house, added the logs to the already well-stocked stack of wood, and wiped his hands on his now-filthy beige trousers.

Focusing on the pulsing pain coming from his side, Flynn knew he had much more healing to do, but he could see the concern in his brother's eyes. "I will survive," Flynn responded, and grimaced as he tried to shift his weight into a more comfortable position. "As soon as I am able to travel, we will finish our mission."

Brennain crinkled his brow and stepped closer. Maggie tittered nervously and got up from the bed swiftly, leaving a trail of rose and lavender in her wake. Flynn's eye shifted to her briefly and he knew she was nervous, being so far away from home and alone with two men.

"About our mission..." Brennain sighed, putting his hands on his hips. "Our king forbade me to allow you to accompany me." He cringed as the words left his lips, and Flynn knew they pained him very much to speak.

"I do not understand. I am forbidden... to accompany *you*? Were you not to accompany *me*? 'Twas my mission to begin with." His ire rose as the consequences of his injury slammed down on him like an avalanche of boulders, squeezing the air from his lungs. So much of his life had been given to this task and he had finally been given the opportunity to do something that matters, and he ruined it by getting himself injured. The mission still needed to be completed and his king knew he was unable to complete the task. Failure gnawed at his gut, making him wish to tear his hair out.

"I shall be well enough to travel in a matter of days—"

"Nay." Maggie came forward and shook her head. "'Twill take a fortnight at the very least, Flynn. You are unwell..."

Anger unlike anything he had ever felt in his entire life flooded his veins. He was not a man prone to temper outbursts, in fact he was hard-pressed to think of a time when he had truly lost his temper at all. Calm, quiet, and calculated—those were the qualities that made him blasted good at what he did. His missions were all he had and now he had lost the most important of them all. After over a year of journeying into the woods, tracking down Mac Rochride, and reporting back to his king, he had finally received the mission he had longed to accomplish. He was made for this, to infiltrate their ranks and gather information. He could not stay here to rot while his brother completed *his* task.

Before he could control his outburst and convince himself to stay calm, he found frustration seeping out of his every pore, manifesting itself into words he knew he would immediately regret. "Stay out of this, Maggie! 'Tis none of your concern!" he roared, causing the wee lass to shake and retreat into the corner. Fear laced her features as her face grew pale.

"Do not speak to her that way! You would be a dead man if not for her!" Brennain bellowed in admonishment.

Flynn deserved it, aye, but he had more anger to spill before he could calm his nerves. "You have grown fond of her, I see," Flynn snarled, feeling envy eat away at his gut. It cut deeper than the wound at his side. Jealousy was a foreign emotion to him. Maggie's praise for Brennain repeated in his mind. She said Brennain had been cutting logs. Brennain had caught the rabbit for the stew. What else had Brennain done to impress his Maggie while Flynn lay like an invalid on this foul, itchy straw mattress? Being helpless did not sit well with Flynn and now he was taking it all out on the only two people he had in this world. He knew he needed to calm himself.

Looking over at Maggie, he saw her back was turned to him as she slowly stirred the cauldron with a large wooden spoon. Her body trembled slightly and he cursed himself a bastard. "Och, I am sorry, Maggie." His throat still burned, but if he had been able to use words to release his anger, he could use them to apologize. She flinched when he spoke her name and he ran a frustrated hand through his tangled black hair.

"Aye. I have grown fond of her, Flynn. She came to you without a thought for herself. She saved your life. I will defend her against you and your pride any cursed day," his brother groused, crossing his arms over his chest.

With a calming deep breath, Flynn tore his gaze away from Maggie's back and focused on the one person who would at least still speak to him. "I am not used to feeling worthless. I suppose my disappointment at my failure mixed with my pride caused me to shout out of turn. I am sorry, brother."

Brennain raised his brow in apparent shock. Flynn almost never had reason to apologize for aught, but he never hesitated to do so, when necessary. Why did his brother look so surprised?

"As I was saying," Brennain continued as if the outburst never happened, and Flynn was thankful for it. "Our King bade me go alone. You know you cannot go, Flynn. Aye, you did much of the work on this and I am sorry to have to go without you, but it must be done."

Flynn held up his hand weakly in defeat and nodded. "Aye, I know. I do not like it but I understand."

"I am sorry, Flynn. I do not wish to go without you, but I have nay choice. Maggie will be here with you." Then Brennain turned to look at Maggie. "You will be all right here until I can return, lass? I shall try to check in, but I do not know how far his camp is from here or how much freedom I shall have."

Flynn looked over at Maggie and saw her spine stiffen. Still, she refused to turn to look at him or his brother. Asking her to stay away from her life for at least a fortnight was asking much of the lass. He would not be able to take her home for a long while and he would need to stay here in case Brennain reported back or needed help. She was as good as trapped, and that made Flynn feel even worse for shouting at her.

"Maggie, I am sorry you are in this position," Flynn added softly. "I have made a mess of everything."

Finally turning, she wrung her hands together nervously in front of her. "I will be quite all right. Do as our king commands. I will take care of Flynn." She spoke directly to Brennain without even acknowledging him and that made his heart ache in a way he had never expected. He rubbed his chest to try to soothe the sudden squeezing pain. Maggie affected him more than he suspected and that thought scared him. He could not afford to grow attached to the lass, yet he found he already was. How could he spend a fortnight in her company and not completely fall in love with her? He looked from her to Brennain. Had Brennain fallen in love with her as well? That ache in his heart persisted at the thought.

Flynn shook his head, determined to keep his thoughts straight and logical. It was just as well she ignored him. Though he found the lass incredibly attractive, he knew little about her aside from the evidence of her being more frightened than a mouse being chased by a cat. He had no time to get involved with a lass such as her. She was clearly innocent in the ways of men, and anything beyond the basic fulfillment of pleasure was more than he could promise to any lass. When he was fully healed, he had every intention of joining his brother to finish their mission.

Brennain bowed his head to her, then turned back to Flynn, shooting him a look with his narrowed gaze. It was a clear warning to behave where Maggie was concerned. His brother need not speak to communicate clearly. He also was a fool for believing Flynn needed any warnings. He had lost his temper, aye, but it was rare and he knew he would not do so again.

"I will enjoy some stew and pack up a few supplies, then I must be on my way. I pray the gods give you a full recovery, brother. I am glad you are as well as you are. We have Maggie to thank for that." Both brothers shifted their gaze to Maggie, who looked at them with wide eyes, as if unsure why they would have need to thank her. She had no idea what a giving, selfless lass she truly was. Very few people would have willingly given up all she had to come so far to help one man.

"I will check in if I can. If I cannot, then I will see you when I see you."

"Be careful, Brennain. Remember what the man in the woods said. He knew we had been on Mal's trail. Mal planted men all around his camp because he knows Tuathal is sending scouts. If there were other men in the trees, they may have seen your face."

Brennain nodded in understanding. "I do not believe there were. I killed the man who took you down and nay men came to his aid. In fact, there is a better chance that they know your face more than my own."

With a raised brow, Flynn said, "You look just like me."

"Nay, wee brother. *You* look just like *me*. I am your elder, and do not forget it." Brennain winked, and Flynn knew his brother was taking his opportunity to get a rise from Flynn while he was unable to do aught about it.

"Then you had better hope nobody knows my face, elder brother. Be safe," he urged. Brennain's smile slid off his face as he grew serious once more. With a nod, his hand gripped the hilt of his sword before he walked over to the cauldron to partake of Maggie's stew.

Flynn still felt bitter that he had to stay behind, but his side was aching terribly and he gritted his teeth against the pain. It was going to be a very painful, and interesting, fortnight alone here with Maggie. He would feel like a fool having her take care of his needs. Flynn had always taken care of himself, despite their mother's constant doting. He was not a lad to stand by while others cared for him. Aye, it would be a struggle, but at least he had Maggie's bonny face to look upon in the meantime.

* * * *

What mess had she gotten herself into? She was completely alone in the middle of the woods with Flynn Mac Greine and she had no idea when she would ever make it home again. His outburst had frightened her more than she wished to admit. Even a man as calm as Flynn was able to lose his temper, but when his temper had flared toward her, her instinct had been to flee. She had not even been alone with him yet and he was already shouting at her the way Papa had shouted at Mama. Papa had always apologized for it afterward, but it always happened again.

She knew Flynn felt awful for shouting at her and she wanted to believe that he had good reasons to be angry. She had no idea what he and Brennain spoke of when they discussed their mission or the king's orders, but it was clearly important to Flynn and he was rightfully upset to lose his chance. That rational thought made her calm down somewhat. He was only a man, capable of anger and disappointment, much like any human. He was injured, bound to a bed, removed from his important mission, and stuck in this dank hut with a lass as plain and most likely as boring as any he had encountered. He was most likely wishing he was stuck with a lass who was bonnier or would take care of his other needs, not simply his wounds.

Och, she knew the ways of the world. Just as Elwynna had been used to satisfy the needs of men, few men would hesitate to take what they wanted when they wanted. While Flynn was incapable of moving, she was safe. But what would happen once he could get out of bed and she was still stuck in this hut with him? Would he keep his boundaries, or would he try to force himself on her? She had never heard a foul word against Flynn in all the time she had been living in Ráth Mór. Still, no woman had ever been stuck in a hut with him for so long. Who knew what he would do?

Breathe, Maggie. She needed to stop torturing herself with the worst possibilities. She hated being so cursed afraid all the time, but she refused to become another victim to any man. Somehow, in a very short time, she had begun to trust Brennain. He had vowed never to hurt her, and he had been quite calm and gentle. He also vowed Flynn would not hurt her, but within moments of being awake, he had lashed out at her. If he had not been bedridden, would he have struck her? She was uncertain. How she wished Brennain had not left. He had quickly become the only other man, besides Àdhamh, whom she could trust.

Thinking of her brother made her heart drop and she had to hold back her tears. She had left without a word to him. She knew she had had no time to locate him and explain why she had to go. She also knew Àdhamh would have tried to make her stay. He protected her fiercely and while she appreciated his constant concern for her, she was a woman: full grown and capable of her own decisions. Looking around the quiet hut, she wondered if her decision to come here had been a bad one. Àdhamh would never find her out here, even if he attempted to. She was trapped here until Brennain could return.

A few hours had passed since he left, taking half the stew with him for his journey. She did not mind. He had caught the rabbit himself and would need the food, considering he had not a clue how long his journey would be. Before he left, Brennain showed Maggie how to use the nets to catch small game and walked her toward a stream that ran just east of the hut. She had access to fresh water, buckets, nets, a small garden of vegetables that were hearty enough to last a fortnight or longer, and enough wood to burn. They would be warm and fed, and Maggie felt an unusual sense of pride knowing she would be the one to gather all the food, build the fires and run the home.

During their walk, she had spotted many berries and herbs she could not wait to get her hands on. Bilberries were everywhere in Ériu at this time of year and not only were they hearty, they were said to be one of the healthiest foods a person could eat. Though it was a bit late in the season and most berries in her village would have been collected, out here in the wilderness, she had all the berries to herself. She could pick wild herbs and mayhap discover new plants.

Her spirits lifted slightly. She had been just telling herself how very badly she wished to get out to see the world. This could be her chance. After all, Flynn did not require her constant attention and would most likely appreciate having her out and about most of the days, allowing him to rest or simply be away from her constant presence.

"Maggie?" Flynn's voice floated over to her from the bed. He sounded weak and slightly hesitant, which made her frown. How could a man as strong and handsome as Flynn possibly be hesitant about anything?

"Aye?" She looked up and turned away from the fire she had been mindlessly staring into for the past several hours while he slept.

"I... need to..." His voice trailed off before she heard the rest of his muffled sentence.

Furrowing her brow, she stood up and slowly walked over to him, making sure to stay out of reaching distance in case he tried to grab her. She was being ridiculous, she knew, but she had grown up always being vigilant. "What do you need, Flynn?"

"I need to piss."

Och. She had not given any thought to this part of caring for him. Looking around the room, she found a bronze pot and swiftly moved to grab it. "Here." She thrust the pot into his hands and turned away.

"I cannot piss lying down," he murmured.

"Right," she agreed hesitantly. Walking back toward him, she looked down at him and sighed. "I can help you sit up but 'twill hurt you terribly."

"I hurt terribly now. And holding my piss for the past three hours has not helped." He sounded irritated and she wanted to scowl at him, but kept her face neutral.

"I never asked you to hold your... piss," she said, and cleared her throat.

"You are too afraid to come near me, and I did not wish to aggrieve you," he countered. "I shall not hurt you, Maggie. I would never hurt or force a lass. Is this what you fear?" Hurt flashed in his eyes. It was the same look she had seen on Brennain's face. These men did not like their honor being questioned. She supposed that was a fine trait in a man, but honor also caused men to do things in the name of pride. Once pride and honor were damaged, men could lose their temper, she knew.

Suddenly, Maggie felt weary of her fears constantly controlling every move she made. In that moment, she made a vow to herself. No more being afraid of her own shadow. She would not allow her fears to control her any longer. What sort of a life was she living when she was too afraid to even speak? And if Flynn dared to hurt her, she would make certain his brother heard about it upon his return. "Nay, I am not afraid of you." She forced the words to sound as confident and calm as she could.

"Then please help me," he said, so desperately that any real fear left her immediately and was replaced by pity and a bit of shame. He was a vulnerable man right now and had not done anything to make her fear him, aside from his one show of anger. He needed her help and she would give it.

Walking over to Flynn, she gently lifted him to a sitting position. He hollered at the pain but there was no way of sitting him up without having to use the injured part of his side. "This will not work, Flynn. Your wound is much too new. We will do this another way."

"'Tis embarrassing," he groaned as he plopped down. "Asking a bonny lass to help me piss is quite humbling."

She paused. He thought her bonny? How could such a handsome, strong, and brave man have ever even noticed she existed? She supposed he had to notice now that they were alone, but to think her bonny was quite a shock. She hid her flush as best she could while she thought of another way to help him with his delicate situation. In all her years healing injured men, never had she been their sole caretaker, having to worry about details such as helping them relieve themselves, nor did she know how to help him now. Just the thought of... that part of him, made her feel an unfamiliar mix of uncertainty and curiosity. What does his look like? She had seen a few in her life, even if she did not wish to. Did she wish to see his? The tingle rolling down her body told her that she did, even if it was shameful to think about Flynn in that manner while he was in her care.

"Maggie?" His questioning voice pulled her thoughts back to the present.

"If you roll over onto your uninjured side, I can hold the pot while you... handle the rest."

He nodded, deciding it was the best option and rolled onto his side away from her. This meant she would have to lean over his body, which was precisely what she did not want to have to do. Bracing herself with one hand against the cold wall, she positioned the pot beside him. He pulled the thick fur away from his body and began to fumble with the tie on his trousers, cursing under his breath as his clumsy hands shook.

After what felt like an eternity, Flynn growled with frustration. "The string is tangled," he murmured.

Maggie looked down to see that he was having a very hard time getting the string from his trousers undone. She almost offered to help, but caught herself just before the words came out. She pursed her lips and crinkled her brow when her gaze caught his. Flynn's eyelids slid shut and he turned away. "I need help," he whispered.

Pity for the man filled Maggie. He was a strong warrior and obviously one of the king's finest to be constantly sent on important missions. For him to be injured and dependent on a lass to untie his trousers so he could relieve himself must be humiliating, and she loathed to add any more discomfort for him.

Silently, Maggie placed the pot down beside him and leaned closer, using her nails to dig into the frayed woolen string of his trousers. He really ought to have these repaired, but that was none of her concern, except that it was now her task to untangle it.

Aside from the popping of the hearth behind her, the entire room was silent as she frantically worked at the knot. The muscles on his bare chest bunched and strained as her hands worked. She tried to concentrate but she was so distracted by his masculine scent and the beauty of him that she had to swallow more than once.

Flynn stayed stiff as a wooden board and averted his eyes when she finally got the last of the knot out and his trousers slackened. The trail of dark hair on his lower abdomen continued below his waistline and she wondered about what else was beneath his trousers, before scolding herself for allowing her mind to wander once more. It was improper to stare at his body, especially that part of him she could see bulging just beneath the fabric of his trousers. She tried not to notice, but it was at eye level as she tugged on the string and it was just so... large. Having spent her entire life avoiding men and therefore, all parts of them, she was flustered at being so close to his male parts. Aye, as a healer she had been close to many men, but never so close to their nether regions where she could see its outline up close, or felt that pulse of excitement in her own body at the thought of seeing more. She tried to focus on her breathing and knew her chest heaved more than normal. She hoped Flynn would not notice her sudden flush or flustered movements.

Finally tearing her gaze away, she looked at his face and gasped at the intensity staring back at her. His green eyes were hooded by heavy lids and he seemed to be memorizing her every feature, just as she did the same. He was the most beautiful man she had ever seen and though it seemed ridiculous for such a large, masculine man to be beautiful, he truly was. Many in his family had bright green eyes, but none more vibrant than Flynn's, or mayhap that was simply her unnerving attraction to him exaggerating their beauty. His tan skin and black hair gave him a dark, mysterious edge that only drew her in more. He was, without a doubt, the most well-made man she had ever met. Still, she knew nothing about him or his mysterious missions, or what he was capable of.

That thought brought her spiraling back down to reality. She was much too close and though he was injured, she would be wise to keep her guard up, especially with the way he was looking at her. "'Tis done," she whispered, and leaned over once more to grab the pot. "Are you... ready?"

Flynn shot up from the bed, standing abruptly and using the wall for balance as his free hand held his trousers around his waist. Maggie gasped and backed away, unsure of what he was doing. He groaned and pushed off the wall, swerving slightly but holding his ground. He turned and stepped toward her with a look in his eyes that was nothing less than pure determination. She wanted to run, but her feet betrayed her and refused to move. Dazed with fear, Maggie's eyes widened as he took another step toward her. He was large, half-naked with his trousers only loosely held in one hand, and obviously powerful enough to ignore the pain of such a terrible wound. As he came closer, his large frame towering above her, she flinched and closed her eyes, awaiting his punishment for whatever she had done wrong. Had she taken too long to undo his string? Her papa would have punished her mama for much less.

When no strike came, she opened her eyes slowly and looked back up at him hesitantly. His brow dropped and a frown pulled at his lips. Putting out one hand, he gestured at the bronze pot she was clutching with white-knuckled intensity in front of her body. "The pot," he growled, just before yanking it out of her hands with force. She screeched and backed up a step. He was going to use the pot to beat her and even when injured, she knew he was much stronger than she was. Why could she not move, or run? What sort of survival instincts had she learned in all these years if the best she could do in the face of an aggressive man was to stare and stand still?

"Leave, Maggie. Make sure Arawn has food and water... please," he forced and winced. Aye, he was in great pain, yet for some reason he was out of bed, ordering her to feed someone named Arawn? Who was Arawn and why was Flynn demanding she leave? "My horse," he clarified through clenched teeth.

She was so frightened by his sudden show of aggression that she did not wait even a moment longer to run for the door, away from him. He confused her more than any man ever had in her life. One moment he was kind and gentle, and she was certain she could trust him. The next moment he was jumping out of bed and storming toward her, demanding she leave. Mayhap he had a fever and was temporarily mad? Maggie had noticed sweat beading on his brow as he tore the pot from her hands. She would check later. For now, her heart beat so fast, she could hardly breathe. She wanted to run far away from Flynn Mac Greine, but knew she was trapped in the middle of nowhere until Brennain came back for them... until then, she would have to be brave, tend Flynn's wound, and avoid him as much as possible.

Chapter Six

The moment Maggie was out of the house, Flynn collapsed back onto the bed and wiped the sweat from his face. His side ached fiercely and it had been a mistake to force himself out of the bed. But when her wee, soft hands kept accidentally grazing the bulge in his trousers as she tried to undo the knot, it had taken every ounce of control he owned not to grow hard before her eyes. She was an innocent lass trying to care for him. She would not appreciate seeing his desire so boldly on display. But then the knot came loose, his trousers slackened, and he saw her gazing upon his body. Her eyes locked on his cock, then moved to his chest. It had been an innocent curious inspection, he knew. Maggie was much too timid to ever boldly stare. And yet, that curiosity from the innocent lass of his dreams had made him go rock hard.

She held that cursed pot in her hands, prepared to help him piss, but she would have swooned had she seen what lay beneath his trousers. There had been no way to hide it and it most definitely was not going to go away. But he could not relieve himself with a hard cock. So, in his panic, he jumped out of the bed and decided to manage the task himself. And to do so, she had to be gone. Before he could relieve his bladder, he had to relieve his desire.

Collapsing on the bed and sprawling on his back, he prayed to all the gods she would stay away long enough to allow him to stroke himself until his pleasure was spent. It was a humiliating moment, but with his desire running rampant and no other relief in sight, he had to take care of his body's base urges if he was to remain near the beautiful Maggie without a huge erection all the cursed time.

Once he was done imagining his own hand was Maggie's, and then waiting several moments before being able to piss in the pot, he pulled his trousers up over his hips and decided to leave them untied. The cursed string was so frayed, it would only knot up again and as much as he enjoyed her hands so near his body, it also led to a situation he could not allow. Once he was healed, he would be off to his solitary life again, running missions for his king. There was simply no place in his life for Maggie and he had to remind himself of that every blasted moment. She was too innocent to simply have a few sweet moments of bliss with him like a serving lass, and he could not offer her marriage... not that she seemed at all interested in him. In fact, she seemed rather terrified of him.

Flynn cursed himself a bastard. His abrupt jump from the bed had frightened the life out of the lass. By the way she froze in place and stared up at him like a cornered animal, he knew she feared him. And when he approached her to grab the pot, she flinched, clearly awaiting some punishment, for what, he had no idea. Had she seen the reason for his behavior straining beneath his trousers, she would have likely been even more frightened.

A sudden realization hit him fast and hard. Maggie was a victim of some form of abuse. No lass flinched as often as Maggie did without cause.

Fool that he was, he always assumed she was simply timid, but now it made sense. When she was around larger groups of people or absorbed in her work, she felt confident and safe; yet when she was alone with just men, she was fearful. He wanted to rip the spine out of whomever had hurt his Maggie. And since when had he started considering her *his* Maggie? He was out of his mind for her and she was scared to death of him. His heart lurched at that realization. It was just as well that she had no attraction to him, but to fear him? Nay, it was not to be borne.

He had behaved like a brute. He was a brute. He needed to control his desire for her, and chasing her away to hide it was not going to work. He could not have Maggie, but could he show her that not all men are violent? Could he make her see she could trust him? This would require him to open up to her, which he had so thoroughly avoided in the past. Keeping people at a distance made his comings and goings much simpler. He knew he could not remain closed to her and earn her trust. It suddenly became the most important goal in his life. Nothing else mattered more than teaching Maggie to trust again. He could not stand to watch her flinch or cower anymore. Mayhap once she learned to trust him, she could open herself up to a real relationship with a man and find love, marriage, and a family.

The thought of Maggie with another man, carrying his child, made his stomach churn with envy. He would essentially be helping her move on to love another and yet, he would make that sacrifice if it meant she did not have to live in the shadows any longer. She was much too sweet, kind, and bonny to be living with her brother and his wife for the rest of her life. This would be Flynn's gift to her, his repayment for her own sacrifices for him.

With new motivation to heal before Brennain returned, he laid in the bed patiently. He realized he had not coughed since Maggie gave him the tea. She was truly wondrous. Aye, he owed her this service, to have a life of love, not fear. And if that life of love was with another man, well, it was worth the sacrifice, but only just barely.

The door opened with a creak and he saw Maggie's bonny face peek through the crack. Her blonde hair glowed as sunlight streamed in from behind her, and her bright blue eyes widened with apprehension. When she noticed he was back in his bed, obvious relief crossed her face and she stepped back in. It stung, but he had to remind himself that it was his own cursed fault for acting like an arse.

"How is the weather, Maggie?" he asked, desperately seeking a topic to discuss with her. He scolded himself for having no experience with small talk. He was not one to bed many lassies, but when he did, it was for the express purpose of pleasure and little talking was ever done. The only women he ever had conversations with were his family. And he could not very well speak about bows or hunting as he would with Aislin, or tease her the way he did Treasa, Alyson, or Queen Leannan, his cousins. Maggie was the first unrelated lass he had ever attempted to truly know, and he feared he was horrible at it.

"'Tis cold," she replied with a bit of an edge. As she came in further, he realized his error. He had chased her away so fast, she had left without her cursed cloak. Her nose was nipped pink from the cold weather and her luscious waves of blonde hair were tousled from the wind. Though she looked good enough to devour, he was certain she was uncomfortable and flustered. How he wished to get out of this bed and help her build up the fire, but he would never recover if he continued to get up. He must allow himself to heal so he could get Maggie out of the house and mayhap earn more trust as they walked. Mayhap he could show interest in her work.

"I apologize. I did not mean to chase you off, Maggie. I was frustrated at my inability to untie my own trousers and see to my own needs." That was the truth, or at least as much as he could give without frightening her.

"I understand," she replied softly. "You are a man used to doing everything by himself. Having a lass care for you must be very hard."

He coughed when she said the word 'hard'. She had no idea how hard it truly was to keep from touching her, or what he had been doing to himself while she was outside. Fortunately, she mistook his cough of shock as a cough from his illness and rushed forward, putting one cold hand on his forehead.

"What are you doing?"

"You had sweat on your brow before I left the house. I was afraid you were catching a fever but you feel all right. Are you feeling hot?"

Aye, he had been hot and sweaty before she left and though part of it had indeed been from his arousal, he knew some of it had been from the searing pain in his side when he stood up. It had been a bad idea to jump out of bed, though he would do it again if it meant shielding Maggie from his obvious lust for her. "I am well. It was from the pain."

Licking her lips, she nodded and backed away slowly, as if she considered him a feral cat ready to pounce on her. He noticed a yellow plant in her other hand and decided to change the subject. "'Tis a nice flower. You enjoy collecting plants?"

She looked down at the flower as if she had forgotten she still clutched the wee yellow plant in her hand. "Oh, aye." She blushed and turned away from him, walking toward the table near the cauldron to place it down.

"Tell me about them." He needed to engage her, make her feel comfortable and safe, and he truly was interested in her knowledge of plants. How she could turn a normal plant that he would otherwise walk past into a healing herb was truly a skill.

Her brows rose as she turned to look at him. "You are interested in plants?"

"I am interested in you, so I am interested in what interests you." She blushed again and he smiled. Och, he wished his life was different. Never before had he wanted anyone or anything other than what he already had. He knew she was not for him, but it still made his chest ache to know he would never truly know her beyond whatever shallow connection they made while he healed.

"These," she held them up for him to see, "are dandelions. They are most hearty. They can grow in all weather, even snow at times. They are also extraordinary. They make the healthiest of teas. I was planning to make you some mixed with mint and honey. 'Twill soothe your cough. I am pleased you have nay fever."

His heart warmed to know that, even though he had chased her away, she still thought of him while collecting those flowers. "My thanks," he replied, feeling humbled and remorseful. "You are a kind lass."

She stayed silent as she prepared his tea. He wanted desperately to know what she was thinking. When she came over to hand him his clay mug, filled to the brim with steaming tea, he inhaled the sweet scent and took it from her hands, gently grazing her fingers with his. He made sure to make it appear accidental, but he had truly wished to feel her soft skin again. He was a fool for her. There had been an inexplicable pull toward her from the first moment he saw her and, even though he knew it was a one-sided interest, he found his desire to know her growing more and more every moment.

"Maggie," he croaked, before taking his first sip. "I truly am sorry that I frightened you earlier. At times I may seem rough or stubborn, but I vow I would never hurt you. I wish you were not afraid of me."

Chewing on her bottom lip as she listened, his heart stopped in his chest as he awaited her reply. Her gaze raked over him slowly and he wondered what she was pondering. Had any other lass looked at him in that manner, he would know precisely what she was thinking, but Maggie was different and that was just one reason Flynn could not seem to get her off his mind. She was unlike any other lass he had ever met.

"Brennain told me I can trust you, and I trust him. He has proven himself gentle with me. I wish to trust you, Flynn. You vow never to strike me or... force yourself upon me?"

Her answer shocked him. She admitted she feared him, but she was willing to try to trust him. It also solidified his belief that she had been violated in some way in the past. His blood boiled with anger but he had to be careful not to upset her.

"I vow it. Maggie, I would never do such a thing. Never."

She nodded and gave him a weak smile in response. "All right, then. I shall work on trusting you, Flynn. I would like that. Believe it or not, I do not enjoy being fearful of men. 'Tis a matter of survival, a learned behavior..." Her voice trailed off and Flynn frowned.

Her words alluded to what he had suspected. Someone had hurt her. She was from Alba and likely her abuser was still there as well. He vowed that once he was well and done with his mission, he would find the bastard and gut him for what he had done to Maggie's spirit. First, he would need her to trust him enough to tell him who her abuser was, and now was not the right time to ask her questions.

He took a sip of his tea and closed his eyes. It was sweet and minty, and it warmed him from the inside out. Maggie moved over to the stack of wood against the other wall and grabbed a log, throwing it into the hearth. He considered their conversation a small victory. He had a long way to go to earn her trust, but he was more determined than ever to do just that.

"Night is approaching and you need your rest. The only reason you were able to get up earlier was from the pain-numbing effects of the poppy juice. You will be in great pain soon enough."

He already was in a great deal of pain. His wound pulsed and his entire side felt as if it was on fire. But pain was part of the life he lived. He would grit his teeth and bear it. Sipping the tea again, the warmth comforted him, and he felt his lids lowering.

Maggie was watching him as she drank a mug of tea, as well. Walking over to him, she took the mug, tucked the furs tightly around his body, and placed her hand on his forehead one more time. "You must rest, Flynn. In the morn, I will change your bandage."

* * * *

A dry, bitter taste coated his mouth and he awoke with a grimace. His throat was still slightly sore, but he could swallow much easier at least. Trying to shift his weight, he groaned at the pulsing pain in his side. Cursed wound. He had actually forgotten about it, he slept so well.

"Be still, Flynn." A soft, warm hand touched his arm and stilled his movements. Maggie. He relaxed under her touch and opened his eyes to look at her. She was wearing naught but her underdress and he swallowed hard. The hearth fire raged behind her and he wondered if she realized how sheer the thin linen fabric was when she was silhouetted in the light. She had the tiniest waist and the most gentle curve to her hips. She was a wee woman, her breasts a touch smaller than most, but they were perfect for her frame. She was the most beautiful woman he had ever seen and he wanted to keep her safe from any man who would hurt her.

"Here," she handed him a clay mug filled with cool water. "You likely have a bitter taste in your mouth. 'Tis an effect of the poppy juice. But it also helped you sleep through the night. May I check your wound?"

Feeling the fresh water slide down his throat, he felt instant relief for his parched mouth. Swallowing the cool liquid and reveling in the easing of his aching throat, he smiled and nodded to Maggie.

Leaning over him, her free blonde waves fell across her face like a curtain and her hands skimmed the bare flesh of his abdomen as she untied the linen wrapped around his wound. Small traces of blood seeped through the bandage and he grimaced as the fabric came off his skin, exposing the now stitched up wound. "How does it feel?" Maggie asked while her fingers slowly grazed over the skin just around her impeccable stitches. "Does it feel overly tender at the wound site?"

He watched her fingers glide over his skin and gooseflesh formed on his arms. She was like a goddess tending him and suddenly being injured was worth the reward of her constant presence. "It does not hurt much on the surface. The pain is within," Flynn replied, shifting his gaze to her soft profile.

72

She nodded at his response and leaned even closer to his wound. Her head was so close to his bare chest, he could feel her warm breath tickling across his skin. If she did not stop, he would soon grow hard for her again. And this time, he would not be able to run away. He had vowed not to frighten her, though he was not certain which would frighten her more: his abruptly leaving the bed again, or his massive erection pushing against his trousers. He never knew he could be so badly injured and still so easily aroused, but she had complete control over him. Her night dress was not helping matters.

"It is not showing any signs of infection. The skin is slightly red, but not alarmingly so, and I see nay signs of unusual drainage." She stood up and put her hands on her hips. A soft smile touched her lips. "I do believe you shall heal well, Flynn Mac Greine. In truth, the wound was not as deep as I had feared. The arrow only hit flesh and the archer must have been several yards away, for the impact was much less severe than a close hit would have been. I will keep a close eye on you, but I do think all will be well. You will likely heal before Brennain returns." He saw her smile falter after she spoke those words, though he could not understand why his swift recovery would alarm her.

"My thanks, Maggie. You are a truly wonderful healer. I feel awful that you have left your brother and Elwynna and must remain stuck here with me." She was utterly trapped, in fact, and he hoped she did not panic or resent him.

Chewing her bottom lip, Maggie shrugged and sat on the edge of the hay mattress he laid on. Her backside bumped his thigh and he enjoyed feeling the warmth of her body seeping into his. Reaching into her satchel at the edge of the bed, she began to rummage for some supplies. "'Tis not so bad, after all. I mean, I would prefer it if you were not injured, of course. But I was only just telling myself the other day that I longed for a bit of... adventure." Her rosy cheeks blushed a brighter red and she opened a jar of salve, gently rubbing the slimy substance over his wound.

Flynn crinkled his nose at the smell of the stuff and she giggled. It was the sweetest sound he had ever heard, especially with her sitting so close. Had she taken his word that he would not harm her? She seemed much more at ease this morn.

"This is a salve of burdock root and garlic. It smells, I know, but they work well to fight infection and heal skin. If there is nay infection of your blood, you should be all right. I would be seeing signs of a fever by now, I believe. You bled a lot, but that is good. Wounds that bleed more tend to become infected less. I do not know why, but... och, look at me, rambling on about things you do not care about."

"That is not true. I am learning so much from you, Maggie, and I love your passion for healing. To think you can find a plant in the wild and know precisely how to use it. You are a rare and wonderful woman."

Her blush increased and she covered her cheeks to try to hide the evidence. He meant every word he said and meant it even deeper than he could express. A tightening in his stomach told him that he was becoming much too attached to the lass. He wanted to know all of her, inside and out. He also knew he would miss her keenly when their time was over, and he had not been with her for more than two days yet. How could he feel this way so quickly? Though his interest in her had developed some time ago, all it had taken was a couple days for him to feel a shift in his heart.

Pulling out a long strip of clean linen from her satchel, she reached around his waist to wrap the fabric tightly. He arched his back slightly to allow her beneath him, and when he did so, she leaned forward for better reach. Their chests bumped and their faces were only inches apart. He had never been so close to Maggie and he suddenly saw the very small freckles that dotted her nose and cheeks. He also noticed that her sky-blue eyes darkened the closer they got to the pupil.

Then, she felt it and her eyes wandered down toward the offending bulge. He looked as well and cursed himself for leaving his trouser loose the night before. Now his desire for her was more than obvious beneath his trousers, and worse yet, they had inched down his hips just enough to allow the tip to peek out of the top.

Taking a deep breath with a slight gasp, Maggie pulled back and continued to tie off the linen with shaky fingers. Flynn stilled, making sure she knew he would not touch her. He enjoyed the trust she was showing and did not want to do aught to destroy it. He berated himself, though he had not meant for such a thing to happen.

He only wanted to prevent another knot in the tie of his trousers, but he could not help it that he grew painfully hard when her breasts grazed his chest.

When she was done, she swiftly stood up from the bed and took a few quick steps backward, just out of arm's reach, he noted. Her survival instincts were practiced and ingrained into her every move. She had had to dodge more than one attack, he suddenly realized. He wanted to ask, but kept his mouth shut.

"Thank you," he softly whispered, as calmly and kindly as he could while he pulled the furs over his groin again.

She nodded and wrung her hands, clearly in some sort of inner battle to be brave and stay, or allow fear to take over and flee.

"If you do not mind, I saw some herbs and other plants I wish to collect when I was out at the stream gathering fresh water and collecting berries yesterday. I would like to take a walk." She was already holding her cloak and attempting to leave, when she realized that she still only wore her underdress. Horror crossed her face and she squealed, running over to her bed, where her blue dress lay crumpled in a heap atop the furs.

With fumbling hands, she pulled the dress over her lithe body, and Flynn made certain to turn away, so she would feel less vulnerable. He tried not to feel discouraged. They had made progress but he knew, realistically, it would require more time for her to trust him. Although, he thought, she had learned to trust his brother in only a few hours riding here from Ráth Mór. That rankled. Flynn was by far the less lusty of the two Mac Greine brothers. How could she fear Flynn and yet feel safe with Brennain, who would bed practically anything in a dress?

He heard her open and shut the door swiftly, and knew she was gone. With a sigh, he accepted his reality. He may not have much to offer sweet Maggie, but he vowed he would teach her to trust in him, and mayhap, men as whole, someday.

Chapter Seven

Oh, by all the gods in Ériu and Alba! She had felt it against her hip at first, when she leaned over to tie off his bandage, but when she looked down, nothing could have prepared her for what she saw. And gods help her, she felt a mixture of both panic and excitement. His manhood had stood straight up in his trousers, but she caught a glimpse of the tip. He must have left his garment loose after the troublesome knot the night before. Though her first instinct had been to back away in fear that he would grab for her, deep inside she believed his vow to keep his hands to himself.

Still, she was a grown woman and knew enough to know a man could not control such a reaction to a woman at times, just as she could not help the achy need pulsing below when she remembered the sight of it. She also knew that many men could not help but take a woman by force when they were filled with such desire. Her papa had forced himself on her mama every time he was in a lusty mood and her mama's screams of terror still rang in her ears. It must be an awful act of violence and she had nay interest in the deed. It would surely destroy her. And yet, her nipples ached and her nether area throbbed. Her body betrayed her.

And when she realized she was still only in her underdress? By the gods, how had she made such an error? She had been ready to get fully dressed for the day when she heard Flynn awaken with a painful groan. All her healer senses had been redirected to caring for his needs, completely forgetting she was wearing a virtually transparent garment. Her cheeks flooded with heat at the thought. No wonder the man had been so aroused. She was leaning her body against him. It was her fault. Her mama always said it was a woman's place to not provoke a man. If he was provoked into violence or lust, 'twas the woman's doing and therefore her deserved punishment. This was precisely why Maggie did aught to stay away from men. She seemed to naturally provoke them.

Perhaps she owed Flynn an apology. He had kept his vow and not touched her. She had to admit that she never thought to be so close to an aroused man, so close that she could see the aroused flesh pointing straight at her, and have him control his need to force her. Flynn had stayed calm, covered himself, and kept his hands at his side. Mayhap he was a different sort of man than her papa, or Gregory, the husband of her sister Paulene. Gregory had misused and eventually killed Paulene. Elwynna had been misused by her own father and many of his men. It seemed hard to fathom that Flynn could be so different, and yet, mayhap he was.

"I need to concentrate," she scolded herself aloud, and she pulled the hood of her cloak over her hair for protection from the frosty morning chill. Her breath came out in tendrils and she had fled so quickly, she had not brought a basket or anything to collect flowers with. She would simply have to hold as much as she could in her hands. She was in no hurry to go back to the wee hut, even though she had left without feeding Flynn a morning meal. Her fears were affecting her skills as a healer, and she could not abide it. He was injured. He would not be able to hurt her, she reminded herself.

After about an hour of walking around the stream collecting more dandelions and finding some nettle, she felt refreshed. The chill had cooled both her cheeks and her nerves. Poor Flynn must be famished, so she decided to go back to the hut. Her hands were full anyway. She would simply have to return another time with a basket.

Making a promise to herself to be strong and brave, she carefully opened the door to the hut, not wanting to disturb Flynn if he had gone back to sleep.

"Maggie," she heard him whisper from the bed. She looked over and saw him trying to prop up on his side, but he winced and crashed back down onto his back.

Putting the flowers down on the table near the hearth, she walked over to him with a frown. "Are you in pain, Flynn? I can give you more poppy juice?"

He shook his head and grimaced. "Nay. I am not in much pain unless I try to sit up. I only wanted to say... I am sorry. I did not mean to make you feel frightened of me. It was an... unfortunate surprise."

Maggie's eyes widened when she realized *he* was apologizing to her about his arousal. She was most uncomfortable discussing this with him, but she supposed it was worth discussing and moving past it if they were to stay here alone together.

"I should be apologizing to you," she murmured. "I was walking around in my underdress. 'Tis nay wonder that happened. I provoked you. I deserve to be... punished."

"What?" Flynn tried to sit up again and this time he did not relent. If he was in pain, he showed no sign of it. "That is absurd, Maggie. How is it your fault that I am attracted to you? Why would I punish you for my own feelings for you?"

Heart beating wildly in her chest, she clutched her cloak tighter to her body. He was not going to blame or punish her? Her brow furrowed. "You find me attractive? You have feelings for me?" No man had ever had feelings for her. It caused a strange fluttering sensation within her stomach. Still, she could do nothing about it in the end. That life was for other lassies. Less damaged lassies. She was not destined for anything resembling a family and so 'twas best to push that fluttering in her stomach away from her mind.

"Who told you a woman should be punished for a man's desire for her?" His abrupt change in demeanor startled her. He seemed angry. She also noticed he intentionally avoided any more talk of his feelings for her. It was just as well. As soon as he healed, he would be off on another mission and she would go home to Elwynna and Àdhamh.

"'Tis just the way it is, Flynn," she responded with exasperation, and put up her hands. "'Tis a lassie's fault if she makes a man... aroused. And she deserves the punishment for her mistake."

"I cannot believe what I am hearing you say, Maggie. Does Àdhamh know you feel this way?"

"What does my brother have to do with it? He did not witness my father's rages nor my mother's punishments for his desire. He knew of it later, but never while they happened."

Flynn took a deep breath and shifted in the bed. "It makes more sense to me now. Maggie, did you father hurt you and your mama?"

Hysteria was bubbling to the surface, as were old wounds, insults, and fears. She had never discussed these things with anyone and could not understand why she was so compelled to speak of them now with Flynn. He would see how damaged she was and be disgusted by her. Mayhap that was best. If he knew she was the unloved daughter of a violent man who had broken her spirit a long time ago, perhaps he would leave her be.

She nodded slowly at Flynn's question and looked away. "Och, Maggie." She could hear the pain in his voice and her gaze went to his. His piercing green eyes were brighter than the grass on the hills just outside the hut and they shimmered with what looked like unshed tears. "'Tis a foul thing to do to a woman and a child."

"We deserved it for angering him," she persisted. "I was not smart enough, fast enough, or useful enough, and Mama could not give him more babes. It was our fault. Even Mama said so."

Swallowing audibly, Flynn shook his head and crinkled his brow, as if every word out of her mouth was worse than the last. "Listen to me, Maggie. A man is responsible for his own actions. Only a coward blames his anger on a woman and a child. Men may be larger, but that only means 'tis our responsibility to protect others, not use our size to force women or hurt children."

What he said made sense and, in a perfect world, it would be correct. However, the world was far from perfect. "Elwynna was used by her papa's men. My sister Paulene was killed by her husband. My mama was... killed by my papa," she trailed off as images of that night flashed in her mind. She had hid under the bed to avoid her father, but she had seen him lift her mother's dress, pull down his trousers and force his manhood into her mama until she sobbed and cried in pain. Then he cut her throat and left her to bleed to death on the floor of their home.

It was too much. Tears ran down Maggie's cheeks as the memory stabbed at her heart again and again. Her mama did not deserve that, but it had happened. Hands shaking, a sob wrenched from her chest and she crumpled to the floor. Her weak, shaking legs could no longer support her heavy heart. Men were cruel and used women to take their pleasure. 'Twas the way of it. Flynn told her this was not true, but it was.

"Maggie..." Flynn struggled to a sitting position, but she signaled for him to stay away by putting out her hands.

"Nay, do not get up. You will hurt yourself." Sniffling, she took a deep breath and scrambled back onto her feet, adjusting her blue dress. It was the only dress she had with her and she needed to take care not to soil it more than necessary. "I am all right," she reassured him, while she swiped imaginary dirt from her sleeves.

The look on Flynn's face told her he did not believe she was all right at all, and he was correct, but she would never tell him so.

"What if..." Flynn's voice broke as he swallowed back some emotion. "What if, once I am able to move about, I teach you to defend yourself."

"What?" Her gaze snapped to his and she wiped her damp cheeks with the long sleeve of her dress. "You would do that for me? Why?"

He took a deep breath and sighed. "You have been through more than any lass should in one lifetime. I can see you are afraid of men, but would not life be a bit easier for you if you could use a dagger? And mayhap a bow? I have mine. Never leave home without it."

A bow and dagger? Just like Aislin. She had admired Aislin for so long. She was fearless and allowed no man to frighten her. Mayhap being stuck in the middle of nowhere with Flynn was her fate, after all. She would take care of his needs for the next several days and use her downtime to search for herbs. Once he was able to get out of bed, he could use their time to teach her self-defense until Brennain came back for them. It was something she had never thought to learn until recently. Àdhamh had spent the last several years protecting her with his body, but he was a married man now and it was time for Maggie to put old demons behind her and learn to protect herself.

The task required her to trust a man enough to be close to him, allow him to guide her. It meant she would be all alone in the woods with an armed man. If he chose to break his vow, he could do precisely what her father had done to her mama... but nay. Looking at the genuine concern on his face and hearing the true kindness of his voice, she suddenly knew, without a doubt, that she could trust Flynn with her life. He truly wished to help her and if she did not take his offer, she may never again find another man she trusted enough to teach her.

"If you truly wish to teach me, I will accept your offer." She squared her shoulders and wiped her wet eyes with her fingertips. She vowed that the tears clinging to her lashes would be the last tears she cried over her past. This was a new start. She would learn to be independent and protect herself. She would no longer live in the shadows of her fear. She felt lighter than she ever had in her life. This man, Flynn Mac Greine, was truly the kindest man she had ever met. He was handsome, strong, and gentle, a combination she never thought to find in her life.

The fluttering in her stomach began again, and she realized with a start that she was developing feelings for him that she never thought possible. She looked forward to being near him, and something about that thought excited and frightened her all at once. He was a traveling warrior. She must learn from him, then learn to live without him. For after these days in the hut, it would all just be a memory. Still, she would leave here a new woman.

"You trust me, Maggie?" Flynn's voice called to her and she snapped out of her thoughts.

With a smile that came from her heart, she realized that she truly did. "Aye, Flynn. I find that I do."

He smiled and the impenetrable wall she had erected around her heart crumbled just a little more. He had a smile that could light up a room. If she was a wise woman, she would make certain no more of that wall fell for the next few sennights.

* * * *

The next sennight passed slowly, but Flynn did not mind, for he had the company of the most beautiful lass in Ériu. He had always been drawn to her light, but learning of her abusive past gave him a greater insight into who she was and why she was so timid. A lass who could live through so much loss and still dedicate her life to healing people, especially wounded warriors whom she truly feared, was a special lass, indeed. He longed to help her any way he could. His recovery was slow, but they fell into an easy rhythm within days.

Maggie tended his wound in the morning, changing the dressing and applying the salve. He noticed that she avoided looking anywhere beyond his waist and he found it endearing that she flushed every time she tended him. He wondered if she thought about that moment as often as he did. Though he had been embarrassed and ashamed at the time, he had not meant for her to see his arousal and he could not apologize for being attracted to her. He only regretted that it had frightened her. Knowing all she had witnessed in life, he made an effort to keep his thoughts clean whenever she was near, which was all the time. Though he found it impossible to keep his eyes or mind from wandering, he had done a fair job hiding his feelings toward her.

He wanted so much more from Maggie than to just teach her to protect herself. He wanted to be the one with her always, protecting her as her man. That thought shook him to the core. When had his thoughts begun to run toward the future? He could not entertain such ideas. He had a mission to finish and many more in the future, he was certain. Even if he could settle down and take a wife, Maggie was not at all interested in such an arrangement, so it was best to remove all thoughts of a future with her from his mind.

When she was not tending his wound, she often walked around the woods and collected plants of various types until her basket was filled to the brim. Her cheeks would be flushed with both the cold and excitement when she arrived back at the hut. Though he would never admit that he missed her presence while she was away, her return was the highlight of his day. She would sit down beside him on the bed, pulling different plants from the basket and explaining to him how each could be used to aid a fever, heal the skin, or cleanse the blood. When she was healing, she was in her element and exuded a confidence he wished she could carry with her always.

Slowly, against her better advice, Flynn began to get out of the bed and walk around the hut for exercise. He was a man of action, and his back had been aching while he lay in bed all day long. Sitting around watching while Maggie lit the hearth fire and made his meals, or cut and dried her herbs was weighing down on his soul, patience, and pride. He found his wound ached, but Maggie had been correct in her assessment that he had been incredibly fortunate and that the shooter had been a great distance away. Most arrow wounds were fatal, yet he was healing remarkably well. He was certain he had Maggie to thank for that. How he wanted to thank her, however, was not an option.

At nightfall, they would eat their simple meals of whatever Maggie had cleverly managed to create, usually consisting of some of the wild berries she had found a few days before, some carrots from the garden that someone had once spent a great deal of time tending before abandoning the home, and some dried meat he had brought along in his satchel. Maggie had successfully caught a hare in one of the nets Brennain taught her to use and Flynn was so proud of her, thrilled by the confidence she felt when she cooked it for him herself, though he had talked her through the process of preparing it.

Maggie had come a long way in just a sennight. She spoke to him openly and laughed frequently. Her level of trust for him seemed to grow more and more with every dawn. And by dusk, they sat together and told stories of their childhood, or pondered the family who had once lived in this hut. He learned so much about where Maggie came from and how hard her childhood had been. She was a stronger lass than she realized, and he made sure to tell her so at every opportunity. His feelings for Maggie had already been enough to distract him, but now he felt as if he may explode from the intense emotions welling up inside him for this wee woman. Aye, she was beautiful, but she was so much more than that. Still, he battled those emotions. Nothing good could come from expressing how he felt. He had a life that could not involve a wife, and she made no indication of wanting a husband, or even any form of physical relationship. She was beginning to truly trust him and he did not want to do anything to ruin that.

"'Tis been just over a sennight and I am done with lying about in this bed," Flynn declared, and he slowly came to a sitting position on the edge of the bed. Maggie put down the wooden spoon she had been using to stir the cauldron of boiling carrots and meat for a stew.

"Let me look at your wound," she said, as she came over to his side. "Do not over-exert yourself." Her warm hands skimmed his chest as they always did when she removed his dressing. He should have been used to it by now, but the sensation always gave him gooseflesh up his arms. Her hands went around to his back as she unwrapped the linen, and he could smell the natural sweetness in her hair. He inhaled deeply, knowing one of these days would be his last chance to be near her, and he wished to remember every detail. The smell of her hair, the freckles dotting her nose, the way her wavy blonde locks framed her face like a feral goddess every morning. She was pure perfection and much too good for a man who would never be around to appreciate her.

"All right, Flynn. I will have to leave the decision up to you. Your wound is healing well on the outside and you have been walking around carefully in the hut. If you feel up to gentle mobility, I shall leave it to you."

"I long for some fresh air. I am a man used to the elements, not a bed covered in furs."

She nodded and regarded him for a moment as he stood and gently stretched to test the wound. It ached still and he knew he must be careful, but he could tolerate the pain if it meant he was free to wander about.

"You will need to dress if you are to go outside. Your cough has gone away completely and I would like it to stay away." Grabbing his tunic that had been folded and unused during his entire stay at the hut, Maggie gathered the fabric in her hand and came close to him. On her tiptoes, she lifted her arms up and slipped the tunic over his head. He hunched over slightly to make the task easier for her. She stood at least two heads shorter than him, but he could not bend much lower and she could not reach much higher.

As the tunic slipped over his face, their eyes were almost level and they locked for the briefest of moments before she shifted her blue eyes back to the tunic around his neck. He read something in her eyes. He was not certain what it was, but it had felt like more than interest. Still, he disregarded any notion that the lass was attracted to him. She simply had to dress him so he could walk outside.

But then her small fingers grazed his shoulders and biceps just before helping him to slip his arms into the garment, and he felt a trail of fire burning in her wake. Her touch was innocent, yet he would do aught to feel it again. He realized that once his time with her was over, he would miss everything about her. He would teach her to be confident and to protect herself, then she would eventually marry a man who could be present in her life.

The thought made him scowl. He did not wish to think of her with another man, but she was not, and never would be, his. Maggie's eyes widened when she saw the sour look on his face and she frowned. "Did I hurt you?" she asked, and stepped back. He already missed her proximity.

Aye, she hurt him simply by being the woman he never knew he needed or wanted. "Nay. My wound is aching, 'tis all." She accepted his explanation with a nod and then fetched his cloak. Once again on her tiptoes, she clasped the cloak around his neck with the small, golden circular brooch his mama had gifted to him years before. The urge to rest his hands on her hips was strong, but he resisted. She was not his to touch and he would do well to remember it.

"You need not dress me, Maggie," he said with a hoarse voice. "I can manage."

His gruff voice must have made her believe he was frustrated and she frowned again. "Oh, I am sorry, Flynn. I was only trying to prevent you from pulling the stitches at your side. I did not mean to take on such intimate duties as a... wife would, or insult your pride," she whispered, and lowered her eyes.

He could not stand to see her become submissive, not to him or anyone else. "Look at me, Maggie." Putting a finger gently under her chin, he prompted her to look up to his height and was more than pleased when she willing did so without a flinch. "I did not mind your help. I appreciate it. You are a good woman."

"Am I?" Her brow furrowed as she considered his words. "I seem to question everything I do when I am close to you..." Maggie's words faded off, as if she meant for her thoughts to be private. But he had heard them. Could it be that she had feelings for him, as well? His heart pounded and his stomach clenched, but he had to keep his excitement from taking over.

"I seem to do the same," Flynn whispered, and looked down at her upturned face. Rosy cheeks and plump pink lips called to him and he knew his eyes were hooded with lust. She would likely not even recognize the look on his face as anything other than companionship, and it was best it remained that way.

"Nonsense," Maggie said, shaking her head. "You have not once shown any signs of questioning yourself this passed sennight." He had questioned nearly every word he said and every emotion he felt. The woman even made him question if he was ready to give up his life as a scout and to take a wife. Not just any wife. Only Maggie would ever do. But that was a ridiculous notion and he knew it. This pull he had toward her could not be allowed to develop further.

Deciding to change the subject before he did what he wanted to do most in this world and take her lips with his own, he stepped back and turned away. "I am ready for my walk. Thank you, Maggie."

"I am coming with you," she said matter-of-factly. "I will not risk you injuring yourself again and being alone in the cold." Wrapping her cloak around her neck, she pulled the large hood over her head and walked toward the door. "Are you ready?"

With a nod, he followed her through the open doorway. If she wanted to accompany him on his walk, he would not say nay to the company of a beautiful lass. They walked in silence for a few moments and he was more than pleased to do so as he absorbed the first bit of fresh air and nature he had witnessed in over a sennight. The air was crisp and heavy, the smell of new rain lingering in the breeze. It would begin to snow soon and that would surely complicate matters if Brennain did not return before then. He could use Arawn to transport Maggie back to Ráth Mór, but he had promised Brennain that they would stay and await his report. If Brennain needed help and Flynn had left to return Maggie, it could mean life or death for his brother. He could not do that, and yet, it meant Maggie was stuck with him indefinitely.

Spotting a plant he now recognized, thanks to Maggie's nightly discussions about her findings, Flynn gently nudged Maggie and pointed to the wet earth floor. "Look, Mags. 'Tis burdock, is it not? You like their roots, aye?"

Her eyes lit up and she clapped her hands with excitement. "Aye! That it is! You have been paying attention to my ramblings, I see," she said with a wide grin. The wind blew her hood off and beautiful blonde waves flew around her face. He could not help it, he had to touch her. Stepping closer to her, he placed his hand on the side of her face and swept the hair back so he could better see her bonny features. He was pleased to see that she did not seem frightened of his touch. Her hair was like the softest silk and he longed to run his fingers through it every night. Her small nose was nipped pink from the wind and her lips parted slightly when he placed her hood back onto her head. Did she wish to kiss him? If it was any other lass, he would believe so, but Maggie was afraid of intimacy and he could not risk it. It was not a matter of bruised pride or fear of rejection. If he moved to kiss her, he may frighten her and ruin all his work to make her trust him.

"I listen to everything you say, Maggie." Stepping away from her, he slowly knelt beside the burdock and began digging in the soft soil to expose the roots, stifling a groan as pain shot through his side. She stayed quietly behind him as he eventually pulled the roots out of the earth. His wound hurt from the pulling motion, but it had not been enough to cause any damage.

"Do be careful, Flynn," she said, just as he stood up, his hands muddied and holding the roots. "My thanks."

One large raindrop fell from the cloud-covered sky and landed on Maggie's cheek. "I think we must head back home before the storm comes." Flynn stepped forward and wiped the raindrop away with his thumb, leaving a dirt smudge from the soil he had just been digging in. Had he imagined it, or did Maggie cradle her face into the curve of his palm when he touched her? Again, he would believe it so if not for the knowledge of her fears.

She nodded at his request to go back and they continued side by side in silence. There was a tension between them that he could feel so keenly, it thrummed through his body like an energy begging to be released. He ached to know her deepest thoughts. She was a mystery to him but every day he understood a little more about her. And, every day he found himself more and more desperate to penetrate her walls, to make her smile and trust him with her life.

The rain began to fall in earnest just as they approached the hut. Maggie squealed as a flash of lightning lit up the sky and she jumped, bumping into Flynn, and causing him to tumble through the open doorway of the hut. Maggie came tumbling down after, landing on top of him with a grunt. His side seared with the pain, but he bit back the urge to shout. He did not want her to feel guilty for harming him, nor did he want to scare her off. He had noticed that she seemed to go into some hidden place in her mind whenever a man raised his voice.

"Oh, Flynn!" she wailed, scrambling to sit up. Her legs were straddling his as she fumbled to pull at his tunic. Was she undressing him? He dropped the muddy burdock root and watched in wonder as her warm hands found their way under his tunic. He licked his lips, pain forgotten as he felt himself grow hard. Her skirts were shoved up past her knees and he could see her slim calves pressed against his large thighs. Silently, he watched as her eyes grew wide with understanding before wandering downward, where his hardness pressed against his trousers painfully.

Pushing to her feet, she heaved and blushed profusely, adjusting her skirt around her legs. "I am so sorry. I only meant to check your wound. Did I hurt you? Are you all right? I did not mean to... to..."

"I am fine, Maggie, though I will need some help up, I am afraid."

"Oh. Right, aye." Shoving her hair behind her ear, she leaned over to brace herself, putting both hands out for him to grab. With a groan, he grabbed her hands and pulled himself up as much as he could without dragging the wee lass back down onto him again. She teetered precariously as she strained back to balance her weight, but together they finally got him to his feet.

To his surprise, she did not flinch, cringe, or back away when he towered over her. "Let us get you into bed, Flynn. 'Tis enough exercise for one day. I fear we have only set your healing back."

"Nonsense, I am well," he lied. His insides felt as if they were on fire, but he would not admit it. He would grit his teeth against the pain if it meant he had more mobility and opportunities to truly interact with Maggie. He allowed her to guide him to the bed, but his mind reeled for more ways to spend time with her. She was quickly becoming a person he was not certain he could live without, and that thought jolted him. He had to remind himself that he had a job to do that would keep him away for longer periods of time and all he could do was help her gain confidence during this small amount of time they had together.

"I would like to start teaching you self-defense on the morrow," he said, just as he positioned himself into a sitting position in the bed.

Her eyes widened and she chewed on her lower lip. "I am not certain. You are still weak. My priority is to help you. 'Tis why I am here. I cannot allow you to harm yourself to help me."

"I want to do this. I need to do this. Do you trust me?" His eyes searched her face for any sign of fear, and he was pleased to see no outward indication. It had been a very long sennight being locked up in a hut with a woman as enticing as Maggie, but he had made certain to remain calm and gentle, and to keep his hands to himself even though he ached to feel her against him. When she stumbled through the door and landed on top of him in such a way that she straddled him, he could not control his body's reaction to her nearness. She was all soft curves, warm, smooth skin, and a body built for pleasure, yet with the mind of a frightened, innocent woman. It was a most challenging combination.

"Aye, I do trust you, Flynn. I am surprised to say so because I did not think it possible, but I do trust you."

His heart beat against his ribs and he released a deep breath. Her words washed over him, giving him a sense of pride that a lass who had lived through so much could find her way to trust him.

"I know you have been through much in your life, Maggie. And I know Àdhamh has always protected you, but 'tis time you learned to protect yourself. I wish to give that gift to you while I can. Do not worry about my wound. I can help you without exerting myself overmuch."

"All right. If you are well enough on the morrow, we shall begin. I suppose it will be a pleasant way to pass time," she smiled sweetly and walked away, leaving him with a perfect view of her swaying backside.

He bit his knuckles to stifle a groan. He could think of much more pleasant ways to pass time, but those thoughts would be left unsaid.

Chapter Eight

Gooseflesh ran up Maggie's arms when Flynn reached around her to adjust her stance. Fortunately, the long sleeves of her dress covered her skin from his view or else he would see the physical evidence of her growing interest in him. Despite her best efforts, Maggie was finding it impossible to ignore the thoughts running through her mind or the sensations coursing through her body. She was a lass of twenty summers, after all. She had not been so much as kissed by a lad due to her aversion to men. But what she felt for Flynn was anything but an aversion.

Once her trust in him began to take root, it felt like a weight had been lifted off her shoulders. Aye, she had trusted Brennain, as well. The two Mac Greine brothers were very similar in both appearance and temperament, and she trusted both, which she found odd. But something about Flynn had always drawn her. She used to wish fervently to be in his presence, but once she was, she would freeze up and act like a frightened mouse. However, the past several days had taught her to speak freely around him and they shared meals, laughter, and stories of their past. He had had a very interesting life as the son of a Sister of Danu.

The Sisters of Danu were renown across the lands of both Alba and Ériu. Not only were they said to be reborn goddesses of the ancient people and have control over the elements, but they had helped King Tuathal defeat his enemy and take the throne.

Aye, Flynn's mother had special skills to control nature and his father was once a king. It was intimidating for Maggie whose father had been an abusive, hateful man, and her mother had defended his actions while also being his victim. They came from two entirely different places in life and yet, she could talk to him easily without fear of judgement. He wanted to help her be a stronger woman, like his cousin Aislin, so she could defend herself. No man had ever taken the time to help her and she felt her heart fluttering wildly in her chest as his hand held onto her wrist, guiding her movements.

The storm from the night before had let up for a few hours, and Flynn decided it was ideal to train outside before the snow began to fall, as he suspected it would very soon.

"There you go, lass. Just like that." His warm breath grazed her neck and a tingle of pleasure ran down her spine. By the gods, she could not concentrate when one of his hands rested on her hip and his thighs pressed against hers from behind. He was only trying to teach her proper form for knife throwing, she knew, but new and exciting energy flowed through his body and into hers.

She knew he found her bonny. She had seen his desire pressing against his trousers on more than one occasion and it did not frighten her as she suspected it would. He had never tried to push himself on her and as grateful as she was, she wished he would at least attempt a kiss. Mayhap he had no further interest in her. He was the most handsome man in their entire tuath and certainly had several bonny lassies to keep him warm at night. Why would he bother with an inexperienced, timid lass like her?

"Like this?" she whispered, flicking her wrist while she still held tightly to the dagger.

"Aye, just so," he replied, stepping back and releasing her from his grip. Her body went cold from the loss of contact and disappointment consumed her. How could she want his touch so much, and what did that even mean? She was frightened of the violent act of love. Her father used to make her mama scream in pain. So what was it that Maggie's body was crying out for? And why did she only hope to achieve it with this one man, and no other?

"You are ready, Maggie. Flick your wrist and aim for that tree trunk," he pointed straight ahead to a towering oak just a few yards away. Most of its leaves rested around the base of its trunk in limp, soggy layers of reds, yellows, and browns. Indeed, winter was well on its way.

With a deep breath, she narrowed her eyes at her target, flicked her wrist and watched in wonder as Flynn's dagger spiraled in the air... and landed with a thwack on the hardened forest floor. Not only had she missed the tree, she did not even stick it into the ground.

Her lip protruded with disappointment and she put her hands on her hips with a huff. She was rotten at this. Flynn would think her pathetic.

Flynn chuckled and bumped her gently with his hip, almost making her lose her balance. "'Tis all right, lass. Nay need to pout. It will come to you." His thumb and forefinger came up quickly to yank playfully on her bottom lip, causing her eyes to go wide and she sucked it in. He laughed at her reaction and carefully bent over to grab his dagger.

"I am nay good at this," she sighed.

"Not true. That was your first attempt. Here, let's try this..." Flynn grabbed her hips with both his hands, and she was mesmerized by how easily his large fingers nearly wrapped around the entirety of her waist. He was truly large, and yet no fear whatsoever took hold of her. She smiled at that realization and he cocked his head in question, clearly wondering how she went from a frown to a smile so quickly. However, he did not ask and she did not say.

"Shift your left foot forward... like so," he used his own foot to push hers outward. "Good. Now twist yer hips this way," his hands maneuvered her body as if she was a cloth doll and she found she enjoyed it entirely. "Put this shoulder back... aye, like that!" Placing the dagger back into her right hand, he wrapped her fingers around the handle of the blade and aimed her arm for her. "That's it. Try again."

He stepped back once more and she did as he commanded, narrowing her eyes and sticking her tongue out to the side in concentration. After a few practice flicks of the wrist, she let it go and watched in slow motion as the blade flew. This time, it hit its mark, the sharp blade wedging itself into the bark of the oak tree.

"I did it!" She jumped into the air and clapped her hands, squealing with excitement. When she turned around to smile up at Flynn, Maggie almost gaped at the look on his face. A crooked, proud grin spread across his beautiful face, his dark beard now framing his jaw after several days without shaving. He looked feral and masculine, but his eyes twinkled with delight. He was a walking contradiction to all things she ever thought about men.

Their gazes locked for a brief moment and she felt the air between them shift. Something had changed about their relationship, though she could not say what, nor was she going to ask. Her body tingled with awareness as he stepped toward her slowly, his large arms crossed over his chest, biceps bulging beneath the fabric. "You are truly something, do you know that, my wee Maggie?"

Her eyes widened and she felt all the blood rushing to her cheeks. Had he just called her *his* Maggie? It should have frightened or upset her, but only anticipation flooded her veins. How she longed for him to lean down and give her a kiss. He stepped closer and her breath hitched in her chest but no words would escape her lips.

Flynn walked past her and yanked the dagger out of the oak's large trunk. Disappointment made her frown. "Why are you frowning, lass? 'Twas amazing what you just did. You are a quick learner. I will have you fighting as well as Aislin by the time my brother returns from his mission."

"Do you ever wonder if he made it safely?" she asked. He barely spoke of the mission his brother was on or made mention of his concerns.

"Of course, I do. But I cannot do much for now and I have to believe he is just as capable as I am. Brennain is an incredibly well-trained warrior, hunter and tracker. If any man could do this, it's him."

She nodded and sighed, her shoulders going limp as she thought about their time together coming to an end. She had so many things she wished to say to him, but she knew it was best to keep her secrets. If she put her heart on the line for the first man she ever truly cared for, and he did not return her feelings, she would leave this hut more damaged than before.

"You look sad," he whispered, and he came forward to tuck her loose blonde waves behind her ears. Her cloak whipped in a sudden gust of wind and he silently regarded her for a moment before speaking. "You care for my brother, don't you, Maggie?"

Her brow creased as she looked at him in confusion. "What do you mean?"

"You trusted him before you trusted me. You mention him frequently and he seemed to be very protective of you when he delivered you here. Are you awaiting his return so you two can... be together?"

His voice was soft and low, almost sad, and she started to wonder if he did, in fact, care for her, but held back for fear of frightening her or being rejected. "Flynn," she grabbed his hand and squeezed, prodding him to look her in the eye. "I do trust Brennain. He earned my trust on the ride here that night, but I do not have feelings for him beyond companionship."

Flynn seemed to perk up slightly at her words. Licking his lips, he hesitated to speak. "You took longer than a few hours to trust me. Why is that?"

How could she explain the truth without making herself appear to be a fool? "Mayhap I was more afraid of you, because you actually have the power to break me, Flynn."

His eyes widened and he jerked away from her grip. "I have given you nay reason to fear me, Maggie. I am out here in the bloody cold trying to teach you survival skills so nay man can ever hurt you again! And you believe I would 'break' you?" he scoffed and spun away, clearly offended by her words. He stormed into the hut, leaving the door open behind him. She ran in after him, shutting the door to keep the heavy winds from filling the house with a chill.

Pacing back and forth in front of the fire, Flynn's jaw clenched and he refused to look her in the eye. "Flynn?" He ignored her and continued to pace. She had to say something to make this right. Though she knew she could never have Flynn in the way she truly wanted, she would die of a broken heart if he despised her. Walking in front of him to block his path, she put her hands out to stop him, forcing him to look at her. "Please, Flynn. I did not mean it like that."

Stopping directly in front of her, his huge body towering over her height, the firelight flickered over his features and she saw clearly that he was much sadder than he was angry. Her stomach bunched in knots, knowing she was about to say more to him than she had ever thought to.

"Then what do you mean when you say I can break you? Curse it, Maggie. I have done all I can to make you feel safe with me."

"I do feel safe!" Maggie threw her arms up in the air, exasperated at her own lack of communication skills. She had never had to discuss her feelings with a man... she had never had feelings to discuss with a man. With a deep sigh, she gripped his forearms and squeezed, silently begging him to listen. "What I meant was... how can I say this?" She felt dizzy and hot as anxiety gripped at her. "You could break me, because of the way I feel about you," she whispered, and hung her head low so he could not see the tears threatening to break through.

His finger went beneath her chin, urging her to look up. A tear escaped from her left eye and slid down her cheek. His brows crinkled as he wiped the tear away with his thumb. "How do you feel about me?"

"Must you make me say it?" she croaked, shaking her head. He would turn away from her. He would think her a silly lass for falling for him when all he meant to do was be kind while she cared for him. She had not taken his need to be kind as any other form of affection, but she had no control over the affection she had developed for him. Somehow, in such a short amount of time, he had begun to mean everything to her.

"I will not make you say or do anything you do not wish. You know that, Maggie."

"Aye, I know that. 'Tis what I love most about you. You are so calm and patient with me. You speak softly and make sure I always feel safe."

"Maggie, I am a man. I sometimes shout and I sometimes fight. And sometimes, as you have seen, I am filled with lust. I am not different from most men in that regard. I simply would never force myself on a woman or hurt her. This does not make me a man worthy of you. It simply makes me a decent man. You have had the misfortune of being surrounded by bastards, who made you believe all men are vile. This is not true. But if you really knew me, you may be frightened by me."

"You could not ever frighten me. I know that now."

"Even if I were to become angry and shout," he asked, stepping closer, but she refused to take a step back.

"Nay," she shook her head.

"Even if I got into a fight with another man to defend your honor?" he questioned, taking one more step until his body was pressed against hers.

She shook her head, "Not even then."

"And... if I were to kiss you?" he whispered, narrowing his eyes at her. "Would I frighten you then?"

Her breath left her body in a rush, her head spinning with the intensity of his words. "Nay. I would not fear your kiss," she whispered, and licked her lips reflexively.

"But, would you welcome it?"

Had her heart ever pounded more wildly in her entire life? She wanted to kiss this man more than she wanted her next breath. "Aye, I would—"

His mouth came down on hers almost violently. A low growl escaped his throat as their lips came together in a mad rush. His hands gripped her hair and held her in place. A thrill unlike anything she ever imagined ran through her body and her arms wrapped around his neck, clinging for dear life as she reached as high as she could on her tiptoes.

His warm tongue swept across her lips and she opened for him, allowing him to teach her all he knew. When their tongues met in a fierce tangle, Maggie moaned at the pulse that grew in her core. How could his mouth illicit such a response from down below? He was not gentle and, though it surprised her to see this aggressive side of Flynn, she was much more surprised by her lack of fear. She trusted him with her entire heart.

"Does this shock you, Mags? That I have been so calm around you, and yet, I want you with such fierce need that I would devour you?"

His tongue slid down the column of her neck and she moaned again, her head spinning with desire. "Aye," she whispered. "I thought you did not want me." His tongue ran back up her neck and slipped into her mouth once more, before he pulled away and nibbled on her lower lip. "Oh, goodness," she groaned. "My knees are weak."

"I would lower you to the ground, Maggie, but that would be a very dangerous move. We are better up here," he whispered while moving over to her earlobe, tugging on the flesh with his teeth. His warm breath grazed her neck, just as it had outside, and she felt her nipples harden beneath her dress. What was this reaction her body had to his touch? She had no idea what to think, do, or say. She only knew how to feel.

Slowly, he backed away, a fire burning in his green eyes that set her body aflame. "I am sorry. I should not have done that."

She frowned. "But, I wanted you to."

"Which makes this all the worse, Maggie. There is something between us, but it can never be anything more. As soon as Brennain returns, I will be taking you back home to your brother and I will be on my way."

She knew his words were true. Still, they may well have been a bucket of freezing stream water being dumped on her overheated body. The sensations that had just been consuming her body now morphed into some torturous ache in her heart. He was like all men, after all. He wanted enough from her to sate his body, but would discard her as soon as he was done.

"You are right." She squared her shoulders and raised a brow, hoping to hide her hurt with indignation. "This can never be." She felt the cursed tears welling up in her eyes as her chin quivered. Flynn had been her first kiss, the first man she had ever trusted to touch her. And when he had, it was as if all the years of pain had melted away in his embrace. But all the hurt came flooding back, now tainted with a new pain. The pain of rejection, from the only man she had ever wanted. He was man enough to push her away before it went too far, at least. Still, mayhap she had wanted it to go a wee bit further. She still could not fathom the act itself, for it was violent and painful, but the soft caresses and kisses? She ached for more of them, but they were not to be.

Flynn ran a frustrated hand through his shaggy black hair and let out a puff of air. "Maggie... do not cry. Please. I am only trying to stop us both from becoming hurt in the end."

"I am not crying. I shall never cry over a man, least of all you, Flynn Mac Greine! But if you think I shall ever favor you with a kiss again, you shall be disappointed. I have never allowed a man to kiss me before and I certainly will not do so again if it is simply to satisfy your base needs!" Her fists clenched into the fabric of her blue dress, the same blue dress she had been stuck with for over a sennight. She had washed it twice in the stream, but she was more than sick of looking at it, as well as the man standing before her now, even if her heart still beat just for him. She would bury those feelings so deep, even she would be unable to find them again. If caring for someone meant only more hurt in the end, she could not afford to care any longer.

"You know, you are mighty feisty when you are angry," he commented with a wink. "I enjoy seeing this side of you."

"Good, because 'tis all you shall see of me until your *handsome* brother comes back to take me home." Her words had the proper affect. Flynn's face morphed from arrogance to jealousy before her eyes. She could not care. Crossing her arms over her chest, she turned her back to him and stormed toward the door.

"Where are you going, Maggie?" he shouted. She was correct. He was a man prone to all the emotions and behaviors of other men. Violence, anger, jealousy. He would never physically hurt her, she knew well, but he was more than able to hurt her heart. Inwardly, she was glad to finally have broken past the polite façade he had been straining to show her all these days. They finally could see each other for who they were. Let him shout at her or be angry. He was nothing to her, nor would he ever be.

"My thanks for your honesty, Flynn. I am most glad you made it clear where I stand in your life before things went any further." She opened the door and stepped outside into the pouring rain. The sky had darkened considerably in the short span of time. Or had they kissed for much longer than she knew? Either way, she needed fresh air, even if that air was currently surrounded by large drops of rain. 'Twas better than being stuck in this hut all night long, staring at the man who rejected her.

"I asked where you are going." Flynn stormed toward her with menace in his eyes and without thinking, her hands flew up to protect her face from his strike. She shrieked and cowered, freezing in place as she awaited his blow.

Several moments passed before she peeked through the space between her upraised arms. He stood frozen before her with the saddest look in his eyes. His arms were at his side and she suddenly realized what she had done. She had sworn to trust him, and she did. Still, years of instinct had taught her to cower and cover when a man came at her with anger in his eyes or voice.

"Maggie..."

His imploring voice called to her, but she had to flee. Her stomach was in a knot. Her feelings for this man were growing out of control. Her past was haunting her, and she was certain she had just hurt him with her sudden need to protect herself. She could not have this man. He belonged to one person: his king. She could not very well have a future with a man who was gone all the time, nor was she capable of giving him what he truly needed in a woman. The act of love was no act of love at all, and she would never bear the pain or torture of it. She was uncertain how other woman ever did. Elwynna seemed to enjoy it very much, but she also had been used so much as a wee lass. Mayhap she had grown accustomed to the pain.

"I need to go, Flynn." She slammed the door behind her and ran into the dark, wet night, feeling the muddy earth squish beneath her leather slippers and splash up her calves. She ran until her side ached and she could hardly breathe. Humiliation flooded her. She had received her first kiss in all her life and it was more than she could have ever hoped for. Flynn had made her entire body melt with just his hands on her hips and the way his tongue nipped at her ear and slid down her throat... for one short moment in time, he had made her question everything she had ever thought about men and lovemaking. Had he lowered her to the ground and taken her, she would have faced her fear of the pain and allowed him to do aught with her body. How could she have been so foolish?

Her initial instinct had been correct. He lusted for her, aye, but could offer her no more. Why should she suddenly care? She knew he could never be with her, but his use of her to simply slake a small bit of lust before pushing her away burned deep into her heart, causing an uncontrollable squeezing pain in her chest. She would have been better off not knowing how it felt to kiss Flynn Mac Greine.

What a pathetic lass she was to think a man like Flynn could ever want more from her. And yet, she had been all right with that. In that moment, she would have let him do anything, just to experience his touch. Her mind feared the act of love, yet her body ached for it. It was the most distressing moment of her life to finally feel as if she could give herself to a man, only to be pushed away. The only thing she could think to do to hide her shame was to run. The night seemed to mourn for her, shedding its cold tears to mingle with her own.

A sob wrenched from her throat and her eyes grew blurry through her continuous stream of tears. It was like a lifetime of pent-up turmoil released all at once, making her forget all sense of herself. Was this the pain her own mama felt every time she begged for affection from her papa? Maggie would never let a man ill-use her as her papa had her mama, but suddenly, she could understand the pain of caring for a man who could not care for her in return, a man bound to his king and the land, a man who could have any lass he wanted. Why would he choose her, pathetic wee lass that she was with her crippling fears, small breasts, and childlike curves, when he could have a real woman who willingly enjoyed the act of coupling? Och, she was a cursed fool.

Through the haze of her misery, Maggie heard the sounds of rushing water up ahead, and she realized she had been running full-speed toward the surging stream. On most days, it was a calm, peacefully flowing body of water and her most favorite place to gather her thoughts. Her mind and body must have instinctively sought out its solace in her pain and anger. However, what she saw ahead was nothing like the peaceful stream she often sought out. The stream overflowed from the relentless rain and churned violently as if angered by the storm destroying its peace. Land and water merged, turning the shore into sludge. Maggie gasped as she slid to a stop, feeling the earth shift beneath her feet, then screamed in horror as she felt her feet give way and her body propel toward the angry stream. Before she could catch her balance, she toppled head first into the rushing water.

She sputtered and gasped as water flooded her lungs. Her dress felt as if it was caught on something, and panic consumed her cold limbs as she flailed her arms, seeking anything to grasp. "Help!" she shouted, knowing nobody was around to hear her, but she shouted anyway and desperately tried to yank at whatever her skirt was caught on. More water rushed into her mouth and she coughed frantically. She wailed in terror. She was going to die out here all alone. She would never see her brother or Elwynna again. She would never see Flynn again. His beautiful green eyes, his flowing black hair and perfect smile. His strong jaw or the way his voice rumbled when he laughed. The way his mouth had felt on hers and how she suddenly realized she longed for so much more from Flynn Mac Greine than she had allowed herself to believe. Now, as the stream threatened to pull her into a dark, watery grave, she gasped for air at the exact moment that the truth struck, like the very lightning still streaking across the sky.

She was in love with Flynn. It had been hopeless from the start. They never stood a chance. She was a broken woman and he was a traveling warrior. He was as brave as she was damaged and yet, he had gone out of his way to make her feel safe and protected. He had kept his vow to teach her self-protection... if only she had ever learned to swim. She would die, but she would die with the knowledge she had accomplished one thing in life she never thought possible. She had learned how to love a man, even if he did not love her in return.

Her limbs stopped flailing as numbness consumed them. The stream felt like an icy vise gripping her body, squeezing the air from her lungs. Her dress insisted on dragging her down and she suddenly had no more strength to fight it. Perhaps this was how she was always meant to leave this earth. She had lived in fear, and now she would die just as a calming peace came over her mind. The roaring stream tried to pull her away, but whatever her dress was caught on, kept her anchored in place as her lungs filled with more water each time her head went under. She stopped fighting. There was no need. She would die. Saying a silent prayer for her brother and Elwynna, she also prayed to the gods that Flynn would someday find love with the right woman. If she must leave this world, she would leave it with prayers of love and peace, not thoughts of anger or fear. Mayhap when she crossed into the Otherworld, she would see her mama once more. That thought almost made her smile as the water dragged her down once more and darkness started to take hold.

Something wrapped around her floating forearm so tightly that she winced at the pain, but she could not see beyond the dark and the rain pelting her face. Her body was lifted and dragged to shore. Sputtering, she rolled to her side and let out a series of violent coughs, feeling water leave her body as air filled her lungs. Forcing her eyes open, she saw Flynn, completely soaked through, towering over her as rain matted his dark locks to his face. He looked almost like a feral beast in this darkness, with glowing green eyes boring into hers. Though her head spun and her lungs burned with the simultaneous release of water and intake of air, her heart squeezed at the sight of him. She never thought to see his face again. He had saved her.

Without a word, Flynn bent over and scooped her into his arms, while her own arms wrapped around his neck for support. Up close, she could see that he clenched his jaw and she knew he was in pain. Her throat was raw and sore from shouting, but she managed to croak out a warning to him. "Flynn... your wound." He did not respond, only tightened his grip on her soaking, frozen body as he took slow, calculated steps back toward the hut. He dodged large puddles, but there was no hope for missing the mud.

Her heart pounded in her chest as she realized how close to death she had truly been. Had Flynn not come to find her, she would surely have been swept away by now, breathed her last breath, and never been found again. The thought sent icy chills down her spine and she instinctively nestled closer to Flynn's body, though he was also cold to the touch.

Kicking the slightly ajar door open with his large, muddy boot, Flynn walked into the house and unceremoniously plopped her onto a pile of furs near the hearth. He held his aching side and grimaced, refusing to look her in the eye.

"My thanks, Flynn," she murmured, but he showed no sign whatsoever of hearing her. Walking away from her, he yanked his soaked tunic over his head, tossing it to the floor with a soggy thump. Even from across the room, she saw that his stitches had ripped open in a few places and she gasped. After several days, the wound had scabbed over and thankfully only small amounts of blood trickled through. She had stopped binding him just a few days ago because it was healing so well.

"Flynn! Your wound!" Scrambling to her feet, she felt heavy and waterlogged with her dress and nightgown clinging to her cold skin. Her cold limbs made her clumsy and weak, causing her to flop back onto the floor on her hands and knees. Her chest labored to breath and her skin tingled as warmth slowly came back to her. Mud covered the bottom of her dress, but that was the least of her worries. Sitting back down on the furs near the hearth, she crossed her arms to stave off the chill. "You should not have carried me."

"You should not have run off!" he barked back, making her jump in surprise. His jaw ticked and she could see true rage in his eyes.

"Well... you should not have shouted at me!" she shot back, clenching her fists. Though her body was frozen, she shook with rage as her blood boiled. How dare he blame her for what had happened after he kissed her with such passion, licking her neck and shoving his tongue down her throat, only to then step back and throw rejection in her face. Her body heated just thinking of it.

"You should not have intentionally made me jealous by calling my brother handsome!"

"Jealous? I did not know you were capable of feeling jealousy over me! You are the one who told me we can never be!"

"You agreed!" he shouted back at her, stepping closer and holding his wound. His bare chest gleamed in the firelight and his wet trousers clung to his large legs... and his male parts, she noticed with wide-eyed perusal and a wildly beating heart.

"I agreed because 'tis the truth. We shall never be anything to one another. I am incapable of having a physical relationship with a man!" she hollered, flushing immediately after having admitted her darkest secret. "'Tis a vile, hateful act and nay man shall ever touch me!"

He stopped in his tracks and stared down at her, all the tension visibly draining from his body. Shame and embarrassment washed over her. She knew her feelings were not the same as most lassies, still she had seen it forced enough on a woman to know how dreadful it was.

"Has a man forced you before?" His tone was calm, yet frightening. "Tell me who and I will run him through with my blade, I vow it."

She shook her head and swallowed hard. Her hair clung to her face and she peeled the offending locks away from her cold neck. "Nay. Not me. My mother, my sister, and Elwynna. I have heard enough... seen enough, to know." His face visibly paled and he propped himself against the bed post for support.

His wound. She needed to repair the stitches. Her wet dress was leaving a trail of water on the hard-packed earthen floor of the hut and would eventually cause the floor to become soggy. Her skirts stuck to her skin as she walked over to her satchel and rummaged for a clean bone needle and some thread.

"Sit," she instructed Flynn as she approached him. He plopped down on a wooden bench, his wet trousers making a sloshing noise when he positioned himself. "'Twill hurt," she murmured, and she expertly threaded the needle and poked him in his side.

"Ouch!" he hollered, but she did not break eye contact with her work.

"I warned you 'twould hurt. Thanks for saving my life, Flynn," she whispered, and she drew the needle through his skin and tugged the thread tightly.

"I would never allow harm to befall you, Maggie," he said with sincerity, and she knew he meant it. Still, she knew he could harm her, for he already had. Some wounds were not visible, but they ran deep and would likely never heal. In her heart, she knew Flynn had saved her from the pain of broken promises and wishful dreams by ending... whatever it was between them, before it even started. Still, her heart ached so painfully that she had to resist the urge to rub at her chest.

"My father used to force himself on my mama in front of me," she confessed as she bit off the last stitch and sighed. "She would scream in pain, cry, and sometimes bleed. But she always said it was a man's right to take what he wanted, when he wanted, from his wife. 'Tis when I vowed to never become a wife. I cannot bear such pain, even to please a man."

She stood back up and walked over, placing the used needle on the table to be boiled later. She had shared her shame with Flynn. He now knew her darkest secret, knew why she was so broken that no man would ever want her.

"Maggie. A man who forces a woman is a beast. Making love should be pleasurable, natural, and mutual. 'Tis a most beautiful thing when a man and a woman come together willingly. I am sorry your mother suffered so, but she was wrong. 'Tis not a man's right to take a woman until she is in pain." He shook his head and stood from the bench.

"You know much of making love?" She knew he must and yet, it brought her close to tears to think of him sharing these same feelings for another lass.

"Nay. I know of bedding a lass, aye. Making love? Nay."

She looked over at him and thought on his words. Had he never loved a woman? Did he know that Maggie already loved him? If his words were true, a man and a woman could find pleasure if they cared for one another. Though she had denied such ideas her entire life, she knew some lassies who did enjoy it. Aislin seemed to be more than satisfied with her husband, as was Elwynna. The thought intrigued her.

"Have..." her voice trailed off and she flushed at the words that were so close to escaping her lips. It was a private thing to ask and she bit her lower lip to prevent herself from asking the question. Mayhap she was better off not knowing his answer.

"Have... what, Maggie? You can ask me anything you want. I swear to be truthful with you. It pains me to see you scared of something that can be so beautiful."

He stepped closer and she wanted to step back, but resisted the urge. "Have the lassies that you bedded found... pleasure? You did not hurt them?" Flynn coughed abruptly at her question and held his newly stitched side to prevent any strain. "I am sorry. I should not ask such questions. I am only curious."

"I believe that they have been most satisfied, aye. I have received nay complaints." His cheeks flushed for the first time ever in her presence, and she shivered in her wet gown.

"You are soaked to the bone, Mags. You must get warm. You will catch a chill if you sit in these wet garments."

"'Tis all I have. You know this." She shivered again and turned to the fire, rubbing her hands furiously near the flames.

"You must take them off," he insisted.

"I cannot!" Maggie groused. "I will not!"

"Mags... be reasonable. We have furs. You can wrap yourself in a woolen blanket and furs. You shall be covered."

"What about you? Your trousers are soaked. And that cursed string is now most assuredly tangled again."

"I can leave them on," he said simply, and she knew then that he would rather suffer in silence than make her uncomfortable.

With a deep sigh, she realized she had to be brave and reasonable. "Nay, you just recovered from a chill. You must get warm."

"As must you," he responded stubbornly. "I shall not if you will not."

She narrowed her eyes and huffed. "Fine. All right. Turn around and I shall remove my garments."

Flynn did as she asked, turning his back and walking away, leaving her to struggle with her clothing. Not only were they sopping wet and muddy, they clung to her stubbornly. Maggie gathered her skirts in her hands, raised them over her hips, and lifted her arms, tugging with all her might. Her underdress was somehow twisted and tangled with her blue dress, and neither would come over her shoulders. With a grunt, she pulled with all her strength and let out a growl of frustration when the cursed fabric refused to release her from their binds.

She heard Flynn growl from behind her, and turned to see what had him so flustered, though she could hardly see with her arms stuck up in the air and the fabric of two dresses now bunched across her breasts, refusing to be removed.

Flynn's head was down and his trousers had slackened just enough that she could see the upper half of his tight backside. His hips tapered and his rear was muscled perfection. She had not meant to stare, but she had also not expected to find him growling with his pants half down his hips.

Turning back around swiftly before he caught her staring, she dropped her skirts in exasperation, feeling the cold cloth wrap around her body once more. Her arms had grown tired form holding them up and tugging so hard.

Like it or not, if she was going to get out of these clothes, she needed help. He was much taller and stronger. He could yank the clothing over her head easily. "Flynn... I need help." She swallowed hard when the words were said, regretting having to say them. "I am stuck. I cannot remove my garments."

Flynn turned to her, holding his loose trousers up with one hand, as his other rested on his hip. "My cursed string is stuck. I cannot loosen them enough to get them down my blasted arse!"

Something bubbled up inside Maggie that she had not felt in such a long time. Laughter. Doubling over, she let out a giggle that morphed into booming laughter, holding her sides as she looked at Flynn's confused face. Tears ran down her cheeks and she wiped them away before she stood back up and walked toward him. "We are a mess." She laughed again and looked down at his hand holding his trousers up.

"I am pleased you find it so humorous," he murmured, but a playful smirk spread across his face and her heart dropped into her stomach. Gods, he was perfect. "What now?"

Straightening her features, she shrugged and chewed her bottom lip. "I think I will require your help," she said shyly. His brows rose and she knew he was suddenly imagining her naked. "You will, of course, close your eyes the entire time," she amended.

"Of course," he said with forced effrontery. "Lift your arms."

"Close your eyes," Maggie reminded him.

He bent down and grabbed at the bottom hem of both her dresses. "Of course. Trust me." And she did. Raising her arms, she watched as Flynn closed his eyes and stood up slowly, gathering the fabric in both hands. Her bare skin instantly warmed from the hearth fire and it felt slightly freeing, and entirely forbidden, for her nether parts to be exposed to the heat of the room while Flynn stood directly in front of her. If he opened his eyes and looked down, he would see parts of her no man had ever seen. Something about that thought made her tingle at her core, just as his kisses had.

With a swift and hard tug, the wet garments pulled over her breasts and head, slowly peeling away from her shoulders and arms. One more tug and she was freed of the cold, wet material... and completely exposed. "Do not open your eyes yet!" she squealed, and she ran in a frantic circle looking for a blanket to wrap around her body. Pulling one off Flynn's bed, she quickly wrapped it around herself and sighed in relief at its warmth. Flynn's natural scent was all over the blanket and now wrapped around her body like a cocoon of protection. She suddenly felt calm and safe. "All right. I am covered."

Flynn opened his eyes and regarded her carefully. She shivered when his gaze roamed up and down her body, pausing at the long, exposed length of her calves and thighs. Heat flushed her body and that familiar ache between her legs grew more intense than ever. She was covered in naught but a woolen blanket and he was holding his trousers up with one hand. It felt so intimate and forbidden for them to be so nearly undressed before one another, but she found she only wished to be closer to him.

The fire crackled in the otherwise silent room. Her mind kept turning over their conversation about making love. She knew he did not love her, but she was more certain than ever she loved him. Would allowing him to show her how a man loved a woman save her from her self-imposed nightmare? She had two choices before her. She could follow her body and heart's guidance and seek out the truth that lay between her and Flynn, discover if he was the man to teach her more about life than she ever thought possible. Or, she could swallow these emotions, hide them away, and walk away from him and any chance at knowing what could exist between a man and a woman forever.

She knew for certain no man would ever replace Flynn in her heart. It felt so sudden, but spending every day and night in his presence had turned out to be exactly what her heart had needed all along. This was the adventure she had begged for in her life. Was there happiness at the end of this journey? Nay. She knew he still had a role to play that would keep him from ever settling down with a family. She was also still not certain she ever wanted to be a wife or have children, and even if she did, Flynn had made no mention of having any feelings for her beyond his lust. And yet... mayhap, for now, in this moment, lust was enough to repair a little of the damage Maggie had been living with for far too long.

His green eyes continued to stare at her with more emotions than she could recognize. He did not speak, nor did he move, but he stood frozen in his place, seeming to memorize every detail of her.

Clutching the blanket around her chest, she slowly stepped closer to Flynn. His pupils dilated little by little with every step she took. Her free hand shook as she stood before Flynn, placing her hand on top of his. "Do you still need help?" she whispered, taking his trouser string in her hand. He nodded slightly and swallowed, and Maggie knew he sensed the new energy that sparked between them. The air had shifted, somewhere between her laughing at their ruined garments and him yanking her dress over her head.

Nothing was funny about the ache she felt to be touched by Flynn. Her hands fumbled with his ties for a moment before she finally made progress on the knot. They slackened further, just enough for him to be able to remove them if he chose.

"Thanks," he mumbled, and stared down at her. "'Tis your turn to turn away while I change."

Nodding, she turned hesitantly, but did not back away from him. Her mind was reeling. She should walk away. Nothing but heartache and rejection could possibly follow. And yet, before her now stood a man who was unlike any other. He was strong, yet gentle.

Loyal, kind, caring, protective, and without a doubt, the only man who had ever made her feel as if her heart would beat out of her chest. She may regret this decision later, but the pull she felt toward him was too strong to deny. She needed, for the first time in her life, to face her fears and she knew he was the one she wanted to face them with.

She heard his trousers being stripped away behind her. She knew Flynn was bared. "Flynn?" she questioned, keeping her back turned and feeling those flutters in her belly again.

"Aye?"

"I was wondering. What would you say if I asked you to... make love to me?"

Chapter Nine

Had he heard correctly, or was his body so filled with lust for the woman standing before him in naught but a wool blanket, that his head was making up fantasies? He stood completely naked behind her, but she had yet to turn around. His erection strained painfully toward her, seeking her heat and longing to give her pleasure. And yet, she was not only an innocent, she was an innocent who had claimed to be terrified of the act of lovemaking. Too many women she loved had been wrongfully used.

"What did you say, Maggie?" he whispered softly and calmly. He was more than shocked, and honored, that Maggie would trust him enough to offer her body to him, but at what cost? It would hurt her to lose her innocence. Would she panic and force him off her? Or worse, would she believe his lovemaking meant they had a future together? As much as he longed to break through all of Maggie's barriers, including the one between her thighs, he was not the right man to take her innocence. He would love her and leave her, with no other choice in the matter. He wanted her more than he wanted anything else in this world. He wanted to promise her a future, bury himself deep within her warmth, and feel her let go for the first time in her life, then get down on his knees and beg the lass to be his wife. But if making love to her meant breaking her heart, he could not do it.

She turned slowly, cheeks flushed with need, chewing on her sweet, plump lower lip. Gods, he wanted to reach out and pull her to him, to tear that blanket away from her body and bare her to his gaze. Instead, he stood still, cock throbbing painfully and mind reeling with possibilities.

Her arms uncrossed as she allowed them to hang at her side. The wool blanket slipped painfully slowly off her shoulders while she stared in wonder at his obvious desire for her. Her beautiful blue eyes took in the entire sight of his body, widening when she focused on his manhood. He was certain she would run away at the sight of his massive, straining erection. He had never been so hard in his life and he gritted his teeth as her lids grew heavy with an obvious lust of her own. She was not showing any signs of the fear he expected to see.

The last of her blanket fell away and he felt whatever blood was left in his brain shoot straight down to his eager cock. She was nothing less than perfection. A small waist with delicate curves and small, yet absolutely enticing breasts. Her wild blonde locks were starting to dry and curl around her face. He was also so proud of her ability to face her fears and trust in him enough to allow him to see her bared. He knew what an honor she was bestowing on him and yet, he did not think it a good idea. It may very well kill him, but he had to make sure she understood what it was she was offering him.

"I trust you, Flynn. I want to do this, with you and only you. Show me it can be beautiful. Prove to me that making love does not need to hurt."

Her words ran through him like warmed mead on a snowy day, heating up his body with more emotions than he was ready to ponder. She wanted him to be the one and, gods, he would give up almost anything to be the one, but it would be selfish to take from her what she owed to her future husband. And he was not that man.

Taking a step back, he shook his head. "Maggie, I... I cannot."

The look on her face crushed his soul. He wanted to take the words back and pretend they had never been spoken. Devastation and embarrassment shone on her bonny face as all the blood drained away, leaving her looking pale. "I see," she whispered, a panicked look in her eyes. Gods, nay. She felt rejected, and he wanted to rip his own heart out and stomp on it for causing her pain.

She turned from him self-consciously, desperate to scoop the blanket off the floor and cover herself up again. He reached out and grabbed her waist, pulling her backside into his throbbing manhood. She gasped and struggled to get away. He almost released her, fearful she would believe he was forcing her, but decided it was her shame and hurt causing her to pull away, not fear. "I won't hurt you, Maggie. And that is what would happen if you allowed me to take you."

Turning swiftly in his arms, she pummeled at his chest with her bare hands. "You have already hurt me, Flynn Mac Greine! I faced my fears! Opened my heart to you! And you rejected me... again! Is it so wrong for me to wish to see the pleasant side of a physical relationship with the only man I trust? Would you prefer I asked your brother?" She punched him one more time in the chest before his hands came up to grip her wrists.

"Stop using my brother against me, Maggie! I know you do not feel for him the way you feel for me! And you have nay idea how much I care for you, either! You mean more to me than aught else. You always have, Maggie! By the gods, have you nay idea how long I have yearned for you?"

Her blue eyes froze as she stared into his, the words of his heart sinking into her soul. "That is impossible."

"It is not. You are kind, talented, beautiful... absolutely perfect." His gaze roamed down her naked body and she squirmed under his scrutiny, but he held her wrists firmly.

"And yet, you refuse me," she growled, her fists unfurling as she tried to claw his chest. She was good and angry, and he much preferred this side of her to the scared lass he had known only days before. He let go of her wrists. If she wanted to claw, kick, bite, or punch him, he would allow it. She had years of anger for men in her blood and she needed to let it out on the one man she knew would not strike her back.

Her nails dug into the flesh of his chest, but he stood still and took it. She roared her anger as she smacked at his shoulders. "I hate you, Flynn! I hate all men!" she wailed furiously.

He wanted to tell her that he knew she loved him, and confess how much he loved her in return, but confessions of love led to promises of a future, and he had no promises to give, so he allowed her wrath to consume her until she began to quake and shiver, tears spilling down her face. Maggie's hands came up to cover her face and she shook with silent tears.

"Maggie, I do not deserve to be the one who takes your innocence. I told you, my life is the king's. I go where he says I go. I am gone more than I am home. How can I take you to my bed, knowing I can offer you naught else? I cannot do that to you, Mags."

Removing her hands, she looked up at him with defeat in her eyes. "I know you can offer me nay future. But am I to live my life fearful of a man's touch? Never knowing what it feels like to be cherished tenderly, or to feel this elusive pleasure everyone else seems to crave? My body craves it as well... but only with you. I shall never touch another man for as long as I live. I am a woman grown and I can decide whom I chose to bed or not. You turn me away. Why? For fear of me expecting more from you? Well, you need not fear. I expect nothing from you. I know 'tis impossible."

"I did not reject you, lass. I only meant to protect you. Your first time will hurt, regardless of how gentle I am. I do not wish to hurt you and make you feel frightened again." Truly, her tears were breaking his heart. He wanted to take her wee body and wrap her in his warmth, take away all her fears. Then it hit him like lightning crashing down upon his head. That was precisely what she was asking him to do. She was asking him to take away her fears and he was, indeed, rejecting her wish, treating her as a child with no mind of her own.

She knew he could not offer her a future, but since when did a future need to be had simply to lay with a woman? He had bedded many women and never felt guilty for offering them no future, so why now? He instinctively knew the answer. With Maggie, it would be anything but simple. And, with Maggie, he wanted her today, her tomorrow, and her forever. He wanted her future. Mayhap he was protecting himself from the pain more than he was protecting her. She seemed to be less concerned about their future than he was. Had he twisted this all around in his own head, thinking she wanted more from him than she truly did?

If being with her now was the only chance he ever had in his entire life, would he regret never once feeling her soft skin against his? Would he regret not showing her a man could truly love a woman with gentleness and attention? The answer resounded in his mind. His wound ached from being ripped open once more, but not as badly as his manhood ached to be inside her, or his heart ached to know Maggie in the most intimate of ways. If he did not make sweet love to Maggie on this night, he would regret it for the rest of his days.

Grabbing Maggie to him, her breasts crushed against his chest, he took her mouth with his, tasting her sweet lips. She groaned, wrapping her arms around his neck as he resisted the urge to dig his fingers into her backside and grind against her. He needed to tame the wildness within, take his time to please her until she had no doubt that lovemaking could be wondrous.

Slipping both hands beneath her backside, he wrapped her thighs around his waist, feeling his cock press against her abdomen. She held on instinctively, trusting his every move. Carrying her over to the bed, he placed her down gently and leaned over her naked form. "I want you, Maggie. Do not ever question it. I was wrong. If you want this as much as I do, I shall gladly make love to you all night." Leaning over, he ran his tongue up the column of her neck.

She arched and groaned as he tasted her salty flesh. "All night?" she squeaked, and he only rumbled with laughter deep in his chest as he continued to glide his tongue down toward her pert nipple, straining for his attention. He took the rosy bud into his mouth and gently sucked, feeling rewarded when her body lifted off the bed, seeking more pleasure.

"All night, Mags. 'Tis how long it shall take to truly show you the many ways a man can pleasure a woman."

His mouth moved over to the other nipple and she fisted her hands in his hair. Her skin was all one shade of milk white, like fresh cream. Aside from the few freckles gracing her nose and cheeks, not a single mark touched her silky skin. "Is there more than one way?" she asked breathlessly, opening her eyes to watch as his tongue played with her hard nipple, flicking back and forth over the sweet peak. Her eyes grew wide, then fell to half-mast as she watched him work with wonder.

"There are many, many ways, and if tonight is my only chance to show you, I suppose I must show you all." She giggled at his words, then gasped as he fluidly roamed lower, trailing his tongue over her abdomen. Her legs fell open for him instinctively and a rush of gratitude that she should be so trusting washed over him. He would take his time, despite the aching in his groin. All his cock wanted was her sweet heat, but he would deny it as long as he could.

Running a finger up her inner thigh, he moved slowly and gently, giving her time to process where his next target lay. His gaze fell between her legs and he groaned at her sweet woman's flesh

116

tempting him to taste of her desire. She did not know it yet, but he was going to make her scream his name at least ten times tonight.

"You are so beautiful, Maggie," he murmured as he settled his face close to her core, using his finger to lightly stroke over the soft pink skin between her legs. Her hips jerked at the sensation and she continued to look down, this time with a slight look of worry on her brow.

"Your face is awfully close to my... nether area," she complained lightly. His finger continued its gentle strokes up and down, feeling her slickness as he began moving in circles. "Oh, Flynn!" she shouted as he touched the sensitive nub at her core. Her hips began to mimic his touch, moving in small, enticing circles.

"One." He murmured, feeling himself slowly losing control.

"One?" she questioned.

"I am counting how many times I can make you scream my name. That was one," he whispered, slipping a finger into her channel.

She whimpered and pushed against his hand. "Flynn!" she wailed as her body writhed.

"Two," he murmured, before lowering his face closer to her core, breathing gently over her hot flesh and feeling dazed at her instinctive responses to his ministrations. His tongue flicked out and ran up her seam. She groaned and watched with wide-eyed wonder as he rotated between gentle licks and sucks before taking her sensitive nub fully into his mouth. She called out his name three more times and he added it to his mental tallies. He was halfway to his goal and he had only just gotten started.

"You taste so good," he growled as he feasted on her, reveling in the moment. He was with Maggie, tasting her, straining to have her. He never thought he would be so fortunate.

"I never knew... this was even... a possibility," she panted, as her hips ground against his face.

"'Tis one of many possibilities, my love," he mumbled as his fingers worked her core and his mouth worked her flesh.

"Oh, Flynn!" he smiled against her skin, feeling proud to be teaching her the pleasures of the flesh and hearing her truly enjoying his touch. He wanted her so badly he was in physical pain, but making her call out his name was enough to sustain him for now.

Her body tensed and he knew she was on the verge of a release. "Let it happen, Maggie. This is the very best part." He flicked his tongue back and forth over her nub and added a second finger into her wet heat. She roared her release, rigid and wild, thrashing beneath him. She rode the wave like a natural. He looked up at her squinted face with delight as she finished. Her small breasts heaved, and he was proud of the redness his beard had left in its wake.

"Oh, my... gods. That was... I have nay words," she panted, looking down at him and he could not help but shoot her a feral grin.

"Did I do well, love?" He gave her core one more gentle kiss before climbing up her body to taste her mouth.

"I would say so," she purred, and he was delighted when she caged him in with her legs. "I have yet to touch you," she whispered, looking down between their bodies to stare at his straining cock. "Would you like me to?"

Her words were a mixture of both innocence and eagerness, making him groan as he buried his face into the crook of her neck. Of course, he wanted her to touch him, but would he survive it? He honestly was not sure. "You may touch it, if you wish. But I warn you... I need it just as it is for the next round, so do not set me off."

She furrowed her brow, as if unsure what he meant, and he had to remember that she was still an innocent until he broke her barrier. She must know what it meant to make love, but mayhap she did not understand what happened to a man when he finished.

Her hand reached down between them and he groaned when her warm finger ran from base to tip. His hips shot forward, and his head dropped onto her chest. "Does that feel all right?" she questioned.

"Too good," he groaned. Her fingers wrapped around him and he had to fight the instinct to pump into her hand. He needed to be inside her sooner than he thought.

"You must stop before I finish, Mags." She gave him that look again. She had no idea how a man finished, but she would know soon. "Are you certain you wish for me to make love to you now?"

Licking her lips, she shifted on the bed and spread her legs wider. "Will it hurt?" she asked with worry in her eyes.

"Only for a moment. I promise to be gentle. I will stop at any time, just say the word." She nodded and smiled as he took himself in hand. Her eyes widened as he stroked himself a few times before placing himself at her center. Gods, he needed to be inside her. It took all his strength to gently rock his hips as he slowly slid in, yet the visual of himself becoming one with her was almost enough to finish him off. Slowly, he buried himself in her until he felt her barrier.

"I must push my way in. Are you ready? 'Twill be the only time we ever must do this." His words gave him pause. He was a fool. This was to be their only time doing this, but he knew better. As long as they dwelled together in this wee hut, he would be burying himself inside her as often as she allowed. Once he knew the bliss of making love to Maggie, how would it ever be enough?

"I am ready, Flynn." With that, he thrust deep, hearing her whimper at the sharp pain. He stopped moving and waited for her to adjust to his girth and for the pain to subside. "I am all right," she promised.

Slowly, his hips began to move again, and he growled at the tightness gripping him as he picked up the pace. He was going to spill himself in her sooner than planned, but he had waited many moons to finally be here with her, and he was not able to last any longer.

"Oh, Flynn... aye, that's so good," she whispered, her heels pushing into his backside and her nails digging into his shoulders.

He adjusted his angle, getting up on his knees and making her arch slightly, placing his thumb on her nub and rubbing in circles until her hips ground against his and she began to tighten around him. Good. He needed her to finish before he did, otherwise he would fail to show her how a man can truly pleasure a woman.

She smelled like sweet wildflowers and he inhaled deeply, always wanting to remember her every detail. His eyes narrowed on hers and they made love wildly as their gazes locked, both refusing to look away. The fire raged in the hearth, heating up the room until a sheen of sweat covered their bodies. His senses were on fire as he made love to the woman who had captured his heart from the start and haunted his dreams. But reality was much better than any dream and he gripped her hips, feeling her tense around him just as he picked up his pace, feeling himself ready to explode. She screamed his name and he roared hers, feeling a shift in his heart that scared the life out of him.

Collapsing on top of her, their slick bodies heaved as they recovered from the most incredible coupling of his life. How had a wee lass, who had been so frightened of a man's physical touch, just blown his mind and ruined him for all others? Her blonde hair stuck to her neck, proof of her exertion.

"Maggie... I don't even know what to say. That was... incredible. Was it for you?" He kissed her neck, peeling her damp hair away and tasting her saltiness.

"It was more than incredible, Flynn. I cannot believe we just made love... and it was beautiful, not at all frightening, because it was with you."

The trust in her eyes was his undoing. He knew in that moment he would never love another woman. Maggie was it for him. Unfortunately, this time together, in this wee hut, was all they had before they went their separate ways. Perhaps bedding her had been a mistake. How would he ever come back from this? He knew he could not and yet, he knew he could not keep her. It was the single worst realization of his life.

"Flynn?" Maggie questioned from beneath him still. "You look upset."

He silently scolded himself for allowing his thoughts to show on his face. He was a cursed informant for the king. Secrecy and control were his greatest assets, and still he could not hide himself from Maggie. He had grown too soft. "I am fine, lass."

He rolled off her with new resolve. For a moment there, he had lost himself to his wandering thoughts. How could he have believed himself capable of bedding her again, when he knew that he would only lose more and more of himself every time. He could not afford that, yet he could not afford to hurt her after what they shared.

She sat up swiftly and climbed out of the bed without a word. Dropping his brow in confusion, he watched as her sweet hips swayed as she walked over to the woolen blanket she had wrapped around her body previously. She bent over to retrieve it, and he caught a glimpse of the red swollen perfection between her legs and her rounded arse. Feeling his new resolve swiftly deteriorating, he bit his fist to stifle a groan. Mayhap just once more...

The blanket wrapped around her body and she turned slowly to face him. Looking suddenly contrite. "I believe I shall get some rest. I want to practice more with the dagger on the morrow."

Dagger? They had just made the best love of his life and she wished to sleep so she could throw a dagger on the morrow? "I will help you." Her words made his heart ache worse than his cursed pulsing wound. He would likely require a few extra days of healing to make up for the damage he had just done, but he could not care.

She shook her head and tucked a blonde curl behind her ear, clutching the blanket to her body with her other hand. "Nay. You are still hurt. I cannot believe I allowed you to do... what we just did, with such an injury."

"You did not allow me to do aught. I did it because I wanted to. We both wanted to. Now you are pulling away from me."

Throwing one hand up in the air, she sighed and shook her head. "I am not pulling away. I am doing what we discussed. There can be nothing between us but this, and to what end? It was wonderful, and I will always remember this moment with you, but that is all we shall have: memories."

He opened his mouth to speak, but she turned and continued toward her bed. "I am your healer. I should not have asked you to couple with me, especially after you tore your stitches."

"It was worth the pain."

"So, you admit you still hurt?"

With a sigh of frustration, he lifted his shoulders. "Of course, it still hurts. But I have had worse than it is now. I can endure this pain. I prefer to be active."

"And, I prefer you to rest and get well. Good night, Flynn."

The curtains to her bed concealed her from his gaze, and he shook his head, wondering what had just happened. Aye, they had agreed naught could come of their feelings, but could she so easily turn away from him? Gods knew he could not, but he would if that was what she truly wanted. She was correct. Nothing had changed.

Och, who was he fooling? Everything had changed. Suddenly, he would give up all he had if it meant he was able to keep Maggie forever.

Chapter Ten

$\mathcal{O}ver$ the next sennight, the storm that had crashed down upon them like an angry siege from the gods swiftly morphed into a relentless snowstorm, preventing Maggie from wandering into the woods to forage for food or practice daggers. The first few days, she had kept her distance from Flynn, forcing him to stay abed while he instructed her on her dagger throwing stance and technique. She was getting much better and a glow of pride had begun to emanate from her.

It had been hard to stay away from Flynn after the incredible experience they had shared. Every night, she longed to feel his body over hers again. He had consumed her inside and out, showing her more pleasure than she ever thought could exist between a man and a woman. In truth, she had only fallen more in love with him during those intimate moments. If she had not seen that fleeting look of regret in his eyes just after he rolled off her aching, sweaty body, she likely would have asked for more. She had seen it, however, and there had been no doubt in Maggie's mind that Flynn had wondered what sort of mistake he had made in bedding her.

Suddenly, the best moment of her life had turned into the most humiliating. She could not stand being a regret to Flynn. The need to flee had caused her to bound out of the bed, but with naught available but a woolen blanket, she had no choice but to retire to her bed. Flynn had told her he could give her naught but that moment, and she had accepted that. To do so, however, she had had to leave before she begged him to show her the other ways he could touch her.

If she was to prevent herself from hoping for more with Flynn Mac Greine, her best chance had been to leave his bed and move on with life, carrying the memory of his touch with her always. It was too late. She harbored such a deep want for more with Flynn that her heart ached in her chest simply from looking at him, which she was forced to do all day, every day, due to this blasted snowstorm.

Food was scarce, and they had survived on what little dried meat, fruit, and grains remained in the wicker storage baskets in the home. The hearth fire burned every hour of the day, not only supplying warmth, but its smoke helped to dry and preserve their foods. Snow had been collected in the bucket and warmed in the cauldron over the hearth, usually supplying them with clean enough water. But porridge and dried boar meat were beginning to churn her stomach. She longed for a chunk of fresh baked bread and a cup of mead.

Two days before, Flynn had refused to stay in bed any longer, claiming his wound no longer bothered him. Maggie did not believe the man, but decided she would likely go mad being stuck in bed every day, as well. He was a man used to wilderness and travel. Surely, he could wander safely about the hut.

If she had harbored any hope for a future with Flynn, those hopes died at the casual way he spoke to her, as if nothing had ever happened between them. Perhaps she was just another lass he had bedded. She had practically begged him to take her. There was a very real chance that he had simply been accepting what she was offering. He had said he wanted her and cared for her deeply, and she believed that to be true, but as he shared more stories of his travels, the sparkle in his eye let her know that his love of adventure would rise above his love for any lass.

He spoke of the war between Tuathal and Elim, and how his family had helped win the High Throne of Ériu for their king. He spoke of his mother, her sisters, and the legend surrounding his family, particularly the one about a faery they all descended from. Faery blood, magical and legendary blood, ran through his veins. The blood of kings and gods. His entire life was one long adventure filled with excitement and she could see he thrived off his travels. It was ingrained into his blood. How had she ever hoped to turn a man with so much passion for adventure into a man who stayed in one place with a wife? She had been a foolish lass and berated herself for ever harboring any hopes where Flynn Mac Greine was concerned. This time together was just another story he would one day tell, if she was even worthy of his memories.

As shameful as she felt, she was desperate for his touch. She would never beg him to bed her again. She had asked for one night with him, and she had received it. Life moved on and yet, watching him move about their wee hut, usually without his tunic on, made it hard for her to concentrate on her practice. It was especially difficult when he came over to put his hands on her, positioning her legs or shifting her hips to improve her aim.

"You have grown quite good at dagger throwing," Flynn nodded, his devastating smile widening beneath a stubbly beard. "I was not well enough before, but 'tis time I showed you how to defend yourself against an enemy. Should a man come upon you, you must know how to do more than throw a dagger."

His hands came down on her shoulders hard and his face grew serious. Widening her eyes, it took her a moment to realize he was suddenly playing the role of an assailant. Heart pounding in her chest, she froze, not sure what to do to protect herself. He kicked her legs out from beneath her, and before she knew it, she was on her back with his weight bearing down on her.

True coward that she was, Maggie covered her face with her arms and stiffened beneath him. She knew Flynn was only doing a demonstration to show her how very quickly a man could have her on her back, but the reality of just how easily she had given in, and how very little she knew about defending herself, shook her to the core.

A sob climbed up her throat as tears prickled her eyes. She had been so confident here in this hut with Flynn, throwing daggers at immobile objects. But in truth, if a man came at her, she would be helpless. That thought destroyed all the confidence she had worked so hard to achieve over the last fortnight with Flynn. He had been too sore to do more than guide her in daggers before but now, even in his weakened state, he had tossed her to the ground as if she were naught but a sack of grain.

"Och, Mags. Do not cry." Flynn got off her and helped her to her feet, wiping a tear away from her lashes. "I did not mean to frighten you, only to demonstrate how swiftly a man can attack. I am sorry, lass." Hurt and regret crossed his face and she knew he was disappointed in her fear of him, after all they had shared.

She shook her head and sniffled. "Nay. I was not afraid of you, Flynn. I trust you. 'Tis only that I had been feeling so brave and proud of my dagger skills that I had not realized how very vulnerable I am to a physical attack. It shook me, is all." She sniffled again and wrapped her arms across her chest to stave off the sudden chill.

"'Tis why I did that. I want you to be prepared. I promised I would teach you to protect yourself, to trust a man's touch..." he paused, and she wondered if he was thinking of their night together. She wondered if he thought of it ever, for he seemed to never give it a second thought. "But I need to also teach you to defend yourself against an attack. I have failed you in this regard and I wish to work on self-defense next."

Something akin to rebellion rose in Maggie, boiling in her blood. She knew Flynn meant well, but it suddenly struck her that she was little more than an obligation to him, perhaps a challenge to boost his ego and make him feel like her savior. How she wished to take his ego down a notch. Aye, Flynn was all those things to her and more, but the thought that he knew it rankled.

Straightening her shoulders and narrowing her eyes, she tapped her foot in irritation. "I am nay more than a project to you, am I? You are trapped in this hut with me and feel somehow indebted for my aid, so you are trying to fix me? You will teach me to throw daggers, protect myself against an attack, teach me to bed a man..." Her voice trailed off, feeling a war between defeat and resentment raging in her mind. "Then you will be done with me and move on with your life feeling like a better man. You were unable to finish your mission, so in your infinite pride, you have turned saving me into a mission while you heal!"

His beautiful green eyes widened at her sudden accusation and his strong jaw locked in irritation. He opened his mouth to speak, then closed it again, considering his words carefully. "'Tis all I can offer you, Maggie. You know that."

"Och! I do know! And how arrogant are you for thinking I wish for more!" she roared, and shoved him back. Her small palms rested on his bare chest and she resisted the urge to run her fingers through the dark hair spattering across his darkened skin. "I got what I wanted from you, Flynn Mac Greine! So, do not feel so sure of yourself!" She shoved him back once more and he remained silent, taking her abuse with stony silence.

"Have you naught to say? You are content with what is to be? Your brother shall arrive and you will go on with your life, our time together nothing more than a distant shadow in the back of your mind? You will forget it was I who saved your life with my own skills, giving up my own life to save yours? Instead, you shall replace that truth with your own arrogant memories of how you helped me?" She shoved him once more, but this time, his hands came up swiftly to grip her small wrists tightly, thwarting her next attack.

"What do you want from me, Maggie?" Flynn asked through gritted teeth, tightening his grip on her wrists and giving her a mild shake. "I have been nothing but honest with you from the start!"

She chortled and tilted her head back in mock laughter. "Och, that you have been. You have made it clear enough that your position with the king is more important than aught else in your life." Without warning, her knee came up to his groin in a feigned attack, making him grunt with surprise as he released her wrists, bending over to protect his nether region from a true attack. With him caught unaware, she kicked his legs from beneath him, watching as a man almost twice her size tumbled to the floor, utter shock and awe written across his every feature.

With a triumphant smile, Maggie leaned over his prone body with her hands on her hips. "Did I do well enough protecting myself, Flynn? Had you been a true threat, I would have kneed you so hard, you would be retching in pain at my feet. So, you see, I need nay help from you to protect my—"

"Is that so?" A feral grin spread across his face as he reached out with lightning-quick reflexes to grip her arms, pulling her down hard against his body. A thrill ran through her as she crashed down onto him, feeling his muscled body beneath her soft one. They seemed to fit together like cream and honey. Separate, they were well enough, but together, they seemed to melt as one, never knowing where one ended and the other began. Her mind reeled as his hot breath fanned across her neck and his hands gripped her waist harder. She felt the rise of his desire and had to catch her breath as her heart threatened to beat out of her chest.

"Very clever, lass," he murmured. "You did very well." His lids were hooded with lust and their mouths were so close, she could almost taste him. How had they suddenly ended up in this position?

And why was she desperate for more? "You are beautiful when you are angry. I like that side of you."

"Do you?" she purred, unable to resist the urge to push her hips into his, increasing the pressure of his stiff manhood against her core. He growled lowly in his throat and she melted further against him. How badly she wanted him again. Only a few thin layers of fabric lay between them. "I have a lifetime's worth of angry. I can gladly share it with you." She sighed, and he pushed himself harder against her, using his large hands braced on her hips as leverage.

Their lips connected in a fierce battle, teeth clashing and tongues urgently seeking each other. Gods, she wanted him, at least once more before they were separated forever. Was that so much to ask?

Moving her hand between their bodies, she sought out his hardness and reveled in her power over his body when he groaned at her contact. "Maggie," he whispered as his hand found its way beneath her dress and immediately cupped her woman's heat. She jerked at first contact, then felt a fire brew within her core. She loved this man. She loved him so much that she ached for a life they could never have and yet, she could never tell him of her feelings. He was not meant to be hers. If all she had was this fleeting moment, she would take it and cherish it with all she was, memorizing the earthy scent of his skin, the hard silk of his muscles, and the feel of his heart beating wildly against her own.

"Maggie," he repeated, "I need to tell you that I—"

The door flew open with a crash, causing Maggie to scream in terror and struggle to climb off Flynn's body, but he held her closely, suddenly sitting up as he wrapped himself protectively around her smaller body.

"What are you doing with my sister?" Maggie gasped, and clutched her heart as her brother stormed into the room.

"Àdhamh!" She tried to run to him, but Flynn continued to hold her captive in his grip. She furrowed her brow and frowned at him, wondering why he would not release her to the comfort of her own brother.

Àdhamh's angry gaze shifted from Flynn to Maggie, and her eyes widened in shock. She had never seen him look at her with such fury. Suddenly, she was glad to be in Flynn's arms, and cuddled closer to him for comfort.

Snow flurried inside the once-warm hut, sending a chill over her body. Brennain stood behind Àdhamh, arms crossed and an unmistakably amused look across his face.

"You... Och! Maggie!" Àdhamh stormed closer to her, ripping her from Flynn's grip painfully, and she hollered out in pain.

Flynn got to his feet and snarled like a wolf at Maggie's brother, his words spoken with a coldness that even made her shiver. "Do not ever touch her that way again. I care not if you are her brother. Nay man shall ever make her yelp in pain again." His fists balled at his side, and Maggie looked between her brother and Flynn, fearful they would start to brawl.

Àdhamh's anger visibly melted, but only slightly, as he regarded Maggie and released her arm. "I am sorry, Maggie. You know I would never hurt you." She nodded and stepped toward him. She loved her brother. He was all things kind and gentle... on most occasions. Then his eyes widened, and he looked back at Flynn with shock. "You have told him? He knows of your... past?"

She nodded and looked up at Flynn, feeling so much trust and love for the man, and a strong sense of wonder that he should feel so protective of her.

She snapped out of the moment when Àdhamh began to shout at her again, causing her to flinch. He recited every curse word in their language for a solid minute, before roaring out his anger at her. "You... you cannot do that! You left the village without telling me! I have been worried out of my cursed mind, wondering where my sister was and how she fared! I am so angry with you, Maggie! How could you do that to me?"

She gulped and felt sudden shame wash over her. She had been in such a rush to save Flynn's life, she had had no time to think about her brother's feelings. "Did not the king tell you where I was off to?" she whispered.

"Aye! He told me my wee innocent sister had climbed on the back of a horse with one Mac Greine brother to ride into the middle of nowhere to save the other Mac Greine brother... and would likely not return for over a fortnight!" He was seething now, and she felt herself on the edge of tears as her body began to quake. How had she been so selfish as to not even spare him a moment for a farewell?

"I am sorry, Àdhamh. I was not thinking about anything beyond my duties as a healer. I had a life to save..."

"Nay." Flynn stepped forward and put himself between her and her brother. "Do not dare to make Mags feel bad for doing the one thing she does best in this world. She is a healer unlike any other. She is selfless and would go to any length to save a life. Do not dare to turn her strength into a failing."

"*Mags*?" Àdhamh repeated incredulously. "Since when do you call my sister by a name so familiar as 'Mags'? And how dare you speak to me about my own sister! Och, I know she is a wee beauty. What I do not know is what you have been doing with her in this hut for over a fortnight! And I will kill you for what I did see when I opened that door!"

"Àdhamh!" Maggie hollered, but he continued as if she was no longer present.

Àdhamh looked Flynn's bare chest up and down with disgust. "I care not who you are, or how powerful your family is! You walk around half naked around my wee sister? You are dishonorable! Have you touched my sister?"

"Àdhamh!" Maggie shouted again before Flynn could answer. "He was shot with an arrow in his side! He could not very well wear a tunic, now could he? He spent most of his days abed in recovery!"

"He looks well recovered now! Especially when he lay beneath you, doing... what was he doing?" her brother roared.

"He was teaching me to defend myself! Something you never took the time to do for me!" she roared back.

That silenced her brother, mayhap too well. His face went ashen and his mouth snapped shut as his body stiffened. "I... I..." he croaked, stumbling on his words. "I was always there to protect you. I knew you had had enough violence in one lifetime. I only ever meant to shield you from that pain, to protect you. I thought teaching you to protect yourself would only bring up more bad memories... Och." Àdhamh ran a flustered hand through his long blond hair. "I am sorry, Maggie. I failed you."

"Àdhamh. You have not failed me. You did what you thought was best for me. In truth, I was not prepared to learn such skills... until Flynn." She looked over her shoulder and locked eyes with Flynn. He gave her a soft smile and stepped up beside her in support. "I never asked you to help me. I was too scared of my past to worry about my present or my future. I never trusted another man, until I met both Brennain and Flynn. They are honorable men, Àdhamh. I trust them both. Have you any idea how powerful it has been for me to learn to trust other men, and to have one of them take the time to teach me to protect myself? I can hunt now and throw daggers. And what you just witnessed as you came in was my successful attempt to throw a grown man to the ground!"

She beamed with pride. It was true. She had truly come a long way and had not even noticed until this moment. And, she owed it all to Flynn.

Narrowing his eyes, Àdhamh looked suspiciously at Flynn. "I am quite certain I saw more between you and Maggie just now than a self-defense lesson."

Flynn began to answer, but Maggie spoke up first. "Nay. There is nothing more between Flynn and me. I treated his wound and in the meantime, he taught me a few other skills." Her cheeks flushed at the thought of exactly which skills he had taught her. "We have simply been awaiting Brennain's return so Flynn could continue his mission for the king. I suppose it is just as well that you have arrived. Now you can take me home with you."

Even as she said the words, her heart shattered to pieces. She had not been prepared to leave Flynn so abruptly, and facing a future without his daily presence suddenly seemed bleak, filling her with despair.

Maggie refused to turn around. Looking at Flynn would only hurt more. What would she see in his eyes if she dared look? Would he be pained to separate from her, or would she see relief that he was finally getting back to his life of service to King Tuathal? Either way, it would not matter. They had their time, and it was over. Her heart ached with the need for more, but it also soared for all she had achieved. She had learned to trust a man, to love him and make love to him. Those were three achievements she never thought to accomplish in her life, and though losing him was the most pain she had ever felt, she also had to use her new strength to overcome her circumstances. She would never be with another man, but she would have her memories with Flynn.

"Why are you with Brennain, anyway, Àdhamh?" Flynn questioned as he looked between her brother and his own. "I thought you were to come straight here if you learned anything important. Did you find Mal's camp, then?"

Brennain had been silent, smugly watching the tension between Flynn and Àdhamh while he leaned against the wall. Now, he stepped forward and his smirk turned into a serious line. "Aye, I found it, and I spent almost a fortnight there, earning their respect and trust until I was able to learn more of Mal's plans. What I learned, however, was that Mal meant to kidnap his daughter back from Ráth Mór, by any means necessary. Forgive me for not coming here straight away, brother, but I felt it was necessary to let Tuathal and Àdhamh know of Mal's plan."

"Elwynna?" Maggie gasped, clutching her heart. Her sweet sister by marriage had been misused terribly by her father. Fleeing to Ráth Mór and meeting Àdhamh had changed her life, but her father apparently was not ready to give her up.

"Aye," Àdhamh growled. "My wife has been through enough. I will not let him near her. But then Brennain informed me that he had to travel back here to collect Flynn... and I knew I had to come with him to make sure my sister was well. I would have come sooner, only I had nay idea where this hut was located, since you simply took off without speaking to me."

Maggie took a deep, steadying breath. Her brother only had two lassies he cared for in this world, and now both had inadvertently caused him grief. "I am sorry, Àdhamh. I wish to get back to Elwynna. I assume you will go to Mal's camp with the men?"

She felt Flynn's gentle touch on the small of her back and she hesitated to look back at him. She did not know what his touch meant, but she had to steel herself against any onslaught of emotion for the man. Their time here was done. It took all her strength, but she kept her eyes determinedly on her brother.

"Aye. We shall all escort you back to Ráth Mór, then we will head to their camp with an army of men," Brennain answered. "I was able to gather information and sneak away without being seen. Even if they suspect I was Tuathal's man and move, I know enough to know where they will travel." His gaze moved to Flynn's and he flashed an arrogant smile. "Are you proud of me, brother?"

Flynn scoffed in a way that only a brother would at his own sibling's boasting. "Aye, that I am, and most glad you did not get yourself killed."

"Never," Brennain said with a smile.

"All right, Maggie. We need to be off," her brother said, changing the subject. "The snow has stopped for now, but there is plenty to contend with and it will slow our travels. Elwynna is distraught that her father is bringing more trouble to our tribe, though 'tis nay fault of her own. I wish to be there to comfort her, as I would have had my sister not run off..."

"Had your sister not run off, I may be dead," Flynn said in her defense. The edge in his voice finally made her resolve to ignore him wane. Looking over her shoulder, his burning gaze on her made a chill run up her spine and she looked away again quickly, before he could see her embarrassing flush. She would never be able to resist a blush when he looked at her that way. But after today, that would not be possible, for they would be separated again.

"Need you time to gather your things?" Àdhamh ignored Flynn's barb and directed his question at Maggie.

"All I have are the clothes on my back, my cloak, and my satchel," she pointed to the leather sack over by her bed. "I suppose we may depart anytime. I should pack rations. I do not have much, but nay sense leaving any behind."

"I am glad to see you at least had your own bed in this hut. I can only hope you truly used it."

"Àdhamh! 'Tis enough of that now!" she scolded. She walked over to the bed, grabbed her cloak, and clasped it around her neck before slinging her satchel over her shoulder. "Let us quit this place."

If her brother saw through her false desire to go back to reality, he was kind enough not to comment on it.

Chapter Eleven

The weather outside was frigid and the air had a sharp bite to it that stung Flynn's ears and nipped at his nose. He was used to such weather, but he feared the elements were not at all suitable for Maggie to travel in. She rode with her brother, slightly behind him and to the left, but Flynn could not help turning in his saddle every once in a while, to make certain she fared well.

"I am with her, Flynn. You need not check on her well-being every moment," her brother groused. Flynn and Àdhamh had been good companions since the man came to Ráth Mór from Alba, yet he could not blame the man for his ire. Flynn had no wee sister, but he would likely be just as protective if he did, even though none of this was his doing. Although Àdhamh's suspicions were, in fact, warranted, given that Flynn did bed the lass... and he likely would have again had her brother not barged into the hut at that exact moment.

With a frustrated growl, Flynn turned back around to face the front, a puff of cold breath escaping his lips. He wished to speak to Maggie, but he needed to do so in private. Before their brothers had both burst into the hut, Flynn had been about to confess to Maggie that he wanted more with her, a possible future. Could he make it so? Would Tuathal allow him to continue his services in a different manner? Though Tuathal was family and knew that love for a woman was essential in life, few men in Ráth Mór were capable of what Flynn was. Could his king allow him a new position in his service? He was not certain, but he was prepared to ask.

That was, however, until Maggie closed off to him the moment her brother arrived. She refused to even look him in the eye. Had she been so prepared to lose him that she never allowed herself the opportunity to grow as attached as he had? He was more than attached. He was irrevocably changed by the powerful love he felt for the lass. He was ready to give up aught just to keep her, something he never thought he was capable of. Her brother stood by like a sentry, waiting to pummel him if he came too close, but Flynn would find a moment to be with her; he had to.

"So…" Brennain said suggestively with a raised black brow.

"So?" Flynn repeated calmly.

"Were you really teaching her self-defense? It appeared you had your hand up her skirt and—"

"Enough!" Flynn groused. "Do not speak of her in that way."

Brennain's other brow went up to meet the first in clear surprise. "Och, you are mighty protective of her. I will take that as an 'aye'."

"An 'aye' to what, exactly?"

"That you have fallen for the lass."

Flynn bit his bottom lip and turned his face away from his brother. This was not a conversation he knew how to have with anyone, but especially not with his brother, who vowed to never love a woman and spent as much time chasing skirts as he did servicing his king. Brennain could not possibly know what it meant to love a lass. Maggie was no ordinary lass. She was brilliant, compassionate, loving, humorous, skilled, caring… all the very best qualities in the world.

"Your silence speaks volumes," Brennain said knowingly. "You can speak to me, you know. I may understand more than you think."

That made Flynn shout with laughter, startling his horse. He patted Arawn comfortingly and rolled his eyes at his brother. "That feeling you experience after bedding a lass and collapsing on top of her, while you are sweaty and heaving with exertion?" Flynn said mockingly to his brother, "That is not love, mate."

His brother reached out and punched him hard in the shoulder. "You believe 'tis all I know of loving a lass?"

"Aye."

"Nay. Do you not remember Morna, from Alba?"

Aye, Flynn remembered the blonde healer from a small village named Miathi on the coast of Alba. They had taken a boat across the sea to retrieve a few warriors from Alba. It was on that journey they brought back Jeoffrey and his wife Clarice, Alastar, Àdhamh and Maggie. He would never forget the first time he set his eyes on Maggie. She was so bonny, yet so timid. Flynn knew even then that she was special, but her brother protected her fiercely, as he did now, and Flynn had hardly had a chance to speak with her. It was only when they arrived home and he discovered Maggie would be their new healer that Flynn began to feign injuries, just so he could be in her calm presence. A ridiculous smile spread across his face and his brother punched his right shoulder again.

"Ouch! Stop that!"

"Nay. You were dreaming of a lass, I am certain of it, and it had better not have been Morna."

"I was not dreaming of Morna!" Flynn scoffed, and punched his brother back.

"So, you admit to dreaming of a lass?" Brennain chuckled.

"What? Nay... I did not."

"Would you two quit bickering like old hens?" Àdhamh bellowed from behind them. "The wind carries, you know. We can hear aught you say. Tell us Flynn, who *were* you dreaming of?" Àdhamh's voice was laced with a warning, and Flynn rolled his eyes and made a mocking face that only his brother could see. Brennain burst out in laughter.

"I will remember that when we stop, Mac Greine. I can see your ugly face."

Flynn only laughed and decided to ignore Àdhamh. There was not much he could say to the man to appease him at the moment, and no sense in trying. He was a grown man and Maggie was a grown woman. What they did or did not do in their own private time was their business alone. Unlike most men, Flynn did not boast of his conquests, nor would he ever view Maggie as such. 'Twas best to remain silent and keep their focus on the road.

The snow was so thick in some areas the entire world seemed to be white, except for the pine needles that showed through in some areas. It also meant enemies could hide behind trees and not be seen until it was too late.

Ráth Mór was only a few more hours away yet with the harsh weather conditions, Flynn knew their progress would be slowed. He hoped they would not require an overnight stop, but if they did not make good time, it would be necessary. It had been late morning when they left and if all went well, they would be home by sundown.

The jostling of the horse made his wounded side throb, but it was much less pain than he had felt over a fortnight ago. Maggie had a true gift and he could not help but feel proud of all she had accomplished during their time together. He wondered if she felt for him, as he did for her. And though he was afraid of the truth, he needed to find out.

"As I was saying," his brother cut off his musings. "Morna."

"Aye... Morna," Flynn responded and gave his brother the side-eye.

"I cared very much for that lass. My time with her was short, and I never even laid with her, but she meant much more to me than just a passing lass. I will likely never see her again, but I do know what it feels like to care for a woman, brother. I am here if you ever wish to speak on it."

Speaking so seriously about lasses with his brother was odd and uncomfortable. Part of him believed Brennain was only setting him up to share his heart so he could laugh at him later. Either way, he was not ready to discuss his feelings for Maggie with anyone, until he discussed them first with her. "My thanks."

"All right. I can see you will refuse to talk. I will let you keep your silence, for now."

Brennain did not know the meaning of silence, but Flynn decided it was a small victory and he would leave it be. He was desperate to get Maggie back to safety and out of this cold.

* * * *

Àdhamh held her tightly around the waist to ensure she was safe on the horse they shared. She truly did not wish to speak to him. She was not entirely mad, but he did persist in treating her as a wee, incapable lass. She was anything but. Maggie was a grown woman in her own right, a healer who saved lives. She did not need to report to him or to anyone else. The way he treated Flynn grated on her nerves, yet she preferred not to get involved. The more she pushed the issue, the more her brother would recognize her love for Flynn, and the more he would question.

"I know something goes on between the two of you, Maggie. I wish you would share with me."

"There is nothing to share, brother. I helped him to heal and while we awaited Brennain's return, he taught me how to protect myself."

"Aye," his brother responded gruffly. "Which means you shared your past with him. You have never told another man about your past or your fear of men."

"I have never been forced to live with a man for over a fortnight. I was quite afraid of him in the beginning. Flynn is a kind man and I quickly learned to trust him. Aye, I did tell him of my fears and their origins. He listened and decided that he would use our time together to help me feel more confident in protecting myself. 'Twas his way of paying me back for my aid... not that I required it. But it was a mutually beneficial situation. He is healing quite well, and I do not feel as if I need to be so frightened every moment of my life. I say you owe Flynn your gratitude, not your ire."

Àdhamh made a guffaw sound that only intensified her annoyance with him. "Elwynna lived with you for a while before you wed. How is it any different? Should I have been angry with her for being alone with you when I was not around? Because I am a lass, you can be angry that I am alone with a man, yet I cannot be mad that you were alone with a lass?"

Her logic made Àdhamh sputter with indignation. "I... well... 'tis just different! She needed my help and I gave it!"

"Aye. Flynn required my help and I gave it. I am still awaiting an argument from you that is not one-sided and illogical. You cannot think of one, I assume?"

"I can think of one! Elwynna had nay protector! Her father had abused her! Without me, she had nobody to speak for her. Besides, she was not an innocent!" he stumbled over his words and she could not help but smirk at his sudden hesitation.

"I need not hear anymore. You have nay excuse for your bluster. 'Tis only your bruised pride. I will not apologize for responding to the call of duty, and I shall do so again if need be."

"You have changed, Maggie. I have to admit, I do like it." She could hear the humor in his voice for the first time all day, and felt herself relax and breathe easier for the first time since his arrival. She loved her brother dearly and knew he only meant well, but she truly felt like a different woman now than she had a fortnight ago. She refused to be coddled any longer, and she refused to stand down. Too many years had been spent fearing what others would think of her, or worse, who would hurt her next.

She was by no means a warrior-lass like Aislin, but she felt confident that she could defend herself at least as well as the next lass, and that was thanks to Flynn. They may never be together, and she may feel a slight resentment toward him for his refusal to change his lifestyle to make room for love, but she could not dislike the man for he had helped her become this new, braver version of herself.

Arriving at Ráth Mór only a couple hours later than normal due to the snow, Maggie was more than happy to dismount from the horse after riding through the towering iron gates. Every limb ached, and she was half frozen through. Her brother helped her down, but she had to hold onto him for a moment to stretch her legs. Flynn and Brennain had carried on in whispered conversations ahead of them for most of the journey, and she could not hear most of what they said, nor was it any of her business, though for some reason she ached to be a part of whatever they had planned.

Now that she had tasted freedom, she was not quite ready to go back to her usual, boring life. Aye, she loved to help heal the sick and wounded but aside from that, little awaited her in this village. Never had she felt more alone or restless. And now that she knew what real love felt like, and what it meant to lay with a man, going back to living in the small roundhouse with Elwynna and Àdhamh felt akin to a nightmare. She did not wish to encroach on their life. Though it was quite normal for family to live together in one home, it usually consisted of larger, extended families. She was simply in their way, even if they would deny it.

"We must report to Tuathal and receive our orders," Flynn said. Hearing his deep voice for the first time in hours made her heart ache. She had grown so accustomed to his presence that even being so close to him all day, yet separated, felt as if a piece of her soul had been torn from her. She supposed she must grow accustomed to living without him. Within days, he would be gone again.

She wanted to look at him, walk beside him, touch him, anything to feel that connection again. Instead, she looked straight ahead and hobbled on her sore legs, using her brother's arm for support.

"I want to get Maggie back to our home to be with Elwynna before I see the king. I shall join you all momentarily." Àdhamh held firmly to her arm and virtually dragged her away, as if he knew she wished to linger in Flynn's company.

"Mags." She stopped dead in her tracks at Flynn's low, pleading voice. Àdhamh tried to yank her forward, but she scowled warningly at him and jerked her arm out of his firm grip.

Swallowing hard, she squared her shoulders, reminding herself that Flynn was never, and would never, be hers. "Aye?" she replied as she slowly turned to look at him. That had been a bad idea. The moment his mesmerizing green eyes focused on hers and she saw his scruffy beard covering his clenched jaw, she felt as if her legs may give way. He was breathtaking and her love for him was debilitating.

"I just wanted to thank you for your tender care and delightful company. You made my recovery much more tolerable." His eyes burned with unsaid words, but she knew he was thinking of their night together and a chill of pleasure ran up her spine. He affected her body in a most shocking way.

She felt her cheeks flushing and somehow, even with the winter's cold surrounding her, she suddenly felt heat rising up her neck. "'Tis my job, Flynn. I was glad to do it." It was all she could think to say, especially with her brother's narrowed gaze shifting between them suspiciously. There was an almost undetectable sadness in his gaze, but Maggie decided she was imaging it, for it had been Flynn who repeatedly reminded her that they could never be more than companions.

Just then their king appeared, bare-chested and heaving as sweat dripped down his chest. Maggie knew Tuathal was a large man and she had seen him many times without a tunic, but this time, she felt no fear and a smile crept up her face. Aye, despite her new confidence and skills, she knew a man like Tuathal could crush or force her, but she had learned more than just self-defense during her time with Flynn. She had learned that men truly could be trusted, and that was a very freeing discovery, considering that her occupation put her in the company of many large, braw warriors.

Swiping his tunic across his forehead to mop up his sweat, Tuathal's long dark hair stuck to his neck. "There you are. I was just informed of your arrival. I left training to meet you." His gaze shifted from the men to Maggie and he bowed his head slightly. "Maggie, what you did for my warrior was the bravest thing any lass has ever done. I am very proud of you."

Her eyes shifted to Flynn and then back to her king. "I only did what was right, my king. 'Tis my job to heal the wounded."

"'Tis your job to heal the wounded aye, but to travel so far to do so, giving up a fortnight of your life? Nay, that is much more."

Àdhamh looked at her and gave her a proud wink. She felt herself flushing. Being the center of attention was never something she enjoyed, even if it came in the form of praise from her king. "My thanks, my king," she murmured, and nervously rubbed the thin woolen fabric of her dress between her fingers.

Tuathal nodded and drew his attention back to the men. "We have much to discuss. Shall we speak in private?" He jerked his head toward his home, and the men began to follow silently. Maggie turned and walked in the opposite direction, toward her home. She was anxious to take a proper bath, change out of this awful dress, and see her sister by marriage. She hoped Elwynna fared well after all that had transpired. It was not her fault that her father was a violent man, hungry for power. Still, she knew Elwynna paid the price time and time again.

"Maggie." Her king's deep voice called to her and she stopped in her tracks, looking over her shoulder in confusion. "I would ask you to join us, lass. This involves you, as well."

Her brow furrowed. What could they possibly discuss that involved her? She knew naught about Flynn and Brennain's private mission, aside from the plan to infiltrate Mal's camp. Sharing her confusion with the king was not her place. Her place was to do as commanded. With a sigh of resignation, Maggie walked toward the men, following them into the king's large rectangular home. Every other home was circular, but his was crafted with corridors, private bed chambers, and enough beds to hold visitors from other tuatha.

As they entered, the sounds of children wailing filled the room and Maggie's instincts went on high alert. "Is your babe still not feeling well?" she asked when she spotted Queen Leannan in the corner rocking Fedlimid frantically to stop his cries.

"Nay. Well, in truth, I do not know. He is happy until he eats. Once he is off the breast, he starts to holler for hours." Tuathal explained. "He seems healthy, but I cannot know why he cries after feeding."

"May I?" Maggie stepped up to Queen Leannan who gladly passed her screaming child over to her, so she could attend to her other screaming child sitting cross-legged in the corner, banging a wooden toy of sorts against the floor. "Is he well?" Maggie nodded to the wee two-year-old child as she took the babe in her arms.

"Och, nay, he likes to fuss whenever his brother does. I assume 'tis for attention, but the more the babe wails, the more we have two wailing children. 'Tis enough to make me wish to run for the hills!" Queen Leannan groused.

Maggie sent her queen a sympathetic smile and lifted the wee linen gown over the babe's belly. His stomach looked slightly distended, but not to the point of concern. Placing him down gently on the bed, Maggie used two fingers to gently poke around his belly button and abdomen. The child made small whimpering sounds and flinched, but otherwise seemed to be calming down as he chewed on his fist, drool dripping down his arm.

"What do you think is the cause?" Leannan asked as she leaned over and observed her child.

"He has pains in his belly from your milk."

"What?" Leannan flinched back and clasped her heart. No mother wanted to hear that her own child could not tolerate her milk.

"'Tis something you are eating, my queen. Whatever you eat shall also be in your milk. Most often, 'tis something most common, such as garlic or buttermilk and cheese."

Leannan looked over her shoulder at Tuathal with contrition on her face. "Och, I put garlic on everything. 'Tis the very best tasting herb we have!"

"Aye, that it is. It also is very hard on most infant's bellies. I am sorry, but I recommend nay more garlic until the lad is able to eat other foods."

"I will gladly do so if it will make my wee one feel better. To think, all this time, 'tis been the garlic. Och, I feel awful." Leannan picked up her now cooing son and cradled him in her arms, whispering sweet apologies while smothering his face with kisses.

Something inside Maggie ached for all Queen Leannan had: a handsome husband who adored her and wee babes to love. These were always things Maggie knew she would never have, therefore she never gave them any thought. Now she loved a man so deeply, she could not help but think of a life as his wife. What would it be like to carry his wee babe within her womb? Shaking her head, she took a deep breath. Such thoughts were foolish and would only lead to greater pain.

"This is precisely why I called you here, Maggie," Tuathal said, pulling her from her thoughts.

"To help wee Fedlimid?" she asked, turning to face him and the three other men.

"Nay. Well, aye, that is fortunate, and I thank you, but I mean to say that I require your further assistance." Then he turned to Flynn, Brennain, and Àdhamh to include them all in the conversation. "I am done chasing Mal around. I am done waiting for him to form a large enough army to attack us. He shall never do so, but in the meantime, he is causing us much grief. He is threatening my people. 'Tis time we gather our warriors and bring the fight to Mal. I want his head."

"Excuse me, my king, but what does this have to do with my sister?" Àdhamh asked. Though Maggie's ire piqued at her brother for, once again, speaking for her as if she was not there or had no voice, she was also curious as to what any of this had to do with her.

"I want Maggie to travel with us to Mal's camp. We will need a healer on hand, in case things escalate, and they likely will, for I mean to put an end to this. She has proven her capabilities time and time again, and she has proven her ability to think under pressure. We need her."

Her heart leapt in her chest. She knew that a fortnight ago, she would have cringed at the offer to travel with the men. She would likely have shaken with fear and even protested. But now? Now her heart longed to go, to be free to travel outside the walls. She had spent so much of her life cowering behind the safety of her brother and her home. She was ready to move forward. She knew it would not all be pleasant. War was terrifying and men would be injured, or worse. She was a healer, the best healer she knew, if she was honest. She wanted this more than she wanted anything... almost. Her gaze locked on Flynn and she breathed deeply at his penetrating gaze. Did he wish her to stay? Or was he silently willing her to go? She was not sure, but she had to remove Flynn from her decision one way or another.

"Nay." Her head jerked away from Flynn and she narrowed her angry eyes at her meddlesome brother. "I am sorry, my king, but I cannot allow my wee sister to travel with a group of men. She is afraid of men and she is an innocent. Besides, the village needs her here."

"Your wife has become quite a skilled healer under Maggie's tutelage. She can handle things here at Ráth Mór. Do not underestimate your sister, Àdhamh."

King Tuathal truly believed in her, and that made all the difference. Her heart soared at the opportunity to be more, do more. She could do this.

"Again, I am sorry, but I cannot allow it," Àdhamh argued.

Something took control of Maggie. She was not sure if it was rage, rebellion, or a sense of betrayal that guided her. Mayhap it was an explosive combination of the three, but she was done standing back silently while her brother made life decisions for her.

"Enough!" She fisted her skirts and flared her nostrils, trying to control her temper. "Do not speak as if I am not here to speak for myself, brother. I know you are used to being my champion and I love you for all you have ever done for me. I am nay longer your 'wee sister', I am nay longer afraid of men, and I certainly am nay longer an innocent! From now on, I make my own decisions, and I am going." She crossed her arms and stomped her slippered foot to drive her point home.

Before she could even process all she had inadvertently confessed, her brother stormed over to Flynn with a growl, planting his right hook into the man's beautiful face. "I knew it! You cursed bastard! You touched my sister! I should kill you!"

Brennain pushed Àdhamh back, causing him to stumble before righting himself. "You fight one Mac Greine brother, you fight both." Brennain's fist connected with Àdhamh's nose, causing blood to spurt out in sickening rivers from his nostrils.

Maggie watched in horror as the men began to brawl. Flynn caught Àdhamh in the belly. "I do not need your help on this, Brennain!" he shouted, just as Àdhamh's fist connected with Flynn's jaw. Flynn staggered back, spit out a wad of blood, and growled as he charged at Àdhamh, knocking her brother to the floor. "You know nothing about your sister, mate!" Flynn shouted as he hovered over Àdhamh's prone body. "You have lived with her all your life and yet you do not see her. She is not yours to command." Flynn backed away, wiping more blood from his mouth with the back of his arm. Brennain stood beside him with his arms crossed while King Tuathal looked on with boredom. Apparently, men breaking out in a fracas in the middle of his home was not a startling occurrence. Even Queen Leannan ignored the commotion as she continued to play on the floor with her two sons.

"You care for her." Àdhamh's voice was soft as he looked up at Flynn. Propping himself up on his elbows, he brought himself to a standing position and rolled his shoulders before looking at Brennain. "Gods, Mac Greine, you hit hard."

Brennain scoffed. "Flynn hits much harder. He simply went easy on you."

"Right," Àdhamh murmured, pushing his long blond hair away from his face. His hazel eyes shone with an emotion Maggie had never seen before, and she swallowed hard and bit her tongue to keep from adding to the insults. "You care for her," Àdhamh repeated, looking directly at Flynn.

It was all too much. She was not ready to hear Flynn's response one way or another. If he denied caring for her, her heart would wither and die, causing her the greatest sorrow of her life, not to mention the utmost embarrassment now that everyone knew she had given herself to him. However, if he admitted to having feelings for her, her heart would only ache for what could never be. They were being sent into a war. Once it was over, she would come back here to continue her work and he would continue to do his work for Tuathal, wherever that would take him.

"I have had enough," she huffed. "None of you, aside from our king, can command me."

"I never commanded you, lass," Tuathal corrected.

"Which is why you are the only man in this room right now that I do not wish to throttle."

"Hey!" Brennain exclaimed, and his lower lip pouted. "What did I do?"

"You punched my brother!" she hollered, and stomped her foot.

"He punched my brother, first!" Brennain countered.

"Your brother took my sister's innocence!" Àdhamh roared, pointing a finger in Flynn's face. Flynn grabbed his finger and twisted it back, making her brother yelp in pain.

Rolling her eyes, she walked toward the door. "You are all fools." Before she left, she turned to address the room. "Àdhamh, Flynn took nothing from me. I *gave* him my innocence... nay, I *begged* him to take it! And I shall never be ashamed. Shame on *you*, for assuming I should remain innocent my entire life." Then her gaze landed on Tuathal, whose huge arms crossed over his chest as he smiled in amusement. "King Tuathal, tell me when to be ready, and I shall be. My thanks for the opportunity."

Maggie wished to slam the door to make her exit more poignant, but remembering two wee children were still within the home, she quietly shut it behind her and walked away from the three most ridiculous lads in all Ériu.

Chapter Twelve

Flynn had been left completely speechless when Maggie shut the door behind her the day before. Not only had she admitted to her brother that they had lain together, she said it with such conviction, he could not help but be proud of the strong woman she had become.

Not so long ago, Maggie was afraid of the world, men, emotions, aught that could bring her pain. Now she was demanding to travel with the warriors, willing to face danger to save lives. His heart bloomed with more feeling than he had ever known he could experience. He could actually feel an ache in his chest when he thought of her, causing him to catch his breath and stand in awe. Nobody had ever affected him so.

To his utter shock, her brother had not further pummeled him or made any threats to Flynn after Maggie had left. He was much too stunned as his sister walked away after publicly berating him for treating her like a wee lass. Àdhamh's jaw had physically dropped and his fair skin flushed with what Flynn had been certain was embarrassment. In a way, Flynn felt bad for Àdhamh. He had done all he knew to do to protect Maggie. Instead of trying to teach her self-defense or to face her fears, he had coddled her, as most good elder brothers would. It had taken another man to teach her the ways of the world. He was proud to have been that man, yet he ached now as he quietly packed provisions for their journey and shoved them in his satchel. He would be so close to Maggie, yet not at all alone, and he had so much he wished to say.

Would she even care to hear what he would say? She seemed to have moved on, no longer being affected by him or the time they shared. It hurt to think he may spend the rest of his life as no more than a shadow in her distant past. Yet, he had been the one to tell her repeatedly that he could offer her naught. She had simply taken him at his word, learned from him what she could, and moved on. He should be relieved that a woman, for once, understood what he meant when he said he could not have a relationship, and yet all he felt was pain. She was the one woman who ever made him question his role in life. She made him want more, want to be more. Instead, he would have to settle for finishing this mission and then seeing what his king required of him next.

"The horses are readied. The question is, are you ready?" His brother always knew more than he should. Even when Flynn did his best to show no emotion, his elder brother knew otherwise.

Turning to face Brennain, Flynn crossed his arms. "Aye. I am ready. I am not one to allow my emotions to affect my work."

Quirking a dark brow, Brennain smirked in triumph. "Emotions? I was simply speaking of your recent injuries, brother. Are there some emotions I should know about?"

Flynn scowled, knowing he had just played into his brother's wily scheme. "Nay. I am only anxious to be rid of Mal once and for all. I have spent over a year of my life tracking the man. You were the one who infiltrated his camp. 'Tis time I did my part."

Brennain looked suspiciously at him through narrowed eyes, as though not at all convinced that there was not more to Flynn's grim mood, but fortunately he kept his peace. "Arawn awaits you outside. He is saddled, watered, and fed."

"My thanks," Flynn murmured, and he tucked a few spare tunics and trousers into his satchel before slinging it over his shoulder. "I am ready."

As they walked out of their family home and toward the stables, Flynn saw about three score warriors and one wee blonde-haired lass who looked as if she would blow away with the wind when her cloak billowed wildly behind her. She certainly did stand out when surrounded by so many large men, and Flynn noticed a few appreciative glances skim over her body. For the first time in his entire life, he was overcome with a sense of possession. He was not at all certain when he had decided she was his, but he had and if he stood any chance of making it so, he had to find a way to get her alone.

As if some imaginary rope pulled him toward her, his legs took several long strides forward, until he stood behind her. "Maggie." He saw her shoulders stiffen when he said her name, and his heart plummeted slightly that she should react so to his presence. "I am glad you will be with us."

She turned slowly and looked up to his height. Her blue eyes settled on his and he could see more emotion in their depths than perhaps she wanted him to see. He could not help but smile. Despite her desire to keep a distance, she still cared for him. He had to make things right. "Maggie, I've been wanting to say that—"

"You have naught to say to my sister. You have done enough." Àdhamh came around his mare and without ceremony, flung Maggie up onto the back of his horse.

She squealed and gripped tightly to the horse, looking at Flynn with shock just before scowling at her brother. "You must cease! I can handle myself."

Her brother scoffed. "Obviously, you cannot where Flynn is concerned." Without another word, Àdhamh mounted his brown mare behind his sister. Flynn wanted to curse Àdhamh and shout that he wanted to make things right with Maggie, and if given the chance, he would make things right forever. But those were sentiments he wished to discuss only with Maggie.

As if in dismissal, the brown mare snorted and pranced a few steps to the right, giving Flynn her backside. He would have almost suspected Àdhamh of teaching his mare such a trick.

"Never mind him," Elwynna came toward Flynn with Aislin by her side. "He is still in shock over the fact that his wee sister is a woman grown. Though he never wanted her to live in fear of all men, having her face her fears without his help has been a bit of a blow to his pride. Discovering that she is no longer innocent in such a public way has not helped."

His fierce cousin Aislin snorted as her red waves blew in the wind. "He needs to get over it. Maggie is a beautiful woman and from what I hear, many men on this journey have their sights set on her. Now that she is no longer so afraid of men, she may soon be faced with more suitors than she knows what to do with."

Flynn was not at all certain if Aislin was intentionally pushing his patience, as she often did, or if she truly had no idea how he felt about Maggie. He supposed that just because he laid with the lass, that was no true indication to others that he wanted more. Yet, to make his intentions known, he needed to speak with her... and her elder brother was making that impossible. Then there was the matter of his king. Flynn could not simply decide to be done with his service. He would need to speak to his king about an assignment that would allow Flynn to be of use, yet maintain a family. And was there truly any sense in speaking with Maggie about his true desires for her until he was free to do so?

He knew the answer. He needed to keep his feelings and needs to himself until he could discuss this with Tuathal, and that could not happen until this mission was over. How he was supposed to be so close to Maggie without allowing his emotions to show, he had no idea. If other lads began to press their suit on her, would he be able to stand by and watch it happen? He also knew the answer to that. There was no way he would do so.

With no way to share his true feelings just yet, and no way to control his emotions for the lass, he found himself in a very unstable position, where love and duty battled for first place in his life. Walking over to Arawn, he tied his satchel to the saddle and swung his leg over his back.

Looking down and snapping out of his daze, he saw Aislin standing before him with her hands on her hips. "You had better figure yourself out before you lose her forever."

"Are you traveling with us, Lin? We can use your archery skills," he responded, to change the subject.

"Nay. Alastar is amongst your party, but I must stay to care for wee Conor. He needs his mama more than this army does."

"You sure have changed, cousin," Flynn said with a smile. "I never thought I would see the day when you are willing to stay behind to care for a child."

Her knowing green eyes, the same shade as his own, penetrated him, as if seeing into his deepest desires. "You have changed, as well, Flynn. I only hope you are not as stubborn as I was. Do not let another claim her heart."

With a sigh, Flynn allowed his shoulders to sag slightly. "I am not certain her heart is mine to claim."

Aislin smacked Arawn on the rump, making Flynn grip the reins to stay steady. "You shall never know if you never try."

* * * *

The snow had relented for the past few days, making travel a lot easier than it had been when they left the hut she had stayed in with Flynn. Snow still covered much of the earth and the chill in the air had a painful bite, but it had been easier to navigate the land without the cold fluffy flakes falling all around. By mid-day, they had stopped to make camp about a mile from where Brennain said Mal had last been located. After his desertion from Mal's camp, it was likely they knew he was a spy and relocated swiftly. With so many trained trackers and hounds, he would not be hard to find on the morrow, and Maggie could not help the anxiety she felt when she thought of all the injuries she would need to tend once they did.

It had only been two days since she had left the hut, but her ache for Flynn already felt like the deepest void, gnawing at her gut and tearing at her chest. She had known living without him would ache, but seeing him in camp and not being able to speak with him was torture. She saw him look for her a few times and she knew he had something he wished to say, but if it was only words of consolation over the abrupt end to... whatever it was they had briefly shared, he could keep his words. They could not soothe the pain of loss she felt, and hearing him rationalize the reasons they cannot be together was a waste of words. If he had wanted her enough, he would have tried to speak with his king. With Àdhamh always hovering over her like a pesky fly, she would most certainly have no time to herself.

Now, as the warriors set up their heavy linen tents and chopped wood to build the fires, she looked up at the sky to gauge the time. 'Twas already growing dark and the days seemed to constantly grow shorter. With the little time she had left of the waning sunlight, she decided to seek what little solace she could and practice with her dagger. It was the one skill she could work on as she wished, and it also helped to clear her mind and pass the time. Being the only woman in the camp, aside from one warrior-woman named Oriana, whom all the men seemed to both respect and fear equally, she was surprised to not feel the all-consuming fear she had once felt in the presence of men. She had Flynn to thank for that.

Pulling her new dagger from inside her winter boots, she stepped to the edge of the camp. Still within view of her brother, who insisted she stay close, she found a large pine towering above her with a thick trunk perfect for practice. Mayhap she should imagine the tree was Flynn's face. Nay, that was unfair. He had helped her become a woman in more ways than one, and she had to admit he had been honest from the start. Aside from the few moments they shared, he had naught to give. Her resentment toward him may be unfounded, but she felt it regardless.

Narrowing her eyes and focusing on the center of the tree trunk that stood several yards away, she took a deep breath and held her dagger's finely engraved bone handle loosely in her grip. Her blue fur-lined cloak suddenly blew to the side with a wild gush of wind, and her green wool skirts tugged at her legs. She ignored the whistle of the wind and the bite of the frost nipping at her nose. Licking her lips, she released her breath and flung the dagger. It spun in rhythmic arcs toward the tree, finally sticking into its bark with a satisfying thwack. Smiling broadly to herself, she squared her shoulders and breathed deeply.

A loud clapping caught her attention from behind and she looked over her shoulder to find the source, hoping to see a braw warrior with raven hair and emerald-green eyes. She would relish even a moment in Flynn's company, even if their parting would destroy her later.

Instead, a tall red-haired lad with bright blue eyes smiled at her and continued to clap. He was almost as large as Flynn with broad shoulders and an alarmingly handsome smile. She had never seen this man, and yet there were so many warriors arriving constantly at Ráth Mór, 'twas impossible to know them all. "Well done, lass. Quite impressive."

He stepped closer and she instinctively stepped back. Her fear of men may have abated, but she had to always use caution. Flynn may have been kind and gentle, making her aware that many men probably were the same... but, not all. She knew well enough that many men would use force to get what they wanted.

"Nay need to fear me, lass. I am a friend of your brother's. Do you not remember me from Alba? My name is Eoghann. We played together when we were wee." Tilting her head and truly taking in the measure of him, she did recall a scraggily wee lad with long stringy hair they used to play with as children. He was four years older than her and often-times played with Àdhamh, but she had a few good times with that lad as well, before he mysteriously left Caledonii, their small village.

"Eoghann? Aye, I do remember you now." His large chest was covered in a thick leather vest and his blue tunic sleeves were rolled up, displaying tribal markings all down his forearms. She recognized the boar's head symbol of their old village and smiled. "'Tis truly you. You disappeared one day. Àdhamh was never quite sure what became of you."

He smiled and stepped forward, carefully this time, and put his hand out to her. Slowly, she allowed him to take her hand. His lips gently grazed the flesh of her hand and then he squeezed his large fingers tightly around hers once, before dropping them. "I am glad you remember me. Aye, my family left Alba abruptly. My father is from Ériu originally, and with the wars raging and Elim Mac Conrach terrorizing his people, my father came over here to fight for Tuathal."

"Did you fight in the battle that secured the High Thone for Tuathal?" she asked, and stepped aside to retrieve her dagger from the tree's trunk.

"Aye. That I did. Once his victory was won, we went back to our small tuath on the coast of Ériu. I was planning on going back to Alba, but once I heard Tuathal was building one large, secured hillfort for his followers, I knew I would prefer to be here."

"Did you only just arrive? We came over from Alba in the spring."

"Aye, just less than a moon ago. My father had been wounded during the battle, by one of our own men, no less. 'Twas chaos out there and many fought against their own, unknowingly. We thought he would recover, though he was weak for several moons. Eventually, he passed."

"I am so sorry, Eoghann. It sounds like an infection of the blood. If the wound is not cleaned properly, it may heal, but an infection takes root in the body, slowly weakening its victim. Seldom will one survive. I am terribly sorry for your loss." And, she truly was. War disgusted her. Too many good men died. She wanted to heal them all and knowing one had died when she could have prevented it, made her stomach go sour.

"Och, your brother did tell me that you have become quite the healer. I thank you for your sympathies. We kept Father as comfortable as we could. Once he passed, I sought my destiny elsewhere and came to Ráth Mór. As soon as I heard your brother was here, I sought him out immediately. I asked about you upon my arrival, but your brother told me you were a timid lass and it was best to keep my distance from you. He also told me you were Ráth Mór's finest healer."

Maggie balked at Eoghann's words. Aye, she had, indeed, been a timid lass, but it was not her brother's place to warn all men away from her. Had he sought to keep her under his wing forever? Could he not have introduced her, at the very least, to their old friend whom they knew to be safe? It may have given her one more person to trust in this world. "Àdhamh has a way of being over-protective at times. I am sorry he kept you away from me. 'Tis the truth that I am... or was... or mayhap still may be, slightly timid, but I am working on it," she smiled.

Eoghann was a nice lad. Though he was quite attractive, he did not give her the same breathless feeling she had when she so much as thought of Flynn. And when he touched her hand and raised it to his lips, she felt amicable toward the man, even nostalgic for their past, but nothing more. Still, 'twas nice to be reunited and have one more friend in her isolated world.

"Do not blame your brother so, Maggie. He has always looked out for you. Your sire was..." he paused, uncertain of how to proceed with his observations.

"A beast. 'Tis all right. I am aware of how vile my sire was."

"Aye, that he was. Your brother was only a lad then and not aware of how much you had suffered. Now, he makes up for it by protecting you fiercely. You left to save one of our dying warriors only

156

a fortnight after my arrival. I have spent much time in the company of your brother and his wife, Elwynna since you left. They have been very hospitable, allowing me to share meals with them and introducing me to many of the other fine people. I quite like Ráth Mór, and now that you are back, I think I shall enjoy it much more."

She blushed under his intense scrutiny and suggestive words. Until that moment, she had not thought him to have any interest in her. She was but a wee lass from his past. Though she would never have any interest in him beyond companionship, she was flattered that a handsome man such as he would be attracted to her. Until Flynn, no man paid her any interest.

"Well, I am glad to have you here with us. 'Tis good to have another familiar face. I admit that I know very few people at this camp."

Just then her brother came up to them with a wide smile on his face. "Ah, I see you both have been reunited, at last."

"At last? I hear he arrived a fortnight before my departure. You were not so eager to reunite us then?" Maggie cocked a dark blonde brow at him and he simply shrugged.

"I am sorry, Maggie. You were not the person you are today. I was trying to protect you." Before Maggie could berate him, he held up his hands to placate her. "I know. I protect you too much. I am working on it, Maggie. Give me some time. I allowed you to travel here with me, did I not?"

Her ire piqued again. Why did he still believe her every move was under his control. "Allowed? Brother, I was coming whether you allowed me to or not. Did I not make that quite clear?"

Eoghann laughed and shook his head. "Some things never change. You two have always argued."

Àdhamh breathed deeply and ran a hand through his hair. "Maggie. I love you. You know that, right?"

"Aye, I know Àdhamh. I love you, too." She truly did. He was the very best elder brother and all she really had left in this world.

"I will attempt to allow you to make your own decisions, but I reserve the right to speak my mind when needed."

"My thanks, Àdhamh." Maggie appreciated that her brother was attempting to step back, so she decided she would allow him to believe he still held some control over her. From now on, she would make her own decisions, but she would listen to his advice if she requested it.

Eoghann stepped forward. "Maggie, may I escort you on a walk?"

"Nay!" Àdhamh shouted reflexively. "The sun is nearly down. Soon 'twill be pitch dark and danger may lurk. I want my sister to stay in my sight."

That was it. Maggie knew he meant well, but he was already controlling her again. Sending him a warning glare first, she then looked over to Eoghann and put out a hand. "I will gladly go with you on a walk, so long as we do stay close to camp. I agree, we never know where danger may lie."

"Agreed," Eoghann put out his arm and she willingly gripped it, feeling a bit lighter now having gained a new companion, another person to feel comfortable around.

As they walked off, Eoghann smiled down at her. "I wish to know all that has transpired between then and now."

She smiled warmly at him, but the hairs on the back of her neck prickled, the instinct that she was being watched suddenly on high alert. It was likely her brother scowling at her, but the need to look over her shoulder took hold. What she saw made her breath catch in her throat.

Green eyes scowled at her and Eoghann from across the camp, sending chills up her spine. Flynn was staring them down as if he wished to charge over and rip her from Eoghann's arms. Part of her wished him to do just that, to stake his claim in front of all and confess his love for her. Of course, she knew this to be her own female folly, hoping for things that did not exist. She was certain he cared for her, just not enough to do aught about it. He was the king's man through and through.

Deciding to focus on the company at hand, she turned away and focused once more on Eoghann, anticipating a night filled with stories and sharing with an old friend.

Chapter Thirteen

Flynn cursed under his breath as he watched that new warrior, Eoghann walk off with Maggie. What was Àdhamh thinking, allowing her to wander off with a man they barely knew? How did they know he was not one of Mal's men who had infiltrated their camp, just as Brennain had infiltrated theirs? Flynn knew better than most that a good scout could convince anyone of good intentions. He had made a life doing the very same thing, earning unwarranted trust, only to report back to his king with all he had learned. All men were suspect, especially tall, strong red-haired warriors who seemed intent on wooing his lass.

"Calm yourself, brother. I can see you ready to explode. Few have seen your true temper and I doubt any will appreciate it," Brennain warned with a firm clap on the back.

"She should not be wandering off with any man," Flynn growled.

"Any man, other than you?" His brother's brow came up knowingly, and Flynn clenched his fists.

"Any man at all. Including myself. This is a war camp. Not the cursed gathering hall! We need to remain focused!"

"Are you focused on war right now, Flynn?"

"Aye! War with that fool Eoghann, and Maggie's fool of a brother for allowing it." Without any further thought, Flynn stormed over to Àdhamh with all the determination of a starving wolf preparing to fight for the last scrap of meat in an otherwise barren forest.

"You fool!" Flynn gave Àdhamh a warning shove from behind, allowing the man to circle around and face him with obvious confusion in his gaze. "You let Maggie wander off with that new warrior? We know nothing of him!"

Putting out a hand to stop Flynn's tirade, Àdhamh surprisingly stayed calm. "He is new to Ráth Mór, but we have known him since we were wee. He used to live in our old tuath over in Alba. We knew him and his family well. He fought for Tuathal during the Wars of Ériu. His family left Alba to fight for the rightful king." Àdhamh sighed and hunched his shoulders. "Mate, you and I have some things to sort out, but do you believe I would allow her to go off with him willingly? I said nay, but the lass has changed since... well, since her time spent with you."

Flynn bristled at the accusation but Àdhamh barreled forward. "Nay, I am not accusing you of aught... aside from bedding my wee sister, which I still wish to destroy you for. The lass has a mind of her own, Flynn. She is acting out, doing all she can, simply to show her own hand. I vowed to try to step back and respect her decisions. I am not certain if she is interested in Eoghann or simply seeking conversation... but I am certain where his interests lie."

"And you are all right with that?" Flynn was only becoming more and more agitated by this conversation, and every second he spent reasoning with Àdhamh was another second Maggie was alone with Eoghann.

"Nay, but at some point, I have to realize 'tis not my choice. I am married and will soon have a child..." His face lit up and Flynn could see the pride in the man's features. "'Tis time I allow my sister the same happiness. And you..." Àdhamh pointed accusingly at Flynn, "You stole her innocence without any promises of a future. I vow, I should gut you. I would have done so already if my sister had not taken full responsibility for it. But we both know you owe her more than you have given."

Aye, he did. Flynn could not fault Àdhamh for his rage. Most brothers would truly have attempted to kill him by now. Flynn came from the most powerful family in all Ériu. His family single-handedly helped Tuathal win the war and save the land. Very few would dare to defy any member of his family. This coupled with his high rank as one of the king's elite warriors made Flynn nearly untouchable. However, his honor was his to bear and he had not honored Maggie at all. Flynn would never allow his position in the tuath to dictate how he interacted with his people, especially not Maggie.

He wanted to confess his love for Maggie to Àdhamh, to vow to try to marry her and do aught to make her happy, but his life was not his own to control and he would not make promises he could not keep. Once this battle was over, he planned to approach the king and ask for a reassignment, but even before that, he realized he needed to speak with Maggie first. She was all that mattered. The lass was on a mission to take charge of her own life, after years spent cowering in corners. Though Flynn was beyond proud of her self-growth over the past moon, he knew for certain she would not appreciate him making arrangements for their future before speaking with her. And he certainly did not appreciate her going off with strange men, even if he was an old companion and verified as an ally.

Flynn shoved his black hair away from his face and scowled at Àdhamh. "I will not discuss my intentions toward your sister with you before I speak with her, but know that I do have intentions." With that, Flynn stormed off in the direction Maggie had left, determined to use his stealth skills to watch the man for any inappropriate behavior and if he needed to step in, he had no issues doing so. Maggie may balk at his interference, but Flynn could only take so much. Àdhamh may trust Eoghann with his sister, but he did not view her as other men did. She was the most beautiful woman in Ráth Mór, nay, in all Ériu, and any man left alone with her would press his advantage.

Pushing through the low-lying barren branches blocking his way, Flynn preferred the cover of bushes and shrubs over the predictable path that they would surely follow leading toward the stream he could hear rushing in the background of the otherwise still night. Stars twinkled overhead, covered intermittently by clouds. An eerie halo circled the full moon, gracing the night with a helpful glow to guide him through the thick woods, fresh snow crunching beneath his feet. Maggie would not appreciate him spying on her and in truth, it was not something he relished. But it was not his jealousy or possessiveness guiding him, he convinced himself. He merely had no trust for this new warrior.

He heard her low sultry laughter drifting in the wind and froze to his spot, feeling his stomach tighten with the very jealousy he swore he did not feel. She laughed in that way only for him. The low rumble of the other man's voice told Flynn they were not far off. Pushing through a thick wall of evergreen bushes, his tunic stuck on a few sharp twigs, but he expertly maneuvered through, coming to the edge of the woods.

The sight before him would almost be beautiful, if not for that cursed Eoghann ruining the view. The stream rushed by swiftly, the moonlight glittering off the surface like small fireflies. A bluish haze surrounded the night, the horizon seeming to go on forever. Maggie sat on a large boulder near the shore, staring down into the frigid water as the wind rippled its surface. Eoghann sat on a separate boulder right next to hers and though the man kept a safe enough distance from Maggie, Flynn could see the man's body tilting slightly toward hers, a clear indication that he wanted to get closer.

Maggie truly was more innocent than she wanted to believe if she did not think Eoghann had his sights set on her. Or, perhaps she did know and encouraged it. That thought made his stomach churn and he grimaced. Eoghann murmured something else that made Maggie tilt her sweet, long, creamy neck back and giggle with delight. It may have been dark outside, but there was enough light for Flynn to see the look of desire on that bastard's face.

Her cloak wrapped around her body, shielding her from the cold, and fortunately from Eoghann's hungry gaze. A few more moments passed as the two spoke amicably, and to Flynn's surprise, Eoghann had not so much as tried to touch Maggie. Mayhap the man truly was only an old companion and they were enjoying a private reunion. Guilt gripped Flynn as he watched in the dark, like a lurking predator. Maggie would be furious with him if she knew he had not trusted her judgement. Still, it was not her he had not trusted.

Just as Flynn was ready to admit he had over-reacted and misjudged Eoghann's intentions, the man stood up and reached out a hand to Maggie. By the sudden stiffening of her back, he could see that she was hesitant but, deciding to trust the man, she stood up from the boulder and took his hand. Flynn tensed, watching the warrior with narrowed eyes. He knew Eoghann was preparing to make a move. If Maggie allowed it, he would have no choice but to turn away and leave her be. Though his heart was in her hands, he had no claim on her and would only lose her if he interfered in her life.

With Maggie's hand in his, Eoghann pulled her away from the shore gently and they walked toward the path, closer to Flynn. Now he could clearly see their features and hear their words.

"Well, Eoghann, 'tis been lovely to speak with you again after all these years. It seems you have lived quite an exciting life. Though I am truly saddened by the death of your father. He was a good man."

Eoghann's smile faltered at the mention of his father and Flynn could understand the man's pain. His own father meant everything to him and Brennain. To lose him would be devastating to all.

"My thanks, Maggie. I miss him dearly. All I can do is honor him by continuing to fight for our country against those who threaten it. 'Tis the very cause that took his life." Taking a deep breath, Eoghann pulled Maggie closer to him in a swift move that had Flynn ready to bound out of the shrubs and pummel the arse. "I cannot believe my fortune to have found you and Àdhamh again after all these years. I hope you will allow me to escort you on another walk on the morrow. I have truly enjoyed your company."

The man was the very image of honor and respect, which only furthered Flynn's agitation. As they walked together onto the path leading back to camp, Flynn decided to push through the woods he had just navigated and meet Maggie on the other side. He was pleased that Eoghann had kept his hands to himself and he truly had only followed them to make sure Maggie was safe. He never meant to invade her privacy. Trust was hard-won when he had seen too many men break the rules of honor.

His own honor dictated that he speak with her immediately. She needed to know how he felt about her before she decided to move on. He had tried enough times, but Àdhamh had interrupted him. He would not allow any further interruptions.

Reaching camp before she did, he settled his hands on his hips and paced back and forth, awaiting her arrival. When he saw her and Eoghann appear at the path leading back to him, he stopped pacing and stood his ground, making certain they both saw him. He sent a warning scowl to Eoghann, who wore a smug, knowing smile on his face before turning to Maggie.

"'Twas a pleasure, Maggie. I have always enjoyed your company. I shall look forward to our walk on the morrow." Confidently, the man took her hand and brought it to his lips, before slowly releasing her and stepping away with a respectable bow.

Maggie's face flushed as she looked at Flynn, and he did his very best not to growl as Eoghann strutted past him with a quirked brow only he could see. Clearly, this man had his mind set on Maggie, and he knew Flynn did as well. Flynn had no time for these games. He would make his intentions toward Maggie known right this very moment.

Stepping forward, Flynn felt his heart pound in overtime as he took in Maggie's windswept beauty. Her cheeks were tinged a soft pink, as was her nose, making her eyes sparkle even more than normal. Hesitation and uncertainty shown in those blue depths, but he would make certain right now that she never doubted his feelings toward her ever again.

"Maggie," he whispered as he stepped forward, drawn to her like a moth is drawn to light. "I would ask to speak with you in private."

Her eyes widened, and he saw her twisting her hands nervously together beneath her cloak. "Àdhamh will be looking for me."

"I am not at all concerned about your brother just now. I have tried to speak with you many times since our last day together at the hut and he repeatedly gets in the way. I have an important matter I wish to discuss. I cannot wait."

Her brow furrowed in concern and he regretted making her worry. "Do not fret, 'tis nothing to worry over." His hand slowly lifted to her face and his knuckles grazed the soft skin on her cheek. To his delight, she leaned in to his touch. With an encouraging smile, he put his hand out. "Come. Please. I shall not keep you long."

With a small sigh that made his stomach clench with emotion, she nodded and allowed him to pull her back onto the secluded path. It was his turn to make Maggie know how he felt and, unlike Eoghann, he was well past slowly wooing her. They had shared much too much for Flynn to be anything other than direct with her.

Standing face to face with her under the shelter of a tall oak tree, Flynn steeled himself for what may be the most important moment of his life.

* * * *

Being so close to Flynn made her stomach do little flips and she found that her chest was rising faster and faster as she tried to regulate her breathing. The intensity in his green eyes frightened her. He had seen her arriving back from her walk with Eoghann and she could tell by the blazing look in his eyes that he had not been happy. His feelings on the matter were a mystery to her, but if he knew he could not be with her, he should not be so angry. Part of her wanted to rage at him for daring to interrupt her life, even if she had no interest in Eoghann. Still, her love for Flynn caused an ache deep inside her chest daily, relentlessly. Being alone with him now, even if his only intention was to berate her for going off alone with a man, made her feel giddy with awareness.

A few pine needles were stuck in his loose hair and she bit back a grin. Had he been using his skills to spy on her and Eoghann? Again, she should be angry with him. She had had enough of men controlling her every move, yet the thought that he cared enough to do so, made her heart lift with hope. The need to reach up and pluck a leaf from his hair was strong, but she resisted the urge. Maggie wanted to see what Flynn had to say for himself and wondered if he would admit to his devious deeds.

"Maggie," Flynn said reverently, running his fingers up and down her neck. It tingled, leaving desire in its wake. Closing her eyes, she swallowed hard and bit back any hope of something more with this man.

"What is it you wish to discuss, Flynn?" She kept her voice as steady as possible, but she knew it quavered nervously. What she desperately wished for him to say warred with what she suspected he would say.

"I wish to discuss us." Both of his large, warm hands cupped her face and she reveled in the rough callused surfaces of his palms against her soft skin. Her breath quickened as his words sank in and her eyes popped open in confusion.

"I thought there could be nay us, Flynn. You told me this often enough."

Determination shone in his gaze. "I was a fool, Maggie. I cannot live without you. My position with the king is meaningless if I must live the rest of my life without you."

She gasped at his powerful declaration and gripped her chest. Her heart ached so profoundly, thumping wildly against her ribs. "What are you saying, Flynn?" she asked tentatively. She knew what it sounded like he was saying, yet it was possible she was only hearing what she wanted to hear, what she had dreamt of hearing since the first day she laid eyes on Flynn Mac Greine.

"I am saying..." Flynn took a deep breath and blew it out slowly. She felt his warm breath fan across her face and gooseflesh covered her body. "I am saying that I love you more than I love anyone or anything. If you will have me, I wish to marry you."

Her knees buckled and, if not for Flynn's strong grip catching her at the waist, she most assuredly would have crumpled into a heap beneath the oak tree. Peace washed over her. This moment meant everything to her. Never had she thought to love a man. Never had she thought to trust a man enough to consider marriage. Everything she ever desired, yet feared, was lain before her now by the only man she could ever love.

A sudden shadow fell across her happiness. "But, what of your duty to the king? I love you, Flynn, but I cannot spend my days alone while you risk your life on missions for moons at a time." She shook her head, trying to focus on reality, not dreams.

"You love me?" His voice cracked with emotion and she realized that she had just told him she loved him without truly questioning it.

"Aye, I love you, Flynn. I never thought to love a man, but I love you with my entire heart and I—"

His lips came down onto hers feverishly. His need took her by surprise and she gasped, then melted into his fervent embrace. She had missed the feel of him, the scent of him, the taste of him. The man spoke to every secret corner of her heart, filling her with yearning and desire. His tongue slipped into her mouth and she opened for him, allowing him to consume her as her body ached for more.

She sighed as he pulled her even closer, crushing her against him. His grip tightened on her waist and she felt him dragging her further into the darkness. "Marry me, Mags. I will do anything," he murmured, and his mouth trailed down her neck.

"I cannot ask you to choose between me and your king," she panted. "I know your duty and honor mean more to you than anything."

Tearing his lips away from her collarbone, he looked down at her and frowned, shaking his head. "You are wrong. They used to mean more to me than anything. Now, you do."

"But... what if the king will not allow you to give up your position? You are very important to the safety of our tribe."

"Allow me to manage those details. I will speak with Tuathal as soon as we arrive back at Ráth Mór."

Her heart plummeted slightly. "So, you admit that he may not agree to let you go?"

"I cannot know what he will say, Maggie. But I want you as my wife, nay matter what."

Despair washed over her. She wanted this more than she wanted to breathe her next breath. Flynn was all she had ever wanted. But opening herself up to a future that may leave her lonely and pining for a man who was seldom ever home... she ached just to think about it. How would she truly feel, going long stretches of time without him? He would arrive home, make love to her, mayhap plant his seed, then be off again? Then what? She would have to live with Àdhamh and Elwynna again, just so she was not alone with his children? Nay, the entire image of such a future made her feel ill.

Pushing away from him, she felt him stiffen as her hands rested on his chest. His heart beat erratically beneath her outstretched palm. "I am sorry. As much as I wish to be your wife, until I know what our future will be, I cannot agree. It breaks my heart to even think about being away from you, desperately awaiting your arrival, wondering if you are even still alive." She gripped her stomach. Just the thought made her queasy.

"Mags, please. What can I do to convince to you wed with me?" Her heart shattered at his desperate plea. She stepped closer and wrapped her hands around his waist.

"Let us just enjoy this moment. We have come a long way in a few short moments. I never thought to love and be loved in return. 'Tis a precious gift you give me. Can we please just be together now and worry about what will happen another day? I want to feel happiness, not despair."

He sighed and tugged her to him. She laughed as he dropped to the ground, pulling her down onto his lap. The area was so well covered by towering pine trees and thick branches, little snow had touched this part of the forest floor. "As you wish, Maggie. Just know that I am determined to be your husband." His tongue flicked out and ran along her ear, causing jolts of desire to run through her body. She groaned at the sensation and nuzzled closer. Being in his arms was all that mattered in the moment.

"And I want nothing more than to be your wife," she whispered, feeling her body quake as his tongue ran down her throat. Her cloak's clasp was apparently in his way, and Flynn grumbled in frustration while his hand came up to undo the hindrance. Her cloak fell away from her shoulders and the night breeze chilled her exposed flesh, but only for a second before Flynn's tongue continued its exploration over her collarbone and the exposed tops of her breasts.

"You must promise me not to consider the suit of any other man, Maggie. I understand why you cannot agree to wed with me yet, and I will do aught to make this right. But I cannot bear to see another man with you."

She sighed as his tongue flicked beneath the neckline of her dress and his free hand slid the wool garment down her shoulder. He pulled one breast out and slowly ran his tongue over the puckering tip. She groaned lowly and watched as he suckled on her flesh, tugging now and then with his teeth. Gods, he touched her with such tenderness and love.

"Are you referring to Eoghann?" she whimpered, and he pulled her other breast free. "I have nay interest in him, Flynn."

"I know," he growled, roughly sucking her other breast into his mouth. The sensation was a cross between pain and pleasure, making her gasp and arch her back. "I followed you both to the stream," he murmured in between little nibbles and licks to her skin.

She giggled at his admission. Somehow the thought of this tall, strong warrior following her out of jealously made her melt inside. She could not be angry, especially not now as he caused such pleasure to spark in her blood.

"I know you did," she panted. Her hands ran through his hair and she pulled a yellowing leaf from his disheveled locks. "You still have pine needles stuck in your hair as evidence."

Looking up at the proffered pine needle between her thumb and forefinger, a rich, deep laugh rumbled in his chest. "I suppose I have been found out. I cannot help it. You drive me mad and I lose all sense where you are concerned."

"I feel the same way," she sighed. "Look at us. I have somehow allowed you to undress me beneath an oak tree where anyone can stumble upon us."

"Thrilling, is it not?" he groaned, and shifting her into a straddling position, he pushed her hips down onto his. She felt his hardness pressing into her bared core, nothing but his wool trousers between them.

"Aye," she whimpered, shuddering as waves of pleasure rocked through her body. The need to move against him repeatedly took over and he more than approved as his hands slid beneath her dress and gripped her bare backside.

Her fingers fumbled between them as she desperately sought out the tie to his trousers. "Are you sure about this lass? If you tug on that string, I will be inside of you so fast, you will have nay time to change your mind." He grinned and waggled his brows tauntingly.

Licking her bottom lip suggestively, she tugged the string and reached inside his loose trousers, pulling his erection out and feeling it pulse with need in her hand. It was hot, hard, and smooth all at the same time and the scent of his musk consumed her senses.

Just as promised, Flynn took no time slipping himself deep inside her, pushing upward as he gripped her backside hard, commanding her body to mold with his.

Her head tilted back as he filled her completely. She had never known of this position, but it was so intimate with her breasts hovering in front of him, his tongue flicking out to graze one rosy tip. His pace was frantic and commanding as he forced her hips down on his, harder and harder. Just before she thought she may explode from pleasure, one of his hands moved in between them, where he found the spot on her womanhood that could make her shudder and groan with pleasure with barely a flick.

His finger caressed her is soft rhythmic circles and it was all she could do to bite her bottom lip to prevent herself from screaming out her pleasure. Thankfully, Flynn leaned over and smothered her groans with his mouth, their hot breath mixing between them as they both tensed, shaking with a release so intense, she somehow felt overheated even in the dead of winter beneath a tree.

"Oh, gods, Maggie," he groaned, and his body went limp beneath her. In that moment, limbs entwined, her chest slick with sweat as she panted to catch her breath, Maggie knew she would never be whole without this man.

"I love you very much, Mags," he whispered in her ear.

"I love you, Flynn. I think I always have."

He looked up at her and smiled, carefully pulling her dress back over her shoulders to protect her from the cold. "Maggie. I went to visit you every time I had the barest scratch. I was desperate to see your face and be near you as often as I could. Do you remember when I came to Alba on a boat to fetch Jeoffrey back to Ériu?" She nodded and smiled as he tucked himself back into his trousers and tied the lace. "I was so struck by your beauty, even then."

"You barely looked at me," she laughed, and swatted his shoulder.

He replied by kissing her hard on the lips before lifting her onto her shaky legs. "I looked, Maggie. Do not forget what I do. I can be very stealthy."

Plucking another leaf from his hair, she quirked a brow and laughed. "Not as stealthy as you think." He picked her up and swung her around, tickling her sides until she burst out with laughter.

"Mayhap I have grown too distracted to continue such work. 'Tis another reason I should give it up. Come," he nodded his head toward the path. "I should get you back before your brother tries to pummel me again."

"Would it stop you from doing it again?"

A mischievous smile crossed his lips. "Never. I would take any beating to be with you. Fortunately, that will not be an issue. You may not yet agree to wed with me, but you are mine, and I plan on making that clear. Right... now!"

With a wicked grin, Flynn scooped her up over his shoulder and she squealed with shock as she felt herself hanging upside down, facing his glorious backside. Flynn laughed as he ran up the path carrying her, and she could not help but laugh as well.

When Maggie heard the hoots and hollers from men all around, she knew they were being watched by all in the camp. Flynn placed her down none too gently and before she could catch her breath, he bent her backward and claimed her lips with a searing kiss. He removed his lips and pulled her to him with force, causing her to gasp. Looking around, everyone in the camp clapped wildly at his antics... all except Eoghann and her brother, who stood side by side with a scowl.

Ready or not, she had now become Flynn's woman, and she could not be happier.

Chapter Fourteen

"You will still be riding with me, Maggie," her brother huffed over his shoulder as he tied his satchel to his horse. Àdhamh had taken Flynn's possessive antics rather well. He may have been angered, but the news of Flynn's marriage proposal soothed his nerves... until he heard that Maggie had not yet accepted.

"I do not know what came over you last night, wandering off into the woods with two warriors, then coming back to camp draped over one of their shoulders. I cannot fathom why you would turn down his proposal after such a show, but until you are wed, you ride with me."

"Fine," she crossed her arms and looked over at Flynn with her pleading gaze. She truly wished to ride with him the rest of the way to Mal's camp. She would feel warm in his embrace and she longed for his touch. Yet, Flynn was doing his best to respect Àdhamh's feelings on the matter, much as Àdhamh was doing the same. She supposed a delicate, silent truce had developed between the two men and she must do what she could to keep it that way.

As for why she had not yet agreed to marry Flynn, that was between them and she need not explain herself to her brother, yet she somehow felt the need to do so. "Flynn is going to request a new assignment from the king upon our return. I will not marry him if he continues to be away on missions for several sennights on end. I cannot do it."

Àdhamh grunted and without warning, grabbed her by the waist and tossed her onto the back of his horse, before mounting behind her. "So, you would ask Flynn to give up his meaning in life, so he can marry you."

Àdhamh's words shocked Maggie, causing the hairs on her neck to prickle. She felt attacked and misunderstood, yet she had not at all stopped to think of it in that manner. "I never asked Flynn to give up his... whatever he does for the king." She knew what he did, but it was not Àdhamh's business. "He told me he wished to give it up, so we can be together."

"Did you ever stop to think how he felt, having to choose between you and his duty? Then, you rejected him, until you are certain you shall have things the way you prefer. What if Tuathal does not agree? Then you and Flynn will... what? Go your separate ways, always miserable and lonely? Or worse, carry on as you are now, having inappropriate meetings together and believing we are all fooled."

Maggie felt her face flush and was glad her brother could not see it. He had known what she was up to in the forest last night with Flynn? Although, that was not her only cause for frustration, his words rang true in the corner of her mind. Was she truly pinning the man she loved between two important roles in his life? Could she somehow find a way to cope with his duties? After all, if Flynn was willing to make changes to make her happy, why could she not do the same?

"Furthermore, your conduct with Eoghann was most hurtful to him. Why would you agree to walk with a man... against my orders, only to turn around to do... what you did with Flynn right after? I am ashamed of you."

She had had quite enough of her brother's unwanted observations and his foul opinions of her. "Àdhamh, I love you, but if you do not leave off, I will box your ears!" she warned. "I have done naught wrong. I told Eoghann from the very beginning that we are companions only. I had not seen him in so many years. I simply wished to speak with him about his life. As for Flynn, we had nay chance to speak since we left the hut, and that is entirely your fault. You made certain to keep him away from me, so how can you blame me for walking in the woods safely with an old companion, then once more when approached by the man who wishes to marry me? Mayhap I would not have needed to seek privacy and peace if you would stop judging every move I make!"

Àdhamh grunted, but did not respond. Good. He was being entirely unfair. She had never once pried into his relationship with Elwynna before they were married. The lass lived with them, and Maggie knew what they did together when she was not home. She

174

never once admonished Àdhamh or Elwynna. Was she suddenly being picked apart for finally finding herself and seeking a life? Because she was a wee lass and he was a strong warrior? The thought made her so angry, she wished to kick her elder brother in the shins! Instead, she decided to keep her peace.

It did not take long before a shout from King Tuathal rang out and the warriors began to dismount. "We have found Mal's camp," Àdhamh explained to Maggie as he helped her down from the horse. "Brennain was correct in his directions. Maggie... this is important. A battle will happen. Men will be injured. Some will die. I trust in your healing talents and I am very proud of you, sister."

Maggie's eyes popped out of her head at his words. Looking up to his height, she saw a lopsided smile on his face. "Truly?" she asked. She wanted Àdhamh's approval. She loved him fiercely. Approval was much more pleasant than his constant displeasure.

"Och, sister. Come here." Roughly pulling her to him, Àdhamh kissed the top of her head and wrapped her in a fierce hug. "Of course, truly. I know I have been an overprotective fool, but I love you and only want what is best for my sister." He released her and held her at arm's length. "You are a woman, full grown. I owe Flynn my thanks for helping you battle your fears. He is a good man."

Tears began to well up in her eyes, but she choked them down. She had no idea how much she wanted his approval of Flynn until right this moment. "My thanks, brother. That means more to me than you know. I love him very much."

"Aye, I know you do. You would not have..." he coughed awkwardly, not able to say the words he was thinking, and she bit back a smile. "... if you did not love him."

"You are correct."

"Listen, Maggie. You will stay safely here at camp, aye? We will bring the injured back to you. Until then, get prepared. We have a few men here who are also decent at stitching or wrapping wounds, so they can help if it becomes too much. But you are all we have for the greater wounds. Tuathal chose you. You can do this."

Swallowing hard, she felt her nerves start to kick in as she wrung her hands. She knew this would be an unpleasant trip. She knew she would see death and gore. It did not sicken her stomach to see blood, but violence always made her feel ill. She was only glad to be away from the fighting. Her thoughts wandered to the safety of her brother, Flynn, Brennain, Tuathal... and now Eoghann. Jeoffrey was here, as were Alastar and Eoin. All the men she had grown to love were here and she suddenly felt her hands begin to quake at the thought of losing any of them. Most of them had wives and children awaiting them. What if they became wounded and 'twas her responsibility to save them? What if she failed?

Nay, nay, nay. She would not fail... She could do this.

"Maggie," she heard Flynn's voice call to her, and she spun on her heels and immediately embraced him when he approached. Wrapping her arms around his neck, she felt comforted when his strong arms enfolded her, gripping her to his body.

"I'm scared for you, Flynn," she murmured into his chest, hearing his heartbeat against her ear.

"Do not be. We have the finest warriors in the land all gathered at Ráth Mór. Mal's army is naught but the last remaining fools who hold on to Elim's disgraceful beliefs. Most are older men who are serfs. They have nay training and even less strength. I wish it had not come to this. It sickens me to think of fighting in an unfair battle. 'Tis impossible for them to win. Tuathal held them off for so long, knowing they are not a threat and cannot penetrate our walls. But now Mal is bent on retrieving his daughter... your sister now. He is sending scouts and spies, and threatening the safety of our women. Now, we have nay choice but to bring this fight to them. I pray they stand down and scatter, but we cannot be certain. We must prepare."

Maggie's heart ached for Elwynna. She had had such a hard life and only wanted peace with Àdhamh. How must Àdhamh feel now, preparing to go to battle with his own father by marriage? Before she could even ask, Àdhamh strode up with his hands on his hips.

"I never thought I would battle against my wife's father. But he continuously threatens her well-being. If he will not give her up to me willingly, and continues to plot her abduction, I must put an end to this."

"Aye. I cannot blame you. I would battle any man who threatened my wife." His eyes locked on Maggie's and she had to catch her breath. He was so intense and focused on her. He considered her his wife, even if she had not yet accepted him, and that made her heart flutter wildly. She wanted nothing more than to be his wife. Suddenly, nothing else felt more important. What sort of life would she live if she decided not to marry him because of his duties? She would never love another. Some time with Flynn was better than no time. She knew that now. Maggie wanted to tell Flynn she would accept him as he was, no matter where his duties took him.

Brennain came up behind Flynn and slapped his back. "Tuathal wishes to speak with you about the details. Mal's camp is just over the hill in the distance. We will raid soon." Brennain looked at Maggie and sent her knowing wink. To think he would be her brother by marriage. Honestly, she could not ask for more.

"Aye. I will be right there," Flynn said to his brother. "I have to go, Maggie. I may not see you until this is all over." He grabbed her arms and kissed her hard before releasing her. "I love you."

"I love you, as well, Flynn. Please be careful," she pled. With a nod, he walked away.

"Maggie, you will be all right?" Àdhamh asked, concern written across his face.

"Aye. I will be."

He reached out and gave her a tight squeeze. "We will return sooner than you think." With that he turned and went to join the other men gathering around Tuathal to receive instruction.

Breathing deeply, her hands shook as she felt her nerves starting to take hold. As soon as the men left, she would be all alone at this camp. She had wanted this, still did, yet the reality was beginning to terrify her. She would worry until she felt ill about every one of her loved ones while they fought against Mal's men. And when they returned, she would be on duty. She prayed it was not her own brother or Flynn who she would have to stitch up.

She needed to calm herself. The sound of a rushing stream called to her, and she desperately wanted to wash the dirt of travel off her hands and face. Perhaps the cool waters would also cool her fears. Looking at the huddled men one last time, she knew standing in one spot would only make her suffering feel like an eternity. Following the sounds, Maggie wrapped her arms around herself to stave off the chill. The wind howling around her had a bite that penetrated through all her layers. The water would be dreadfully cold, but her hands were covered in a layer of grime that she could only assume also covered her face. She could not treat injured men with dirty hands, nor could she begin to touch her boiled tools until she properly cleansed herself with the special soap in her satchel.

Leaning over to cup some freezing water into her palms, she splashed it on her face and cringed as it stung her chapped skin.

"Thinking to sneak away before saying farewell?" She heard Eoghann behind her and stood up swiftly to face him.

"Oh. I am sorry. I thought you were with Tuathal discussing strategy."

A strange, mischievous look crossed his face and her stomach churned with foreboding. "Oh, I was. I learned just enough to report back."

Taking a step back, she felt the hem of her dress dragging in the water behind her. "Report back?" she questioned, wishing she had more room to back away.

"Report back to Mal!" His arms shot out so fast, she had no time to react. One arm encircled her waist while the other wrapped around her mouth. "You're coming with me."

She kicked and thrashed, trying unsuccessfully to bite his hand and kick his shins. What was happening? Why was he taking her? She tried to scream, but his hand muffled any sound.

"I am sorry, Maggie. It has to be this way," he said, dragging her away from the water and through the brush. "We need a lass of great import to use against Tuathal. Mal wanted his daughter back. I infiltrated Ráth Mór under the guise of finally joining Tuathal's army, but my mission all along was to get close to Elwynna."

Maggie gasped and kicked out again, hitting him square in the shin. He hissed through his teeth but did not dare release his grip on her. She could barely breathe with his hand covering her mouth and half her nose. Her chest heaved with panic. This could not be happening, after a lifetime spent avoiding dangerous men, she had too easily trusted an old familiar face. He had fought for Tuathal, not against. Why would he do this?

"Och, do you think 'tis only your future husband who can spy on the enemy camp? I knew Tuathal had spies, I just was not certain who until I arrived," he grunted, and he struggled to control her. Panic caused her to buck like a wild mare and she made contact more than once, but the man was tall, strong, and obviously trained to manage more pain than she could inflict at the moment.

Once they were hidden beneath a cluster of towering pine trees, he sat down beside a thick round trunk, pulling her down with him. She sat on his lap and felt herself growing ill. What would he do to her? To think she once believed herself capable of defending against a strong man. She was completely helpless.

"Your warriors will be leaving soon. By the time they realize I am no longer with them, we will already be on our way to Mal. I know a shortcut that will get us there before Tuathal's party, and now that I know they plan to attack from the south... well, I am afraid most of the men you love will likely die today. I am sorry for that, Maggie."

Tears slid down her cheeks as she struggled even more against him. Nay. This was a nightmare. In the distance, they could hear the pounding of hoofbeats as all the men took off from camp, heading toward Mal. Finally, Eoghann removed his hand from her mouth and she took a deep breath before releasing a shuddering sob.

"Why?" she cried, knowing that nobody would hear her now. She had been the only one to stay behind at camp. "You fought against Elim! You are friends with my brother! Why would you do this? You lied to me about... everything!"

"Maggie, sometimes a man must change his allegiances, especially when the man he once fought for, is the man who killed his father. I did not lie to you about anything."

"What? I do not understand!" She could hear the panic rising in her voice and her limbs quaked as he stood up quickly and began dragging her through the forest. "Where are you taking me?"

"I have a horse stowed away. He is tied to a tree over here. We will be at Mal's camp quite soon. I shall do my best to insure your safety, but I cannot promise anything."

Finding the brown-and-white spotted horse well-hidden in the thickness of the trees, he grabbed her around the waist and hoisted her on top of it before swinging his own leg up. He mounted so swiftly, she never stood a chance at escape. "You took advantage of my brother's friendship, just so you could try to steal his wife? You are a terrible person, Eoghann!"

Maggie was past caring if he struck her for shouting back at him or throwing insults. She was in a state of shock and still not certain what was happening. It had all happened so swiftly.

"I am not a terrible person!" he shouted, kicking the horse and they took off so quickly she squealed and panicked, looking for something to cling to. Eoghann's strong arm came around to steady her before she fell. "I am a warrior, Maggie, and I am loyal to my family! I watched my father suffer terribly for many moons after being sliced through by the very king he fought for! We left everything we knew behind in Alba so we could fight for our rightful king! And he killed my father!"

"What? Nay!" she roared while the world whipped past them in a blur, the wind stinging her face. She was not so sure he could hear her words, but she heard his clearly against her ear as they rode in a different direction than the other warriors.

His voice came more softly than before. "It was chaos. Elim's men mixed with Tuathal's. Few men had leather vests with Tuathal's crest on it. Most of us wore rags or soiled garments. It was hard to know friend from foe. Still, my father fought hard, taking down many men so he could help Tuathal secure his throne. But Tuatha cut my father down. We tried to save him, but he suffered, dying slowly before our eyes. Had we stayed in Alba, he would still be alive! Tuathal never came to visit, though I know he knew what he had done. No apology came. I wanted to believe that it had all been an accident, but I know now that Tuathal intentionally cut down my father, though I

180

cannot understand why. I vowed on the day he died that I would seek revenge for my father's death."

Slowing the horse slightly, Eoghann looked around to make sure they were out of sight of Tuathal's warriors. "Mal was Elim's greatest warrior. We knew he was building an army against Tuathal, so I sought him out and joined his ranks, eager to take Tuathal down. When Elwynna left camp and married a warrior at Ráth Mór, Mal was determined to get her back. When I found out that the man she married was my old companion, Àdhamh, I was sent to join Tuathal's army and learn all I could while attempting to steal Elwynna away."

"Why does Mal want his daughter back so badly? She is happy with my people and with my brother! Her father hurt her, used her for his own purposes. He does not love her. You would bring her back to that man, to be abused again? Now you bring me to him instead? Why?" How could she have so wrongly judged his character, after years of caution?

"Tuathal claims to be a man of honor. We know he will not attack if we have a lass who is under his protection. Our army is not strong enough to fight him. We need time. Gaining Elwynna back would have given us a chance to bargain with Tuathal until we could find his weaknesses. But Elwynna was too well protected. Your over-protective brother does not let her out of his sight while he is home. I could not get to her. When I heard that you were the healer, I knew I could get to you instead. I knew you would trust me once we reunited. Taking you was just as well. Neither Tuathal nor Àdhamh will allow harm to befall you. Once I learned Flynn was the informant, always tracking Mal's every move as he tried to gain power, I knew stealing you away would give even more encouragement for him to back off Mal."

Maggie silently shook her head, listening as Eoghann described their plan in detail. They now had Ráth Mór's healer at their mercy. She knew she did not mean much to most people, but she meant all to Àdhamh and Flynn. While she knew Tuathal and his warriors would do aught to save her, she also felt like a fool, allowing herself to be used as a pawn and placing all those she loved in danger.

"Tuathal would never kill an innocent man intentionally, Eoghann. Surely, as a warrior, you understand that accidents happen in battle. How can you put so many people in harm's way?" She tried to reason with him. He was not insane, she knew this much was true. He was a man driven by revenge, but not madness.

"That does not bring my father back, does it?" Eoghann growled. "I am fatherless because of Tuathal Techtmar! I will do all I need to, to take him down. And if those men die in the process, 'tis their own fault for following a power-hungry fool!"

"Elim was power hungry! Mal is power hungry! All Tuathal ever did was try to save this land and its people, and now you are helping Mal take power! He will ruin Ériu, Eoghann! And most of these men are also fathers! How many children will you leave without a father, just to avenge your own? Tuathal has a wife and two children. Adhamh will have a child next summer. Alastar has a wee lad. Jeoffrey has two wee lads. Freyne also has two, Eoin has two! I could go on—"

"Do not! You bore me with details. You believe I do not know this already? This is war! I shall do what is needed. And right now, what is needed is getting you to Mal. When Tuathal arrives and realizes we have stolen his healer, sister to one of his best warriors and future wife of his best informant, they will scramble to gain the upper hand. Then, we will attack. Mal has plans to weaken Tuathal's army with this battle, then seek shelter in Alba as he recruits more warriors. When he arrives on Ériu's soil once more, he will be ready for the final battle."

A chill ran up Maggie's spine and she sealed her lips from speaking further. She was wrong. Eoghann was mad. Mad with grief? Mad with power? She was not certain, but the man was not to be reasoned with. Her best chances of survival now were to stay silent and think of a plan. She still had her dagger in her boot. She could pull it out and try to attack Eoghann, but she needed him for now. He knew which way the camp was, and she would never find Flynn and the rest of the men without Eoghann.

Once they were there, she had no choice but to allow him to take her to Mal. She knew he was several times stronger than her. Eoghann had not attempted to harm her, even as she thrashed at him. Mayhap he was not prone to violence toward women. If so, she would need to use that to her advantage.

Based on his information, Tuathal's army was taking a longer route to Mal's camp, circling around to the south for an attack. Normally, this would take Mal's men by surprise, expecting them to come from the west. But once Eoghann arrived and informed Mal of their plans, everyone she loved would be in grave danger.

Heart aching and stomach roiling, Maggie struggled to keep her mind clear. She had to stay calm. One thing was for certain: she had spent too many years cowering from the power of men. She would cower no more.

* * * *

"Something is not right," Tuathal growled lowly as he held up a hand to still his warriors. "I feel it in my gut."

Arawn pranced nervously beneath Flynn and he shushed soothingly to his faithful horse, hoping to calm him.

"What is the matter, my king?" Flynn's uncle Liam urged his horse forward to face Tuathal. Since his daughter had married the king, Liam had become a close confidant and well-respected advisor.

"I have fought in many wars, more than I care to know. When we reach a camp in a surprise attack, there should be certain sounds in the distance. Men practicing with swords, laughter, shouting, the sounds of their blacksmith... something. 'Tis much too quiet. They knew we were coming." He narrowed his eyes and took a frustrated breath.

"But, that means—"

Tuathal cut Liam's words off with a slow nod. "Aye. It means someone in our ranks betrayed us. They could not have known of our arrival otherwise."

Flynn looked over at his brother on his left, then to his cousin Eoin on his right. They all shrugged and widened their eyes, wondering who amongst them would dare to betray their king.

Turning his horse to face his men, Tuathal's eyes skimmed his group of three score soldiers, some on horseback and some on foot. His large war horse stood a few hands taller than any other, and coupled with his own massive height, he easily looked down at his men with accusation in his eyes, yet he seemed to be searching the group for a particular man.

"Eoghann. He is missing."

Flynn growled. Eoghann had given him a bad feeling from the start. He was a new warrior to Ráth Mór and had fought for Tuathal, so he had no real reason to accuse Eoghann other than a deep sense of something sinister he felt emanating from the man. Yet, he had not said a word, suspecting the ripple in his usually honed instincts was due to his jealousy over the man's relationship with Maggie.

Àdhamh looked around and visibly paled as he realized that, indeed, his childhood companion, and the man he had allowed around his family, was not to be found. He cursed under his breath and ruffled his hair anxiously.

"When was the last time anyone saw Eoghann?" The king roared. The tendons in his thick neck corded and bulged as blood flooded his face. "Who saw him last?"

"I saw him in our group while we discussed our attack to the south, my king," Brennain said, and a few men confirmed with nods of their heads or responding with a chorus of "ayes".

"So, he knows our battle plan!" Tuathal clenched his fists. "Fall back, men. We have lost the element of surprise. If he arrived before we did, and he most likely did since we took the longer way around to the south, they are awaiting us. I will not risk the lives of my men. We shall come up with another plan."

An arrow whizzed through the air, flying just passed Tuathal's ear and sticking into the ground near his horse's right front hoof. His horse whinnied and reared its front legs. Tuathal held on tightly, gripping the sides of his panicked horse with his huge thighs.

Chaos reigned as men shouted and turned around to face their attacker, all prepared to fight to the death to protect their king.

"I would not fall back if I were you!" a loud shout from high in a tree called down to them. "We have something you may wish to retrieve... or, someone."

Everyone went silent at the archer's words. Flynn's stomach clenched. Who did they have? Perhaps they had found a way to get Elwynna after all. Flynn shifted his gaze to Àdhamh and saw the man go pale. Clearly, he was thinking the same thing.

Freyne, Flynn's cousin by marriage and one of Ráth Mór's most skilled archers, nocked an arrow in his bow and aimed, ready to release on his king's command.

"Hold," Tuathal said, eyeing the archer in the tree. "What do you speak of?" he addressed the man.

A rustling of leaves made the men shift their gazes to a thick cluster of trees behind them. Flynn knew Mal's camp was just over the hill in that direction. Tuathal's army was much too far away for Mal's camp to have been prepared for the attack, unless they had been previously informed. Tuathal's army had approached quietly from the south, but it was obvious Mal had been planting a trap.

A tall man stepped forward, holding a lass with blonde hair in his grasp, his arm wrapped around her waist and the other holding a dagger to her throat. Though her features were concealed beneath the large hood of her cloak, Flynn's heart dropped into his stomach when he recognized the bright blue fabric lined with fur.

"Maggie!" Àdhamh shouted, and rushed forward before Tuathal put out a hand to stay him. Nothing was going to stay Flynn.

Propelling off Arawn's back, Flynn rushed toward the man holding Maggie at knifepoint. He knew he could not get to Maggie and he also knew he must be careful to prevent her neck from being sliced, but that gleaming dagger stood between him and all that mattered most in his world.

"Stay back, Flynn!" Maggie shouted, clear panic in her voice, though he still could not see her features. She must be incredibly frightened. He blamed himself. In his quest to teach her to face her fears, she had decided to join them on this dangerous mission. Now, she was held captive by the enemy.

"Cut my sister and I vow I will split you from throat to bollocks!" Àdhamh shouted from behind Tuathal, straining to get closer.

The tall blond-haired man sniggered at Àdhamh's threat. He knew nobody would harm him while he held Maggie at his blade's point.

"Restrain Àdhamh and Flynn!" Tuathal shouted, and without hesitation, five warriors rushed over to pull them back, preventing their anger and fear from causing further harm. Though his desperate need to save Maggie caused him to thrash in rebellion, Flynn understood his king's need to manage the situation and trusted Tuathal to handle it with proper care. Àdhamh did not seem to be as level-headed, and curses flew while he kicked several warriors in the shin. One man punched him in the gut hard enough to drop him to his knees. Àdhamh fell, but his curses continued to fly.

"What does Mal want?" Tuathal shouted to the man in a clear, commanding voice.

"Fall back. Return to Ráth Mór, collect his daughter, and bring her back to him. Only then will you get your prized healer back. I doubt she will be in the same condition she is in now... but she will be alive."

Flynn clenched his fists repeatedly and locked his jaw so hard, his teeth ached. Panic rose but he fought it down, knowing well that panic would not help him in the moment. Àdhamh was panicking enough for the both of them, and Flynn felt guilt and pity wash over him. The two women Àdhamh loved most were being used as bait in a war brought on by a petty, unstable man.

Staring hard at Maggie, he hoped she was watching him, hoped she could see the determination and promise in his eyes. He would save her. He would never leave this camp until she was safely in his arms. Her face was obscured by darkness and her chest rose and fell rapidly beneath her cloak.

"I will save you," he mouthed to her. A very slight movement that looked like a nod moved beneath the hood of her cloak. She could not dare move much, risking a slit to the throat, but he was certain then that she had understood his silent promise.

"Nay! They cannot have my sister nor my wife! Tuathal! Do not allow this!"

"Carry Àdhamh away!" Tuathal groaned, running a hand through his hair. Flynn knew his king was trying to think of a plan, and Àdhamh's frantic pleas were only distracting him.

"Tell Eoghann I will kill him! I will hunt him down and gut him like a boar!" Àdhamh shouted as he thrashed and kicked, being dragged back by several warriors until he disappeared from sight.

Flynn's mind was reeling with possible strategic plans to get Maggie back safely, but it was hard to think past his fury and the increasing need to vomit. The man holding Maggie shook her hard and she squealed when her hood slipped off her head. Terror shone in her eyes and the blade at her neck gleamed in the light of the high-noon sun. They must be surrounded. They already knew at least one archer was in the tree above them. One wrong step and any of them could be dead. Why they did not kill Tuathal on sight, Flynn could not understand. Mal must truly have wanted his daughter back before the battle began, and would not risk losing his opportunity.

According to Elwynna, her father never showed her love. She was there merely for the purpose of keeping the army pleased with her body, though unwillingly. Why was the man so desperate to have her back? Was it nothing more than a power struggle, wanting her only because she had run away and sought refuge?

"You have three days to deliver Elwynna Mac Rochride back to her father, or your wee bonny healer will be disposed of... but not until every man in camp has satiated himself. I may go first." The blond man winked at Flynn just before running his tongue up Maggie's cheek. She cried out and jerked away, squeezing her eyes shut with disgust, and the man gripped the blade harder.

"Our camp is almost a two-day ride away!" Tuathal argued, but the man only sneered.

"Three days... ride hard."

"Aye. We will bring her to you," Tuathal glared at the man, "but only if you vow that nay harm will come to Maggie. She is not to be touched by any man. If, upon my arrival, Maggie claims to have been violated, I will not surrender Elwynna."

Flynn stared at his king in bewilderment. He was agreeing to give up Elwynna? There had to be another way. "My king... this is... we cannot..." Flynn was at a loss for words, Àdhamh would surely kill Tuathal, leading to his own death. Nothing but grief, death, and despair would come of this.

"'Tis the only way, Flynn! Do you not want your future bride back? She is one of us, and our healer. I am sorry. I tried to keep Elwynna safe, but 'tis not worth the loss of lives we shall have if we battle over her."

Tuathal turned to the blond man holding Maggie captive. "Three days. Mal shall have his daughter back. Remember my conditions."

With that, the man smiled with malice and nodded before he let a shrill whistle out and backed into the bushes behind him. Five archers dismounted from surrounding trees, some smiling with mirth, others sneering in disdain. Flynn's instincts had been correct. They were set up by Eoghann and surrounded the entire time. They never stood a chance at succeeding in their attack. They kept Tuathal alive, if only until Mal had Elwynna.

Rage, all consuming, boiled in Flynn's blood. The fear in Maggie's eyes, the way she shook with terror and cringed with disgust at the man's touch. Nothing felt right. How could they sacrifice an innocent woman, one who carried a child, to the vile hands of her father? Why would Tuathal allow this? His conviction was stronger than ever. He would not leave this camp. He would stay to save Maggie and, somehow, find a way to save Elwynna as well.

"My king. I will stay here. I will not leave until I have Maggie."

Àdhamh, finally being released and allowed his tirade, shouted all the curses he could up at the gods, spitting in the dirt beneath his feet and glowering at his king. "I came all the way from Alba to fight for you! I took my wee sister with me to give her a better life! And you allow the enemy to take her away without a fight? Then you offer my wife up in exchange? You are a bastard!" Àdhamh spat at King Tuathal once more, looking as if he were ready to murder the man.

A few men hissed at his words and many more backed away, just in case Tuathal unsheathed his sword. Instead, Tuathal measured Àdhamh, looking him up and down with narrowed eyes. "You are one of my best warriors, Àdhamh, so I will let this go, only because I would be equally upset if my wife and sister were threatened. However, the next time you speak to me with disrespect, we will fight to the death... and I shall be the victor. Do you understand?"

Glaring back at Tuathal, Àdhamh's nostrils flared and his lips pursed, fists clenched at his side. Flynn had grown quite close to Àdhamh before their animosity over Maggie. Though Àdhamh had acted as an overprotective brother, he was a good, fair man, and Flynn ached to help him. Only, he could not show any sign of his intentions in front of Tuathal. He was loyal to his king, but he would never stand back and allow a woman to be sacrificed. It was not Tuathal's way either, and the entire situation left Flynn baffled to find answers.

"I am staying here. I will break into the camp and get Maggie back." Flynn said with his hand on the hilt of his sword. "Even if I have to watch from the shadows, I will not leave her."

"I will stay with my brother. I know their camp well and I have met many of the men."

Tuathal stepped forward and nodded. "You two may stay. I cannot allow any more than that. My plan is to retreat and—"

"Truly? You will leave my sister here, at the mercy of these men?" Àdhamh shouted. "Nay! You plan on collecting my wife as well? Does it not matter that she is carrying my child?"

Never in his entire time serving his king, had Flynn seen such fire blaze in Tuathal's eyes. Roughly, Tuathal shoved Àdhamh to the ground, towering over him like a feral cat ready to pounce on its prey. Leaning over Àdhamh, Tuathal reached down and took him by the collar of his dirty green tunic. "You start to anger me, lad. Never interrupt me again! Never question my tactics or my loyalty again!" he shouted and shoved Àdhamh to the ground. "Now, shut your mouth before you ruin everything!"

Flynn, Brennain, and Àdhamh all looked at Tuathal questioningly. Ruin everything? He sounded as if he had a plan. He also sounded much calmer than expected, considering Maggie's life

189

was being threatened. Suddenly, all the pieces came together in Flynn's mind. Tuathal was a man of many strategies, yet he would never be so aloof in a situation like this, unless...

"That man who had Maggie, is he... who I think he is?" Flynn whispered carefully so only Tuathal, Brennain, and Àdhamh could hear.

Tuathal helped Àdhamh back onto his feet and looked around the remaining men. "Head back to camp! We retreat!" Tuathal shouted loud enough to rattle the trees. Their men looked confused to hear their powerful king pulling away without a plan to save Maggie, but dutifully, they did as they were commanded.

Once the men cleared, Tuathal nodded toward Flynn. "Come. Mount up. We shall speak as we ride. We must appear to be making haste." He marched over to his large black horse and mounted easily as the rest of them did the same. Following alongside Tuathal as they traveled away from Mal's camp, they could see the rest of their army riding away in the distance.

"I must catch up with them soon. We shall not truly retreat. I had to make it appear that we were cooperating until I can get a plan together." Tuathal looked over at Àdhamh with his steely blue gaze. "I would never give your wife up! After all we have been through, you believe I would allow that? I know you are distressed, Àdhamh and I cannot blame you, but your impertinence almost ruined everything!"

Before Àdhamh could offer up a rebuttal, Tuathal turned to Flynn and raised a knowing brow. "Aye. That man is who you think he is. 'Tis why I am slightly comforted that Maggie is safe. I will still allow you and Brennain to hang back and observe, but I want you to do nothing unless absolutely necessary. As long as Maggie is safe, you stay quiet and unseen."

Brennain laughed and clapped his king on the back. "You truly are a man of strategy. You have men everywhere, do you not?"

"Aye, I do. 'Tis imperative if I am to keep my people safe."

Àdhamh growled through clenched teeth and sent a scathing look at them all. "Will you stop speaking in cursed riddles and tell me who that bastard was who held a blade to my sister's throat?"

"He is one of my men, Àdhamh. I have many more than anyone knows. Even Flynn and Brennain did not know his face. They knew I had another man in Mal's camp, but they did not know who. Nor did he know of them. 'Tis the best way to keep everyone in line and out of danger."

"So, you are saying that man was not truly going to harm my sister?" Àdhamh said in bewilderment.

Shaking his head, Tuathal replied, "Nay. He has made quite a name for himself at Mal's camp. He is trusted and had to keep his men believing he is loyal to them. But, he answers to me. As long as Maggie is in his care, she is safe."

"He is one man! He cannot keep all the other men away from her!" Àdhamh argued. "I still do not like this. We need to get Maggie out!"

"Aye. And we shall. As soon as we catch up to our warriors, we will rest, eat, regroup... then, we attack tonight, much sooner than they anticipate. They will be unprepared for our attack. Brennain and Flynn, turn around now and quietly scout the camp. Learn where Maggie is being kept and come up with ways to get her out. When we all arrive again after sundown, we will rescue Maggie. After she is safe, we attack."

"Aye," both Flynn and Brennain said in unison.

"I am coming with them," Àdhamh demanded, slowing his horse and preparing to turn around.

"I would not expect anything less from you, Àdhamh," Tuathal smiled. "You are a faithful, good man. The sooner you learn that I am, as well, the better off we shall be."

Contrition marred Àdhamh's face as he scooped his long blond hair away from his eyes. "Aye, my king. I am sorry I doubted you."

"I am a man with a wife and two children. Had I heard another man offer them up to the enemy, I would have killed him before he had a chance to explain. I am only sorry I had to put you through that while I came up with a plan. 'Tis not easy being a king, overseeing so many innocent lives, and having to come up with strategies without notice. All it took was one man, Eoghann, to fool us. We could have all died. 'Tis also why I keep men of my own hidden and scattered in the shadows," he grinned. "Now, be gone. I shall return with our men at nightfall."

With a knicker to his horse, Tuathal took off at full speed, ready to catch up with his men and prepare them, once more for battle.

Fear for Maggie still niggled at Flynn. He was relieved to hear that she was currently in the hands of one of Tuathal's men, yet men were fallible, and that man had licked her cheek and frightened her. After all she had endured in life, to have a man treat her in such a way, even if only playing a role, was enough to enrage Flynn. Friend or nay. That man would feel Flynn's fist for frightening his love.

Desperate to watch over Maggie's safety, Flynn turned Arawn in her direction and sprinted back toward camp, Brennain and Àdhamh on his heels.

Chapter Fifteen

A small fire burned in the large tent Maggie had been unceremoniously tossed into by Eoghann. Once they had pulled her away, the dagger at her throat had been removed and the large blond man had switched to a gentler version of himself. Baffled, Maggie bit her lower lip and stayed silent, wrapping her cloak tighter around her shivering body. Old fears were hard to shed. Aye, she had learned to protect herself in certain ways, and had also learned that not all men were cruel, but now she was held captive by many men and threatened with violation, the very fear she had faced her entire life. Panic bubbled to the surface and she clenched the fabric of her cloak to hide her quaking hands.

She had promised herself not to cower in fear, and she would not. For some odd reason, her captor was being much nicer now that he was alone with her. "Here, drink this," he smiled as he handed her a mug of hot tea. She stared at it warily, wondering if the man meant to drug her. Taking the mug in her hands, she was at least pleased by the warmth it offered her frozen fingers. A tentative whiff of the rising steam revealed the healing scents of dandelion and mint. She smelled no bitterness or malicious herbs mixed in, but to be certain, she dipped her pinky into the hot liquid and sampled a taste. Honey had been added for sweetener, but no other surprises.

"'Tis naught but what you smell and taste, I vow. I am to keep you safe."

Maggie could not help but scoff at his words. Had he not just been holding a cold sharp dagger to her throat, licked her cheek, then threatened to take her by force and share her with other men before killing her if Elwynna was not delivered? She shivered at the thought and looked away from the man. He had kind hazel eyes and a surprisingly genuine smile, yet she knew a handsome face could hide a beastly man. Her father had been quite handsome, yet he had destroyed her mother.

Taking a sip of the tea, she sighed at its warmth. "I am not who you think I am," the man said softly, as if not wanting to be overheard. Two men stood at the entrance of the tent, one of them her own companion, Eoghann. Och, she hated him for using their past to form trust between them, then betraying her. She understood Flynn's promised whisper to come for her, but he was only one man. What could he possibly do? Tuathal had willingly left her behind and that thought stung enough to make her eyes water. He had ordered her brother seized when he tried to save her, then had him dragged away. She had saved so many of Tuathal's men from illness and injury that his betrayal broke her heart. He had been one of the very few men in this world that she could trust. Yet, she now realized that he was like most men, willing to do what was best for him, sacrificing a weak woman for his own needs.

She appreciated Tuathal's demand to Mal's man to keep her safe and untouched, but he had to know that his threat to keep Elwynna if Maggie was hurt was hollow. Mal knew how valuable Maggie was. They could misuse her and Tuathal would still give over Elwynna to retrieve her. And hearing Tuathal agree to give over her sister made her heart break. Elwynna was just as valuable to this world as she was, but it was just like a man to put a price on a woman's worth, depending on how useful she was to him. This only made Maggie more furious with her supposedly fair king.

All she could do now was be brave, bury her fears, defend herself as best as she could, and pray Flynn came back soon. But, three days was a long time to be alone in this camp, and this man kept saying things that made her brows crinkle with unvoiced questions. "Who are you?" she whispered, before taking another sip of tea.

"I work for Tuathal," he mouthed, and she gasped. "Hush." He covered her mouth with his hand. "I will keep you safe as best as I can, but when others are around, I will need to treat you like a prisoner. Understand?" she nodded slowly, only slightly relieved. This man may try to protect her, and he did not seem like he was eager to force himself upon her, yet he could not stay by her side for three entire days. At some point, she would be vulnerable, relying only on her own very new survival instincts. She was not fool enough to believe that she could hold off a man who wanted to harm her.

Thinking of the dagger still strapped into the side of her left boot, she itched to feel for it and reassure herself that it was still in place. However, she decided to wait. She did not know this man and he had licked her... no man in this camp suspected she was armed with a dagger, and surely none suspected she could throw it accurately at most targets, as long as they were not moving... and not too far away... curse it. Her skills were nothing compared to these men.

A sudden realization made all the blood drain from her face. Eoghann had seen her dagger. He had also seen where she strapped it to her boot. If he chose to, he could disarm her immediately, leaving her helpless. As if he knew she was thinking of him, Eoghann's face appeared in the opening of the tent, sending her a salacious smile. He was certainly smug at having tricked her into his trap, the bastard.

"Reaghan, Mal is asking to speak with you." So, the man who held her hostage had a name. She looked at him and his hazel eyes widened. She knew he was torn between staying to protect her or obeying the man he was meant to be loyal to.

"Aye, I shall be right there," Reaghan said with a nod to Eoghann, who sent her a wink before exiting the tent. She wanted to kick Eoghann in the bollocks, and vowed she would if given the opportunity. He had taken her away from Flynn just as they had finally found their way to one another. She ached to be with Flynn and suddenly, nothing in this entire world seemed more important than being the woman fortunate enough to call him husband. She cared not if his duties to Tuathal kept him away for long periods of time. As long as she was the lass he came home to, her heart would be content.

Reaghan looked at her before exiting the tent, as if he wanted to reassure her, but doing so would be suspicious to Eoghann and the other tall dark-haired guard just outside. Instead, he exited and shouted at the guards. "She is to remain unharmed and untouched! Remember, Tuathal will only give Elwynna back to Mal if Maggie is not harmed... in any way."

The dark-haired guard turned and stuck his head into the tent, narrowing his eyes at her as if deciding whether or not she was worth the trouble. The slow smile that spread across his lips told her that he thought she was.

Reaghan stormed off with a scowl of warning just before the dark guard leaned over to speak to Eoghann. "He says she is not to be harmed in in any. I assure you, I can accomplish what I wish with her and she will not be harmed." He laughed lowly and the hairs on the back of Maggie's neck rose at the scent of danger. "She will scream my name and beg for more by the time I'm done with her, aye?" She could see the silhouette of the huge dark guard as he made thrust motions just outside the tent.

"Do not touch her!" Eoghann warned the man with a growl. "I will gut you myself. She is our prisoner, not our slave."

The other man gave a grunt that told Maggie he was not at all convinced that Eoghann would follow through with his threat and that worried her most of all.

Breathe, Maggie, Breathe. Losing her head now and going into a panic would not help, just as it had never helped in the past. She had come much too far to lose control now. Still, she clutched her hands together nervously and closed her eyes as she paced listlessly. How long would Reaghan leave her alone? Could she truly trust him? She thought she could trust Eoghann and that had not turned out well. She could only trust herself, she decided.

As several moments passed, Maggie finally sat down on the floor of the tent, tucking her legs up to her chest as she nervously twirled a blade of grass between her fingers, pondering her options.

Reaghan appeared again, this time with a stocky man with long red hair and a matching beard. Looking up at the large man, Maggie scrambled to her feet and adjusted her dress, backing up a few paces to give herself more room. The look on Reaghan's face was blank and she knew he was playing the role of faithful servant again, but if Mal forced him to hurt Maggie, would he do it to keep himself in his good graces? She was honestly unsure and that thought had her backing up one more step. Self-defense or not, she could not fight off the two men standing in her tent if they tried to harm her.

"Do you know who I am, lass?" The large man's deep voice filled the room with commanding authority.

Swallowing hard, she urged her hands to stop shaking as she nodded, "I... I believe so."

"I am Mal Mac Rochride, leader of this camp. I hear my daughter is now married to your brother." Maggie did not like the knowing glare in his black eyes or the slight curve of his chapped lips. His skin was ruddy from too much sun exposure and wind. A large nose with broken vessels adorned a rather round face, though his body seemed more muscle than fat. His leather vest covered the expanse of his chest and she shivered, remembering all the stories Elwynna had shared about her sire. He had not cared for her at all, aside from what use she was to his men. If he were so cruel to his own daughter, what might he do with Maggie?

"Answer me, lass!" he boomed, causing her to shrink back a few more steps. Her back was against the tent's wall now.

Nodding, she answered, "Aye. 'Tis true."

He cackled and rubbed his large hands together eagerly. "Your false king would not give me back my daughter. How fortunate I was to have Eoghann join my ranks and infiltrate your village. He knows your brother well and, while he was busy trying to find a way to bring my daughter back to me, he discovered it would be much easier to take you. Your brother is much too busy rutting with my daughter to pay any attention to you."

She knew he spoke to hurt her, but his words hit their mark. While Àdhamh loved her very much and protected her more than she cared for, he had been rather distracted with his new wife. It had been a lonely place to live, feeling like an outsider day in and day out... until she fell in love with Flynn. Now she understood why Elwynna always wanted to be in Àdhamh's presence and why they were both so distracted. She was distracted right now just imagining Flynn's embrace. She hoped she survived long enough to see Flynn again and tell him she would marry him, no matter what his circumstances were.

"I am also most pleased to hear I caused your brother pain. He stole my daughter and if he will not give her up, then he will lose his beloved wee sister," the man chuckled. "That you are the healer of Ráth Mór, well that only made this more interesting. I am most excited to see how far Tuathal will go to save you."

Looking her up and down, Mal grunted and stepped closer, running his knuckles down her cheek. She flinched and tried to turn away, but he gripped her chin tightly and forced her to face him. "You are a wee bonny lass. My men have not had the company of a woman in many moons, not since my daughter was taken from me." He licked his lips and grinned, and his yellow teeth caused Maggie to grimace.

"You are vile!" she shouted, shaking with rage. How dare he use his daughter so foully, and not care at all how he hurt her. "You used Elwynna!"

Mal only shrugged, not releasing his grip. "Men are predatorial by nature, lass! They have needs, and they are much more loyal and hardworking when those needs are met! I never allowed a man to hurt her, simply sate themselves with her body. You think I am a terrible father? Mayhap, but I am a leader of men and know how to keep them happy. Since she left, the men have been restless. Och, they are loyal and will not abandon me, and for that, they deserve a... sweet reward."

"Nay!" Maggie slapped his arm as hard as she could, jerking out of his grip. Reaghan stood behind Mal with a look of warning on his face. Was he worried Mal would strike her, or worse? Well, keeping her mouth shut clearly was not helping her or preventing him from leering. "I know what men are capable of! I have grown up watching the women I love be used for the pleasure of men!"

"Good. Then you understand why I must allow my men to seek their pleasure from you. Do not worry, lass, 'tis not all my men, only a handful of my most trusted warriors. They will not hurt you... overmuch."

Reaghan cleared his throat from behind Mal and licked his lips before speaking. "My lord, Tuathal said if any harm came to Maggie, he would not give back your daughter. She must remain untouched or the deal is off."

Mal rocked back and forth on his heels, rubbing his beard with one hand. "He said if Maggie claims to have been harmed, he will not give us Elwynna, but I hear this lass is the best healer in Ériu. Tuathal will give me my daughter, for she is not worth what Maggie is worth. I believe Tuathal is bluffing. We can do whatever we wish with this bonny lass, and Tuathal will still give up Elwynna. After all, she is Àdhamh's sister and from what I gather, one of his finest warriors is in love with her."

Maggie gasped at all Mal knew of her and it made her stomach clench painfully. Eoghann truly had reported well back to Mal, and now Maggie was a pawn in the games of men.

"Och, I know all about you, lass. I know Flynn Mac Greine will do aught to have you back. Eoghann did well to bring you to me, mayhap he should have the first taste." The man roared with laughter and Maggie felt panic rise in her throat. Her very worst fears were going to come true and she could not stop them.

"With all due respect, my lord, Eoghann may have a turn, but I believe I deserve her first. I am the one who made the deal with Tuathal to get Elwynna back." Maggie's eyes grew wide at Reaghan's declaration and she clutched her chest to try to stop her heart from beating out of her ribs.

"Nay... nay..." she murmured, looking around for a way to escape, but she was cornered in the tent with two large warriors in front of her and two just outside.

As if she had not spoken at all, Mal nodded at Reaghan's request. "I care not which order you take her. Just make sure there is enough of her left for a few other men when you are finished."

"Aye, my chief," Reaghan agreed; he stepped forward and gripped her arms tightly, pulling her to him.

All of her will not to panic disappeared as her blood ran cold with fear. "Let go of me!" she wailed, struggling to get out of his grip. "Do not touch me!" She felt as if she may be sick.

His lips crashed down on hers forcefully and she let out a terrified scream, clawing at his face. Mal only laughed with amusement before stepping out of the tent and telling the two guards to follow him to his tent. She was completely alone with Reaghan, fear gripping her.

Suddenly, he released her. In outrage, she slapped him across the jaw so hard her hand stung. Rubbing his face, he did not seem angry or surprised by her outburst. "I just saved you, lass. We will not be bothered for some time. I am sorry I frightened you."

Crossing her arms tightly across her body, she moved away and shivered as all her pent-up fear finally started to come to a head. She truly thought he was about to violate her and it cause her stomach to churn as images of her own mother being forced and beaten filled her mind. "I just want to go home," she sobbed into her hands, feeling relieved, frightened, and disappointed in her inability to stay calm or protect herself when it mattered most.

"Tuathal will come for you," Reaghan said with assurance. No words could say how terrified she was, so she only nodded and sat down on the ground, the earthen floor beneath her rear spreading coldness through her body.

"Reaghan!" A loud voice bellowed from outside the tent. "We are under attack!" a man yelled.

Turning to look at Maggie fiercely, he pointed a finger in her direction. "'Tis Tuathal. He came faster than I expected. Stay here."

Maggie only nodded. Where else could she go? She prayed he was correct and the men attacking were her people, not another clan fighting for power. The shouts of men filled the air outside, but she was determined to stay where she was. Being thrown into the middle of a battle was the last thing she wished for. She prayed Flynn was with the other men and that he would be safe.

The flap of her tent opened and the overly large dark-haired guard from earlier crept toward her, a sneer on his face. His hand reached out for her, but she shifted quickly, avoiding his grip. He was a giant man and if he got his hands on her, she may not stand a chance, but she was slight and quick on her feet. Her heart beat wildly, but she remained vigilant.

"Come here, lass. 'Tis my turn to have ye." He lunged for her again, and again she evaded him.

"Should you not be helping Mal fight?" Maggie questioned, trying not to sound as if her fear was choking her from within. In truth, she could hardly breathe through her panic as the warrior circled her like a vulture, waiting to devour its prey.

"What? While you are in here unattended? Nay, lass. As I said, 'tis my turn. We have more than enough fighting men to handle a small raid," he scoffed.

He stepped one way and she dodged, but he feinted and stepped back in the other direction, wrapping his huge arms around her small waist with a steel-like grip. She squealed just before all the air was squeezed from her lungs. His grip tightened around her middle with a crushing force, but she shot her leg out and connected with his shin.

"Ow! Ye wee bitch!" The large warrior slapped her across the face with the back of his hand, causing her to reel back from the pain and scream in terror before he dropped her to the ground and bore his entire weight down on her. "Stop yer moving. Ye are only making this harder than it needs to be."

It all happened so fast, yet Maggie felt as if every heartbeat, every movement, was in slow motion as her mind switched from panic to survival. His rough fingers skimmed up her leg as he gripped the hem of her dress, forcing the fabric upward.

Nay. She would not be this man's victim. She would not allow a man to ever use her the way her mother, sister, and sister by marriage had been. Maggie had lived a life of torment, worrying about every glance from a man, preferring to stay close to her brother instead of facing her fears.

Falling in love with Flynn had been the beginning of a new life for her. He had taught her that good men truly did exist, and he was the best man on earth. He had taken time out of his life, even while wounded and recovering, to teach her self-defense, dagger throwing, to face her fears... and to know true love for a man. The time to prove to herself that she was nobody's victim was... now!

Sliding her right hand down her leg, she leaned forward slightly, crinkling her nose at the foul smell of the man leaning over her. He must not have bathed in over a fortnight and his breath smelled of onions and garlic. But she needed to lean only slightly further to reach the dagger in her boot. Feeling the fine bone hilt with her fingers, Maggie carefully pulled the dagger out of her boot's leather straps.

With all her strength, she lifted her knees hard and fast, connecting with their target directly between the large man's legs. With a howl of pain, the man loosened his grip on her, instead cupping his now-bruised bollocks and leaning over unsteadily. "You will pay for that!" he roared, but made no attempt to grab her again.

Seeing her opportunity, she sat up quickly and pushed him backward with all her strength. She could feel the hard ridges of muscle beneath his tunic and knew she would never have been able to make him budge if he was not writhing in pain. Fortunately, he was so off balance by the unexpected blow to his nether region, he toppled over with a groan, still holding himself as he rolled into a fetal position.

It was almost humorous to behold a full grown, overly-large man wail, and rock back and forth like a wee child on the ground, yet she had no time to further think on him. The sounds of shouting men and clanging metal had grown much closer since her attack and if she were to escape this man before he recovered, she needed to check her surroundings and run away without being detected.

Just as she stepped up to the tent opening, the flap pulled open from the outside and she stepped back with a shriek, nearly plowing into a towering man. If one of Mal's men found her in here and saw the man on the ground, surely they would punish her. Lifting her dagger high in a defensive stance, she was ready to strike if needed.

The most beautiful green eyes she had ever seen stared back at her with intensity and she gasped with relief. "Flynn!" she cried and ran into his arms, clutching him around the neck and silently thanking the gods that he was safe and with her again. Brennain stood beside them and peeked into the tent. Seeing the man readying himself to stand once more, he nudged them out of the tent. "Good work lass, but we must keep moving!" he shouted over the sounds of reigning chaos.

"I heard you scream. I fought my way from the entrance of this camp to get to you. Are you all right?" Flynn pulled back and placed his hands on either side of her face, narrowing his eyes as he inspected her for injuries. "Did he hurt you?" She knew he referred to more than just physical wounds.

"Nay. He tried, but I... well, I kicked him in the bollocks." She shrugged, much too distracted to think of a more proper way of saying it. Brennain grunted with amusement beside her and she could not help but smirk herself.

"Good," Flynn said, and he kissed her forehead before releasing her. "Come. Our men are taking this battle but with the darkness, 'tis always hard to fight. I need you out of harm's way before I can rejoin my men."

She had so many questions, so many things she longed to say. She wanted to tell him how much she loved him and thank him for always believing in her. If not for him, she would not have been brave enough to take on that man. But, most importantly, she wanted to tell him that she would marry him, no matter if he decided to travel for Tuathal in the future. Mayhap she could join him and they could seek a life of adventure?

Before he could drag her further from the tent, her attacker came through the doorway and charged at Brennain. With the two men beside her engaged in a sudden brawl and with the darkness of the night, Maggie almost missed the gleam of a sword just behind Flynn as one of Mal's men charged him from the back. Had it not been for the fire burning just to the left of the man, the metal of his sword would not have glittered in the light and caught her gaze.

"Flynn!" she wailed, and pointed with her left hand. "Behind you!" It was too late. There was no way Flynn could turn and draw his sword quickly enough to defend himself against the fast-approaching enemy. Her stomach plummeted. Flynn would die trying to save her and she would be forced to watch it happen before her eyes.

* * * *

Maggie's warning had him spinning on his heels and reaching for his sword, but as soon as he saw Mal's man, he knew there was not time enough to save himself. He would never get to marry Maggie or have a family. He would never get the opportunity to tell her he chose her. He had already decided he would give up the life of an informant, traveling all over Ériu in search of Mal, if it meant he could be with her every day. If their king refused, they would leave and seek a life elsewhere, for no life was worth living without his wee bonny Maggie and her sweet smile. Nay, he would die here on this day. He only prayed Maggie would move on with her life, face her fears and find love. She deserved that.

A dagger whizzed past his nose, the sound of its blade cutting through the air as it repeatedly arced seemed to consume him, despite the sounds of battle all around. All his senses were on high alert. The scent of pine wafted in the night breeze, the stars glittered brightly overhead, surrounded by the gray haze of clouds. The sound of the blade piercing the warrior's flesh just before he roared with pain and toppled to the ground, only inches away from reaching Flynn. The man's sword clattered to the ground and Flynn's neck snapped back to seek the source of the dagger.

Maggie. His Maggie. Her right hand still extended out in front of her as she watched the warrior fall. A swelling of pride for this woman hit him hard in the gut. She had saved him, and had she even hesitated for a split second, he would be dead. But he did not have time to thank her just yet. That would come later. For now, they needed to move.

Grabbing her by the wrist, he pulled her through the chaos. "My dagger!" she hollered as he pulled her along behind him.

"I grabbed it for you, lass," Brennain said, trailing behind her, searching the area for a safe place to take her. "There, that cluster of trees. You can hide in there while we finish this."

Flynn pulled her into the edge of the forest where a thick cluster of pines formed a rather formidable wall. She would be safe here.

"Nay. I do not wish to hide. I wish to fight," Maggie argued, trying to remove his firm grip from her wrist.

"Absolutely not!" Flynn shouted before clearing his throat to soothe his voice. "You saved my life back there, Mags. You saved yourself from that man. I am beyond proud of you. But besides your one dagger, you have nay defense. That dagger cannot fight off a sword. I cannot allow it."

Brennain handed her the dagger and nodded. "I am sorry lass, but he is right. 'Tis not safe. You must stay here."

"I will not! Why should I stay here, simply because I am a woman, while you risk your life? I think not!"

Flynn opened his mouth to scold the stubborn lass for not understanding the ways of the world. She was a brave lass, but she was wee compared to these towering men. One dagger and a dose of bravery would not be enough to save her if a man was bent on attacking. Before he could think of a proper way to convince her to stay safely hidden, a loud whistle broke through the air, stilling all other sounds almost instantaneously. He knew that sound. 'Twas the signal of their king, to stop fighting and put down their swords.

"Mal has fled," their king's voice dominated the night. "Coward that he is, he left his men to fight in his stead, while he, Eoghann and a few other men seek out safety." He spat into the earth and looked at Reaghan, who stood beside him. "This man is not the enemy. He is my warrior and is to be treated with respect. Anything he is guilty of, including holding the dagger to Maggie's throat, he did to serve me in Mal's camp. Aye?"

A chorus of voices shouted, "aye," in understanding. Maggie stepped forward and out of the shadow of the trees once she knew it was safe, but Flynn looked down at her and scowled.

"Did Reaghan touch you?" Her eyes grew wide and even in the dark, he knew her suddenly diverted gaze meant he had. "What did he do to you? I will kill him!"

Maggie grabbed his sleeve and pulled him toward her. "Nay! He saved me. He kissed me, but he had to—"

"Had to?" Flynn roared, and stormed away from Maggie, ready to defend her honor, even if it meant disobeying their king.

"Mal was going to give me to his men," Maggie whispered, and Flynn stopped in his tracks. He could hear the fear and hurt in her voice. Of course, she had been frightened. "He wanted Eoghann to take me first as a reward for stealing me, but Reaghan demanded that he deserved me first, because he had been the man to negotiate the terms. Mal agreed, but Reaghan had to kiss me... to make it appear he was going to... take his turn."

Heart lodged in his throat and stomach churning with distaste, Flynn focused on breathing before he murdered every single one of Mal's men in this filthy camp. What made men believe they could treat women so horribly? How dare Mal try to give his Maggie to his men. If the man had not run off like a coward, Flynn would be first in line to gut him. "I am sorry for all you have been through, my love." Flynn turned and pulled her against him, wrapping his arms tightly around her waist and inhaling her sweet floral scent.

"I was so afraid," she murmured against his chest, then pressed her ear to his heart. "I thought Reaghan truly meant to force himself on me, but as soon as Mal and the other guards left us, he released me. And, I slapped him."

Flynn's laughter rumbled low in his chest. "That's my feisty wee lass," he said before kissing the top of her head.

"Nobody has ever referred to me as 'feisty' before," she giggled, and looked up at him. Her golden hair lit up in the light of the dying bonfire and her blue eyes sparkled with amusement.

"You are feisty," he assured her. "You are spirited, brave, strong, and a true survivor. And if I am the only man in the world who sees this, then I am truly the most fortunate man alive."

"What are we to do with Mal's remaining men?" someone asked Tuathal from the crowd of warriors surrounding him.

"We take them prisoner. At one time, I would have invited them to join my ranks, but these men are the shite on the bottom of my boot who turned their backs on a true chance to fight for right. I stand for Ériu. They stand for power and greed. I say they use that power to our benefit by serving as our slaves." Flynn could not help but agree with Tuathal, and based on the murmurs of approval all around, everyone else agreed. When he had first won the war against the false High King Elim Mac Conrach, Tuathal gave all enemy warriors a chance to fight for him, to defend Ériu alongside her rightful heir. Most men had willingly agreed. As Tuathal had expected, those men had been forced to fight by their tyrannical leader at the time. Elim would have killed a man and all his family if he felt the slightest bit of resistance. Not surprisingly, those men had been more than willing to fight under a true leader and for a better cause once Elim was defeated.

These men, however, the ones who still fought for Mal, were the ones who never truly had Ériu's best interests at heart. Nay, they wanted land, power, and riches, never minding whose blood they spilled to obtain it. Each of them deserved to be enslaved and forced to toil the land they had betrayed. Flynn also knew that, even though being a slave could mean abuse, starvation, and even death at the hands of a cruel master, Tuathal was not that man. He would make these men work hard and keep a close eye on them, but he would treat them fairly, as human beings. Tuathal was no tyrant, and that was precisely why he earned respect from his men.

"Maggie!" Àdhamh ran out of the group of warriors beginning to round up Mal's men when he saw Maggie enfolded safely within Flynn's grasp.

"Brother!" she laughed, when she saw him coming her way. Releasing Flynn, she ran into her brother's arms and shrieked with delight as he swung her around. "You are hale?" she asked, and he gently put her down on the ground.

"Aye, that I am. My wife is safe at home with my child in her womb and my wee sister is safe in the arms of a good man." He hugged her close and winked at Flynn over her shoulder.

Flynn's heart soared to have Maggie's elder brother's approval. It mattered to him that Àdhamh respected him and trusted him with his sister. Grabbing Maggie's hand, Àdhamh walked over to Flynn and Brennain, bowing his head in greeting. "I have been an arse and I wish to apologize. My sister means everything to me, as you know, and I would do aught for her. Years of protecting her turned me into a man who refused to let her go, but she has chosen a fine man and I cannot speak for her decision to marry you or not, but I can say that I do support your marriage."

A sense of peace washed over Flynn. He wanted to whisk Maggie away and beg her to marry him right now, but he was still a warrior and Mal had left behind a score or more of men who needed to be detained. Now, surrounded by death and violence, was not the time to beg her once more to marry him. Though every part of him longed to carry her away into the deserted forest and make sweet love to her, he knew he must wait. To have Àdhamh's blessing would have to suffice, for now.

Looking over Àdhamh's shoulder, Flynn saw that bastard Reaghan walking toward them with his arrogant stride. He knew the man was loyal to Tuathal, but he had been out of line when he licked Maggie's cheek before, then kissed her in that tent. Maggie had been frightened, and that made Flynn want to injure the lout.

"What do you want?" Flynn barked at the man as he stepped into their circle.

Reaghan cocked an arrogant brow, which only annoyed Flynn further. "I came to make my peace with you. We are on the same side, after all."

"I wonder why you assume we must make peace?" Flynn stepped forward and fisted his hands, trying his best to not punch the fool in the nose. "Mayhap because you held a knife to my lass's throat? Or because you licked her cheek and frightened her? Or perhaps because you kissed her in the tent?" Flynn groused. Aye, he was definitely growing closer and closer to pummeling the man with every second that passed.

With a scoff, Reaghan shook his head. "You know as well as I that I had nay choice but to pretend she was my captive. I am sorry she was frightened, but I did what had to be done for my king. I kept her safe and, in case she did not inform you, she already paid me back for that kiss. My jaw still aches from the sting of her palm," Reaghan said, and he rubbed the tender spot. "Had I not been there to protect her, much worse would have happened."

Flynn did not want to think on that. He was still fuming at the memory of the man licking her. "Did you need to run your tongue up her cheek?" Flynn asked through clenched teeth.

A thoughtful look crossed Reaghan's face and he tapped his finger to his lips in mock contemplation. "Nay, I suppose I did not need to do that. I simply got lost in the moment and—"

"Wrong answer!" Flynn's right hook flew straight at the bastard's nose and he reveled in the sound of the man's cartilage cracking with the force of his rage.

"Flynn!" Maggie wailed, and tried to step forward, but Brennain held her back and whispered something about "allowing the men to work it out" in her ear. Fortunately, she listened.

Reaghan, to Flynn's astonishment, took his punishment rather well, holding on to his bleeding nose with one hand as he nodded in understanding. "Aye, I deserved that," he conceded.

"Aye, you did," Flynn agreed. Then he put his arm out to Reaghan and begrudgingly smirked. "My thanks for keeping my Maggie safe. I owe you a debt."

"Fine way of showing it," Reaghan said wryly, before putting a hand out to clasp Flynn's outstretched forearm.

With that, their peace was made. Now that Flynn had successfully defended his woman's honor, he had other business to tend to, such as helping to round up Mal's men. Then, he would find time to speak to Tuathal about his position as an informant. No matter what, he was determined to convince Maggie to marry him.

Chapter Sixteen

As soon as Mal's remaining men were secured within a few larger tents and well-guarded, Tuathal decided that they would do best to use the deserted camp for the night. It was slightly past midnight before everyone settled in, hoping to get a few hours of sleep before heading back to Ráth Mór in the morning. Once Flynn found Maggie safe in Mal's camp, he refused to let her out of his sight. While she did not mind one bit being in his presence, they never truly had a private moment to discuss their future. Furthermore, Maggie had something of great import she wished to discuss with King Tuathal, and to do so, she needed to find a way to leave Flynn's side. Based on his grip around her waist as he securely held her on his lap, Flynn was not going to let her get away so easily.

Maggie could not help the fluttering in her stomach. She would marry Flynn Mac Greine. He was loyal, kind, hardworking, yet gentle... and the most handsome man she had ever known. And he wanted her. Gods help her, she wanted him with a fierceness that consumed her body in flames and her mind with thoughts that would send her elder brother into a fit of rage.

Àdhamh and Reaghan sat across from Maggie and Flynn around the fire, with Brennain, Alastar, Jeoffrey, Freyne, and Eoin also close by, enjoying the flickering of the dying flames.

"I was so worried about you, Mags. I cannot tell you how my heart squeezed in my chest when I saw... *him*," he shot look of disgust at Reaghan, "holding you captive. I know he is not the enemy and we made our peace. Still, the image of that dagger to your throat haunts me. Then your terrified screams inside the tent. Och, I thought I had lost you ten times over this day. I never want to be away from you again," he murmured in her ear, causing chills to race up her spine. He cherished her in a way that she never thought possible and she loved how openly he shared his affections with her.

"I never wish to leave your side either," she whispered back, placing a soft kiss on his cheek. Maggie wished to shout her love for him and proclaim that she would marry him, but she still had unfinished business with Tuathal. "However, the night grows late. We must get some rest before our journey home."

"Then allow me to carry you to our tent." Flynn said suggestively with a waggle of his brows.

Maggie gave him a reprimanding look. "We shall be sharing a tent with many men, including my brother who will likely lay between the two of us and sleep with one eye open. I do not believe we can do aught in such cramped, occupied quarters. Furthermore, I do know how to walk. You need not carry me."

"What if I wish to carry you?" Flynn retorted, leaning in to nibble on her throat. He felt so good. His touch put her under a spell, and caused her to lose all sense. She could almost see herself hiking her skirt up to her waist, straddling his lap and taking him now, forgetting anyone else existed. But, nay. And though they were surrounded by men, she knew Flynn would not relent so easily. She had to come up with an excuse to leave his side that he could not deny her. "You wish to carry me to the place where I shall relieve myself?" She smiled wickedly and tilted her head.

With a sigh of resignation, Flynn loosened his grip on her waist to allow her up. "I shall not be long, *mo chroí*," she said as she ran her hand through the dark stubble across his strong jaw. "I love you, Flynn." With that, she hopped off his lap and ventured toward a distant and thickly wooded area where he would believe she was... busy.

But once she knew he had started up a conversation with Alastar around the fire, Maggie swung back around to the cluster of tents where she knew Tuathal was staying with a few of his men to guard their prisoners. As late as it was, and as much as they needed rest, it seemed few men actually slept. Mal running off had been a blow to Tuathal. Though much bloodshed was prevented and none of their own had been killed, it felt like failure. For several moons, Flynn watched Mal from a distance, gathering information and traveling back to Tuathal. It had been a balance requiring enough information and correct timing. Just when Tuathal decided the time was right to snuff out Mal once and for all, Eoghann had infiltrated their lives, stealing information for Mal and learning all of Tuathal's plans.

These were the games men played during war, and yet none of it was a game at all to Maggie. It made her feel ill to think of Flynn gone for sennights at a time, risking his life... and for what? For Mal to flee once more? How long would it take to track Mal down again? Would Flynn be sent to find him? This last question was the very one burning into her mind, and it was the reason she needed to speak to her king.

Whispered voices could be heard coming from within a large tent just ahead of her, and two large men stood guard. Swallowing her trepidation, Maggie squared her shoulders and took a deep breath. If she could fell a large warrior with just her knee, and take another down with the flick of her wrist, certainly she could manage a conversation with her intimidating king.

Both guards ignored her as she approached. This only added to her determination. Wee woman or not, she was the best cursed healer in all Ériu and she had saved one of their best warriors with her skills. Och, she had saved the very man standing before her now, averting his gaze as if she were not worth the effort of a simple acknowledgment. "Greetings, Findmall." The two brothers guarding Tuathal now, Findmall and Fiacha, had grown up with Tuathal while he was in exile in Alba. When Tuathal had been ready to claim his rightful place as the High King of Ériu, it had been these two brothers who journeyed to Ériu first, learning the land and later guiding the way for Tuathal. Without their help, he may not have ever succeeded with his plans. But, without Maggie, Findmall would have died from an infected wound. Perhaps the man had forgotten this and needed a reminder. "How is your leg?" she asked sweetly, raising a brow in question.

Findmall cleared his throat, but kept his gaze straight ahead. Fiacha, fortunately, was not as stubborn as his brother. "He still limps, but he lives, thanks to your healing touch, Maggie." Fiacha's praise made her smile and she was suddenly overcome with a sense of pride. Several moons ago, when she had been brought to Findmall's side to help him, she had been internally terrified of the large, imposing brothers. Either one of them could snap her in half like a twig. They frightened her terribly not so long ago, yet here she was with her shoulders held high, a sense of self-worth and dignity bolstering her bravery. Nay, these men were not so frightening after all.

"'Tis my greatest pleasure to heal the ill or wounded. I am most glad he is well. Now, I would like to please speak with King Tuathal," she said with a smile.

Findmall snorted. "Not happening. He is inside with his advisors."

"And, you are not one of them, Findmall? Fallen from favor, have you?" she jibed. He always had a serious and sour disposition. It used to intimidate her. Now, she found it most entertaining to try to break through his aloof personality. His brother sniggered and winked at her, causing Findmall to bristle.

"You have a cheeky tongue, healer." Findmall groused.

"Her name is Maggie," she heard through the thin tent fabric as the front flap opened wide enough for Maggie to see King Tuathal surrounded by his advisors, the three husbands of the Sisters of Danu. Liam and Garreth were Flynn's uncles, and Liam was also Tuathal's father by marriage. Flynn's huge father, Brocc Mac Greine, smiled widely when he saw her standing outside, then faltered when he saw her shiver.

"Findmall! You left Maggie out in the cold to shiver? I shall inform my son about your improper treatment of his future wife." His voice held no true threat, yet Findmall's eyes grew wide and he frowned. Findmall feared Flynn? She had come to know him as a gentle lover and kind soul, but she supposed, to other men, he was quite fierce and intimidating with his size and skills on the battlefield. Few knew of the role he played as an informant for Tuathal, but he was always at the king's side, which must give him quite the reputation. Factor in that he was a son of one of the legendary Sisters of Danu, son of a king who was also well known as a descendant of the first High Kings of Ériu, and she supposed Flynn could send terror into any man... even one as arrogant as Findmall.

"She has not yet agreed to marry the lad, have you, Maggie?" Garreth said with a wide grin and a shove at his brother by marriage. Liam grunted and winked at her, flashing a handsome smile and two dimples her way. The three men must be nearing their fiftieth year, yet all of them still appeared to be made of stone with their strong builds and robust health. Aside from the gray strands shimmering in their hair and a few laugh lines around their eyes, they seemed youthful and filled with spirit. Perhaps being married to the three Sisters of Danu had kept them happy all these years. They were all rumored to hold their wives in the very highest regard, counting them as equals and openly doting on them. Was that why Flynn had no issues about attempting to ravish her publicly? It seemed to be in his blood, his own father having openly chased his mother, Una. for many moons before she finally gave in. Aye, Flynn was born from a powerful love and she felt her cheeks warm, knowing that same love flowed through him, into her, enveloping them both in a heat that knocked them on their backsides.

"Do not tease my future daughter. She may well be the only daughter I ever have. You have three of your own, Liam. Do not chase mine away!" Brocc guffawed, and she blushed even brighter. He already considered her a daughter? She had hardly spoken to him in all the time she was at Ráth Mór, due to her cursed fear of men. Now, she was surrounded by large men and all she felt was love and respect for them, and from them in return.

"Maggie. You wished to speak with me?" Tuathal said gently, scowling playfully at his advisors.

"Aye, my king... if it is not poor timing. It is rather... private."

Raising his brow, he got the hint and shooed his three rambunctious family members out of his tent. Before Brocc left, he looked down at her and smiled, placing a hand on her shoulder. "Flynn has never shown an interest in any lass before you. I knew he would love a lass one day, but I never expected him to love the way he loves you," Flynn's father nodded and left the tent. Her heart fluttered even more, if it were possible. It was as if a hundred butterflies took flight within her, making her feel light and tingly all over.

"Have a seat, Maggie," Tuathal offered, gesturing to a small stump of wood near the center of the tent. He sat beside her on another stump. "What can I do for you?"

Now that she had his full attention, Maggie was not quite certain how to begin. "Well... you see... when Flynn first asked me to marry him, I told him it depended on whether or not he continued to serve as an informant for you." Tuathal raised a brow in question, yet stayed silent. "He is loyal to you, as am I. He enjoys his work for you, as well. I realized during all that has transpired that I was not being fair when I asked him to give up his position with you, to stay home and start a family with me."

"I see," Tuathal said, rubbing his dark bearded chin and boring his blue gaze into hers. "What did Flynn say to that?"

"He accepted my conditions and promised to speak with you about another position. Only, I wanted to speak with you first. I know Flynn would give up everything to be with me, but should he have to? My conditions were most unfair, not only to him, but to you. He is good at what he does."

"Aye, that he is," her king agreed, and shifted his large body on the uncomfortable stump he sat on. "Why are you telling me this, Maggie?"

"Flynn is not the only one willing to sacrifice," she pressed. "I realized that I want to marry him, no matter what, even if he stayed in your service as an informant. However, I still cannot stomach the thought of him being away from me for sennights at a time, so I came to a decision."

Nodding his head, Tuathal let a small smile slide across his face. "What decision is that, lass?"

"I wish to be allowed to go with him. I would be giving up my place at Ráth Mór as your healer, but Elwynna has made great strides and with only a little more practice, she can easily replace me. Aside from my brother, I do not have much else tying me to this land. I love Ráth Mór, but I love Flynn more. I will go where he goes... If you will allow me to give up my place as healer."

"Do you truly believe you are that replaceable, Maggie?" Tuathal asked with a furrowed brow. "Your talent as a healer comes from more than just training. You have a natural instinct and a fervent love of it. I see you chasing herbs about the village and beaming like a child who was just given a sweet tart every time you find more wild mint." He grunted in amusement. "'Tis not easy to give up one's passion, lass."

"Flynn is my passion," she insisted.

"And what if you could have Flynn and be a healer? Would you not prefer that?"

She shook her head and looked away. "Not if it meant he had to sacrifice his own happiness for mine. I cannot allow it. I cannot deny that I love being a healer, but healing never filled the emptiness that lay dormant inside me my entire life. Only love can fill that, and Flynn has. I feared men my entire life. Before now, I would never have dared wander off alone or speak to a man without my brother to attend me. I still have much to learn, but with Flynn's guidance, I can be helpful to your cause if I accompany him."

Tuathal took a deep breath and stood from his seat. "I know, lass. I hope you do not mind, but Àdhamh has told me much about your life. You watched your mother be forced and abused by your father, then your sister was neglected and killed by her husband..." his voice trailed off and he began to pace. "And then Elwynna's father used her terribly," he murmured. "You know many lasses who have been harmed by the worst sort of men, but if you truly pay attention, you will see that most of the women around you are in healthy marriages. I treat Leannan like a queen, and not because she is one. 'Tis because she means everything to me. Aislin is Alastar's entire world. If anything, she is the one with the power in that relationship," he grunted, and Maggie could not help but crack a smile at the truth of his observation. "Treasa, Alyson, Clarice, the Sisters of Danu... they are all revered by their husbands, as they should be. You have met an unfortunate number of bastards in your life. 'Tis time you are treated with love and respect. I am glad you and Flynn found one another."

His demeanor switched suddenly, and he almost looked contrite. "May I ask you a question, Maggie?" Swallowing hard and crinkling her brow, she nodded. "Does your desire to leave have anything to do with me?"

Her heart beat wildly in her chest. Could he see that she had been hurt by his sudden turn on her and Elwynna earlier that day? "What?" she asked, trying to buy time to think of an answer.

"Please be honest, lass. Earlier today, your perception of events had been much different than the truth. You heard me offer up your brother's wife as a trade. You watched me allow Reaghan to drag you away. You must have felt betrayed by me."

Taking a deep breath, Maggie shook her head. "You are my king. 'Tis not my place to question you. But I admit, I was hurt that you seemed to allow me and Elwynna to be treated as spoils of war. I did not know then that Reaghan was one of your informants, keeping me safe. I felt as if my life was at risk and I was being abandoned. I thought you were going to give my sister back to her horrible father. He tried to give me to his men, as well. If not for Reaghan, I can only imagine what would have become of me. Nay, I now understand your reasoning. However, I do have a question for you... about Eoghann's father."

"Ah." Tuathal nodded and continued to pace. "I had a feeling Eoghann would mention his father's death to you while he had you in his clutches. I assume he named me his father's murderer?"

"Aye, he did. He said his father left Alba to fight for you, but you killed him. I told Eoghann you would never do such a thing, but he believes very much that you intentionally killed his father."

"I did intentionally kill him."

Maggie gasped and clutched her heart, never having expected such a thing from her honorable king, nor such an open admission. "What? Why?" If this was true, mayhap she could not blame Eoghann for being bent on revenge. He had kept his word and never harmed her. She had simply been his way of getting Elwynna back to Mal.

"Eoghann's father was not fighting for me. I believe he told his family that lie, so they would not turn on him or be disappointed in him, but make nay mistake: Domnall O'Connel came across the sea from Alba to fight for Elim Mac Conrach. During the final battle, his father came directly at me in attack. Worse, he tried to strike me down from behind, like a coward. Had I not turned at the right moment, I would have perished. Instead, I was able to deflect his sword, causing him to cut his own leg. My only regret is that I did not finish him then and there. I hear he suffered from his wound for many moons, and though I am not sorry he died, I am sorry he suffered, and that his family had to watch him perish."

Maggie listened intently, suddenly wondering how she could have ever doubted her king. "I wanted to believe Eoghann," Tuathal continued. "Truthfully, I did believe he meant to join our cause. His friendship with your brother made me trust him. He played me for a fool, and because of that, you were put into harm's way and I cannot apologize enough. Sometimes even a king is fallible. I have a weakness, you see. I try to always believe the best in everyone, but I must learn my lesson. 'Tis precisely why I took the rest of Mal's men as slaves. I have already offered them peace once and they refused it. I have nay choice now but to keep them close at hand, under our watchful eyes. As for Eoghann, a part of me wishes he knew the truth of his father's betrayal, although a larger part of me does not believe he would ever believe it."

Maggie twisted her hands in the fabric of her skirt. "I am sorry I ever doubted you," she said sincerely. "I know you are a good man and a great king."

"My thanks, Maggie, I appreciate that. I try my best to protect my people. 'Tis why losing Mal is such a blow."

Before Maggie could respond that perhaps she could accompany Flynn on his next mission to track down Mal, the guards announced as Flynn entered the tent.

"Maggie?" Flynn's green eyes widened as he looked between her and Tuathal. She stood up quickly from the wooden stump and rubbed her sweaty palms on her dress. She only just now realized that she must have been gone for much longer than she intended. "I have been looking for you. You said you had to—"

She cut him off before he could complete his statement. "Aye. I am sorry Flynn. I lied. I had a serious matter to discuss with our king and I lost track of time. I hope you were not worried."

Flynn stepped closer to her and her heart raced as it always did when he was near. "I was worried a bit, but I trusted you were safe here at camp." He tucked a blonde hair behind her ear and smiled down at her. "I also have something important to speak to our king about," he said, before shifting his gaze to Tuathal. "Have you a moment?"

"Aye, I do, Flynn. Would you like Maggie to leave?"

218

Shaking his head adamantly, Flynn gripped her hand and pulled her closer to him. "Nay. In fact, what I need to say involves her... I hope." He looked down at her and smiled, causing those butterflies to flutter wildly again.

"Go on," Tuathal urged. "What have you to say?"

"I love Maggie with my whole heart, King Tuathal. This is hard for me to say, but 'tis time I consider serving you in another way, in Ráth Mór. I can travel from time to time, but what I wish above all else is to settle down on this land, marry the lass I love, and start a family. I do not wish to leave that family for long periods of time. I do not think I could bear it." Maggie felt Flynn squeeze her hand and she squeezed back, feeling as if she may burst with love for him. Still, she did not want him to give up his life for her. "I want to see her face every day and watch our children grow."

Tuathal chuckled to himself and looked at Maggie with amusement. "This is an interesting turn of events, for your lass has just offered to give up her position as Ráth Mór's healer so she can travel with you on your missions."

"What?" Flynn's gaze snapped to her and his brow crinkled. "Why? You said you would not marry me if I continued to be an informant."

"Flynn, I was wrong to say such a thing. I know that now. I love you, and that means I wish for you to do what makes you happy. If being an informant for Tuathal is what you love, then I shall love doing it with you. I can learn more defensive moves, more use of weapons. You can train me to gather information... I can learn." She was desperate to convince him to accept her offer. She preferred to stay here and live a safer, quieter life with him, but if that was not an option, she would be happy anywhere, so long as they were together. "We can do this," she added with a forced smile.

"So, you will marry me, Maggie, nay matter what?" he said, gripping her hips and pulling her flush with his body.

"Aye, nay matter what, Flynn." Her eyes closed as he placed a sweet kiss on her forehead.

"I love you, Maggie. But I meant what I said. I would like to stay put and raise a family with you, if our king will allow it."

Both of them went silent and looked at Tuathal as he stared in wonderment at them. His long dark hair was tied in a braid draped over his shoulder and a slow smile spread across his handsome face, blue eyes sparking with amusement. "I have a feeling that you two will be very happy together, nay matter where you end up. Maggie is willing to give up her place to be with you," he pointed to Flynn, "and you are willing to give up your place to be with her."

"Flynn..." Maggie begged, looking up to his height. "I cannot be responsible for you giving up something you love."

"And I cannot be responsible for you giving up your dream of a safe life and a family. You deserve that. I want to give you that. I do not wish to travel anymore, truly. I only wish to be with you, at Ráth Mór. I love you more than anything, Maggie. I am so proud of the brave lass you have become. I am proud that you have faced your fears and would continue to do so, just to be with me. You are a strong woman and you should continue to use that strength to help our people with your healing talents..."

"Have I nay say in any of this?" Tuathal mused. Maggie and Flynn looked back at their king. "I presume you both could argue your point for a lifetime, so allow me to decide what is best. Is that fair? After all, did you both not seek me out for that very purpose?"

"Aye," both Maggie and Flynn said at the same time.

"Flynn, the information you have gathered for me over the past year has been incredibly accurate and beneficial. Because of you, we have kept a watchful eye on Mal and his locations and plans. We were safe because you kept up on his whereabouts. I can never thank you enough for your work. A better informant, I may never find. However, one of the biggest assets to your missions was your anonymity. Mal did not know your face or who you worked for. Brennain was able to infiltrate their camp, which also now makes him too well known to the enemy to continue. Because of Eoghann, Mal knows your name and your face. He also knows you are an informant for me. I am sorry Flynn, but for your own safety, I can nay longer allow you to continue your missions. You did well, and I will be honored to have you here with me as one of my finest warriors... and mayhap you shall even join the ranks as an advisor with your father and your uncles. Would you like that?

Maggie felt as if she was floating on air with happiness, but she prayed Flynn would be equally content with Tuathal's decision. She could not bear his disappointment at being forced to stay.

"My king," Flynn said, with a smile that lit up his face. "Naught would make me happier than to become one of your advisors. I vow to always be faithful and loyal."

"Och, I already know that, Flynn," Tuathal waved him off. "Are we not family? I am your cousin by marriage after all. More than that, we have fought beside one another, and you have proven your worth. I would be honored to have you by my side. I would also be honored to stand beside the Druid who will marry you to Maggie. Never have I seen two people willing to sacrifice all, simply for the happiness of the other."

Flynn nodded and clasped arms with his king as Maggie watched on with such pride. Then, without warning, Flynn got down on both knees in front of her, gripping both hands tightly in his. The look of pure, honest love in his eyes as he looked up at her nearly sucked all the air out of her lungs. Never had she thought to find a man who would cherish her as Flynn did. And never did she know that love could actually ache physically in her chest, squeezing her from the inside out until tears began to run down her face.

"My sweet Maggie. The moment I saw you when I came over to Alba with my men, I lost a piece of my heart. When you boarded that ship and came back to Ériu with us, I knew my life would never be the same. You were timid and scared, but I saw the strength you buried deep within. I feigned more than one injury just so I could be in your company."

Through her tears, Maggie laughed with joy, remembering the times he came to her with wee scratches that hardly needed tending at all. "I thank all the gods in Alba and Ériu that I was shot with that arrow. It brought you to my side, and I would not give up those days of pain for all the world, for every moment of recovery was filled with memories of you. I already loved you then. But now..." he shook his head, trying to think of the right words. "Now, there are just nay words to describe my love for you. I only want you... and a home filled with wee children. Maggie, will you marry me?"

"Aye!" she cried, choking back a sob as she launched herself into his arms, knocking him backward with the force. "I will marry you, and I am sorry I did not accept the first time. I am such a fool!" She sprinkled every corner of his face with kisses, savoring his musky scent and the feel of his strong arms embracing her. Love was a greater emotion than she ever thought existed, but she knew she need not try to describe it with words, for Flynn felt it, as well.

In her elated state of mind, she only faintly heard Tuathal grunt with humor as she lay sprawled across Flynn, smothering him with affection. "Perhaps I should find another tent for the night. You need this one more than I do."

Chapter Seventeen

Five moons later

"*That* smells wonderful, Maggie. Your gift with herbs is beneficial for both healing and cooking, it seems," Flynn's mother, Una said to Maggie as she stepped up beside her and smelled the mixture of root vegetables and herbs Maggie had been busy cutting up. With a genuine smile, Maggie looked at his mother and blushed at the praise before continuing her preparation. Flynn watched the two most important women in his life chat amicably and felt a tug on his heart. The hearth fire popped and sizzled in the middle of the room as his father turned a boar on the spit, plenty of meat to feed their entire family, who would be arriving soon to share in a large meal together before enjoying the Beltane festivities.

"You have had a ridiculous smile on your face for far too long, brother. I am beginning to think marriage has turned you into a soft fool."

Flynn grunted at his brother's remarks. Perhaps Brennain was correct. Flynn had gone soft. He still practiced daily with Tuathal and the other warriors, ready for a fight in case Mal ever caused trouble again, but so far there has been no word from Tuathal's other informants. They had sought out any clue of Mal's whereabouts but his sudden disappearance without a trace meant that he likely had planned to flee all along. No rest would be had by Ráth Mór until the threat of Mal was gone, and though Elwynna had had her child only a sennight ago, he knew that she and Àdhamh felt the weight of her father bearing down on them. Their family would never rest at ease until Mal was found.

Aye, he was still a well-trained warrior and he would do what his king commanded of him. Thankfully, his king allowed him to stay close to family, so Flynn was able to come home to his bonny wife every night. Though it was customary to live as a large family within one home, Flynn had offered to build a small home in the village for just he and Maggie. He knew she was used to living with just her brother previously and wondered if moving in with his loud brother and overly-affectionate parents would intimidate her. To his delight, Maggie had insisted they live with his family, thankful to have a family of her own and to feel useful and part of a unit.

After their small marriage ceremony five moons ago, he was pleased to see how quickly his mother and Maggie took to one another. His mother was the soft-spoken sister of the three Sisters of Danu. Her element was earth, and he believed her innate calmness had something to do with her connection to the world. She was not as fiery as his Aunt Ceara or as easily shaken as his Aunt Gwynneth, whose moods could shift like the very waters she controlled. His mother took all in stride and had welcomed Maggie into her home, making her feel like a true daughter.

Flynn smiled to himself. His mother would be even more elated when he and Maggie announced the news that— "Och... there is that smile again, you dolt." Brennain said, catching Flynn off guard as he punched his shoulder harder than necessary.

"Leave your brother alone," his mother chided. She stepped away from Maggie and over to the hearth, wrapping her arms around his father's waist from behind. "He is finally happy, and I wish the same for you, Brennain. 'Tis truly all that matters in life." His father grinned widely, his large hazel eyes twinkling as they did every time his mother showed him affection.

Turning to face Una, Brocc grabbed her close and stared down into her green eyes, the eyes she had passed on to her sons. "Your mother, as usual, is correct. I almost lost her more than once. Brennain, you were already kicking within your mother's womb before she finally gave me a real chance."

Brennain made a gagging noise and rolled his eyes. "Must I hear the story of how I was created every year? I understand! She was your foster sister. You loved her! She loved you! You... bedded one another," Brennain made a gagging sound again and scrunched up his nose, "and created me. Then a horrible woman tried to split you up and made Mama leave you. I know! 'Tis disgusting!"

Flynn laughed at his brother's ire, thankful that the story of his creation, though told often enough, was not nearly as detailed as

Brennain's. Mama and Papa always said that Brennain was born of a passionate love affair and Flynn knew they wanted that same sort of love for their sons. Flynn had found it. Without Maggie, he was nothing. A wife was never anything he expected to have, or ever sought out. But in his heart, he knew that only Maggie could have claimed his heart so fiercely that he would willingly give up his life of traveling to start a family. Which reminded him...

"Speaking of creating a child..." his eyes shifted to Maggie and he smiled, her face visibly turning red and her eyes grew wide. The knife in her hand stilled, carrots forgotten, and the room went silent. "Come here, Mags," he smiled, and beckoned her with his finger. She put the knife down carefully, wiping her hands on the linen apron around her waist. As small as ever, nobody could possibly have noticed the changes to her body quite yet, but the time had come to share their news.

Maggie shyly walked over to him, tucking a wisp of blonde hair behind her ear before wrapping an arm around his waist. He looked down at her and felt that same flutter in his belly that he felt every time he saw her. He would never tire of his beautiful wife.

Looking up at his parents, he wanted to laugh at the expressions on their faces. His mother's green eyes were as wide as he had ever seen them, and she fervently wrung her hands together while his father tried to look casual, but could not hide his stifled grin beneath his short black and gray beard.

"My beautiful wife has informed me only a fortnight ago that we shall have our first child."

A shrill screech filled the room as his mother literally jumped into the air and waved her hands before punching his father in the arm.

"Ouch!" His huge father grimaced as he rubbed his aching bicep. "That hurt, woman."

"I told you! I told you so!" she screeched again, before she turned to Maggie and embraced her so hard he half wondered if he should pry his wife away before his mother suffocated her. "I am so very pleased, Maggie!" She made a gasping sound and clutched her heart. "I am going to be a grandmama! Oh!"

Then his mother turned her delight on Flynn, and his eyes grew wide as he watched her lunge at him next, wrapping her arms tightly around his body, trapping his arms to his side. "You will be the very best father, Flynn Mac Greine. I am so proud of you." His mother was wee, and her head only went up to the center of his chest, but that did not stop her from kissing his arms, chest and any part of him she could reach. His arms were still pinned at his side. He could shrug her off if he wanted to, but his mother's reaction to his news was much too charming to try to stop. He felt his cursed stupid smile spreading over his face again.

"Och, Una. Give them some space," his father said lazily.

"You owe me a back rub," Una said with a grin. "I was right."

"You were placing wagers upon my wife's womb?" Flynn asked in shock, pulling Maggie into a tight, protective embrace. Maggie just watched the chaos silently with a proud grin across her face.

"Aye. I knew she was with child... I just knew it! Your father thought I was only being overbearing and dreaming of wee babes. I decided I might as well get something out of my over-sensitive intuitions."

"As if I would ever turn down giving you a back rub," Brocc said suggestively to his wife. "You need not make wagers to earn one."

Brennain gagged again and Flynn pursed his lips to prevent himself from laughing at his brother. He felt Brennain cuff him hard on the shoulder from behind. "I am very happy for you both. Maggie is a true treasure. She is just what you needed in this world, brother."

"May I say something?" Maggie's sweet, timid voice whispered beside him.

"Of course," Flynn said. "You should always speak your mind in this family, *mo chroí*."

Maggie turned to look at Brennain before taking his large right hand in hers. Brennain's brow furrowed as he clearly wondered what Maggie was going to say. Flynn could not help but wonder as well.

"Before the day you approached me and asked if I could leave Ráth Mór to save Flynn, I was scared of all men. I could not even stand to be alone with one. I always wanted a family, but it had seemed so far out of reach. How could a man ever love me if I was incapable of speaking to one? But Flynn was always special to me, and though I admit I did fear him as well, my heart was still drawn to him." She looked up at Flynn and gave him a sweet smile that made him feel as if he was melting from within. Aye, his brother was right. He had become a soft fool for this woman and cared naught who knew it.

"When you told me he was dying and needed my help, I did not even hesitate. The healer in me could never allow a man to die. But in truth, the love I already bore Flynn could never allow me not to go to him. Once I was on that horse with you, I was frightened, traveling alone with a giant of a man, your arm wrapped tightly around me for several hours. You could have snapped me in two or done any number of awful things to me. I began to wonder why I had put myself in such a position."

"I would never do such a thing to any lass, Maggie," Brennain said, with obvious hurt in his voice.

"Aye, I know that, Brennain. 'Tis my very point. I knew within just a short time in your presence that I was safe. You were the first man besides my brother I ever truly trusted. It was because of your goodness that I knew men could be kind. It helped me while I was alone with Flynn..." her cheeks pinked and Flynn hid a proud grin, knowing she thought of their time together, especially the love they had shared. "I would have eventually trusted Flynn on my own, but that trust I bore for you, because of your honor, made it easier for me to accept that he was also honorable. I thank you, Brennain, for bringing me to Flynn. The Mac Greine's are a family full of honor and I am proud to now be one."

Releasing Brennain's hand, she wrapped herself around Flynn again and faced his parents, rubbing her abdomen with a sigh. "And now I shall be adding to the Mac Greine clan. I never thought I would see the day. I thank you all for taking me in and accepting me as one of your own. I love your son so much and vow to always be a faithful, loyal wife and a loving mother to many babes... we hope." She said with a hesitant look in her eyes.

"Aye... many more, Mags," Flynn said, feeling as if he would burst from happiness. Was it possible to actually die of love for a woman? How could he ache so deeply inside?

"Oh! You are such a blessing to us all!" his mother cried, and scooped Maggie up in her arms, once again nearly suffocating her. "Maggie, I know you had an awful life and you lost your mama. I know your papa was also very unkind. Brocc and I can never replace your parents, but I want you to know we both truly love you as our daughter."

"Aye, Maggie. 'Tis the truth," his father said, and he opened his arms wide, ready to envelop both his wife and Maggie in one strong embrace. Flynn watched, stunned as his parents devoured his pregnant wife. Had they truly wished for his happiness so profoundly? They never said a word to him about settling down or starting a family, and yet it clearly made them happier than anything had in a very long time. A sense of calm came over him. He felt whole in a way he never expected.

"I think you are their favorite son," Brennain pushed him playfully.

"Nay, 'tis not me they love so," Flynn said wryly as his parents finally released Maggie.

Just then the door burst open as their entire family poured into their home, shouts and loud laughter filling the air with familiarity. His family was not a quiet one. In fact, he was the quietest of all, yet it was not so much a lack of things to say; it was more a need to observe. It had always been his greatest skill: to observe his surroundings, the actions of people, study them until he knew their every move before they even made it. It was what made him the best informant Tuathal had. Those skills would still come into use for his king. For now, he was quite content to observe his family, especially Maggie.

"Greetings!" His loudest uncle, Garreth boomed from the door as his equally loud Aunt Ceara followed in his wake, laughing at something Aislin had said. Alastar trailed in after Aislin, carrying their wee son Conor. Eoin and Treasa followed next with Neassa and their newest child, a son named Colin.

"I hope you cooked enough food for an army, because half of Ériu is coming through!" His Uncle Liam laughed as he and Aunt Gwynneth followed through with Alyson, Freyne, their three children, King Tuathal, Queen Leannan and their two children, and their youngest son, wee Duncan who always trailed in the very back as if he had no idea what to make of his own family.

"We have plenty!" His mother cheered as she guided her sisters and their families through. "Beltane is my very favorite night of the year!"

"'Tis also the anniversary of your births, do not forget," Garreth informed Una as he looked from her to Gwynneth and then his wife.

"Aye... thirty summers ago, on the eve of Beltane, we were born," Aunt Ceara said nostalgically.

"Thirty?" Wee Duncan furrowed his brow and opened his mouth to remind his aunt that she was well beyond thirty summers of age, before she sent him a scathing look of warning.

"Maggie is with child!" Brocc announced unceremoniously, clearly trying to change the subject before Ceara boxed wee Duncan's ears.

"That was not your news to tell!" Una scolded, wagging her finger in her husband's face.

A round of shouts and cheers boomed in their small home as everyone Flynn loved huddled together in one small space, patting him on the back and hugging Maggie, who seemed stunned by the sudden onslaught of attention, yet flushed with happiness.

"I knew you had it in you!" Alastar shouted above the din. "The quiet ones are always the most virile," he winked. Flynn just shook his head at his cousin's husband. Alastar was always full of words to speak, yet did tend to make Flynn chuckle on most occasions. Aislin whapped Alastar upside the head and took wee Conor from him with a wink to Maggie.

Once the celebratory words were exchanged and everyone settled down, the women, as usual convened in one area of the house while the men convened in another. A serious look came over Tuathal's face and Flynn knew he had ominous news to share. Though it was a celebration, the state of the tuath's safety was always on Tuathal's mind.

"We've had news of Mal," Tuathal whispered, so only his men could hear. Flynn looked wearily from his king, to his brother. "He fled to Alba with a score of men, Eoghann included. He means to gather a following and return with an army."

"But, you are from Alba," Flynn's cousin Eoin interjected. "Alba supports you entirely."

"Not entirely," Àdhamh said with a sigh. "I grew up there, and my tuath is most loyal to Tuathal, as are most. But as with any land, people are divided. There are always those ready to start a war if it means more power for them. My wife must not learn of any of this. She has been quite weepy since our daughter was born. She cannot be bothered with news of her father," Àdhamh warned the men with a scowl. Everyone nodded their understanding.

"I need to send two men over to Alba to seek more information," Tuathal groaned, and ran a hand through his dark hair. "My informants are all currently scattered across the land. I must call them back and refocus our efforts."

"Not all," Brennain said with a smirk. "I am more than willing to go across the sea to Alba. I learned a lot about the man while in his camp. I have nothing holding me here for now. I am free to journey, and I think I can track him down."

Flynn looked sideways at his brother. He seemed over-eager to head back to Alba. "Mal knows your face, Brennain. Is it wise to take this on?"

"This is not an undercover mission," Tuathal shrugged. "It matters not if Mal knows their faces, so long as they can avoid trouble, find the man, gain support, send word back to me, and stay on his heels. Can you do that, Brennain?"

"Of course, I can. I am itching to go," he smiled widely, green eyes shining with the prospect of adventure. Flynn's brother had always been much wilder and more prone to getting wrapped up in trouble. That was precisely what worried him.

With a decisive nod, Tuathal clasped forearms with Brennain. "I appreciate your eagerness to go. You are a fine warrior and I trust you. You shall travel with Reaghan."

"What?" Flynn growled. Och, he still hated that man for touching his wife, even if he was only playing a role. He played it over-well. His brother would be gone for several moons with that lout?

"Reaghan is good at what he does, brother," Brennain slugged him in the shoulder. "'Tis why you hate him so. He even convinced you that he wanted your wife and you cannot let it go."

Flynn wanted to defend his reasoning, but decided to let it go. He had Maggie as his wife, and that was all that mattered. If Reaghan was safely away in Alba, even better.

"Shall we all go out to the Beltane festival?" Queen Leannan stood from her bench seat and slowly walked over to Tuathal, putting a hand out to him. She looked like a true queen with her dress of dark blue silk that Tuathal had searched the land and juggled many trades to procure for her, and a sparkling gold circlet upon her head, golden blonde curls tumbling about her face. His cousin had once been a timid, self-conscious lass before Tuathal fell desperately in love with her. Now, true happiness and radiance shone off her and she fit the role of a queen quite well.

"Aye, we must light the fires and begin the festivities," Tuathal grinned.

"Let the ale flow!" Brennain cheered, and most of the family responded in kind as they rushed through the door of his family home. They were ready to celebrate the beginning of spring, a time of renewal and fertility.

Looking at his beautiful wife standing on the other side of the house in her flowing yellow linen dress, her wavy blonde hair tied back into a braid, he was struck by the happiness that flowed through his body, tingling his skin all over. Maggie had only meant to save his life, yet somehow along the way, she saved his soul. And now, she carried his child. Telling their family had made it all feel so real and a sense of rightness filled him.

Walking over to him slowly, Maggie crinkled her brow. "Are you all right, Flynn? Are you disappointed to be staying behind while your brother goes on a journey?"

Shaking his head as his wife's sweet scent filled his senses, he pulled her to him gently and leaned his forehead against hers. "I am more than all right. I do not wish to be anywhere other than right here, right now. How have I gone from a traveling informant with nay future aside from service to my king, to husband of the most beautiful woman in all Ériu, and soon to be a father? You have made me happier than I can say, Mags."

A mischievous glint twinkled in her blue eyes as she licked her lips before looking around the empty room. "If words are not enough, perhaps you can show me in... other ways," she whispered, grabbing his backside and pulling him closer to her.

"Other ways?" he cocked a brow. "I can think of several more ways..."

"I am certain we will be alone for quite a while now. Shall we see how many times I can make you call out my name?" she said seductively, cupping his desire in her hands with a proud grin.

"Och, Maggie," he groaned.

"That is one..." she purred.

"This is not fair. That is my game," he murmured against her lips as she slowly walked him backward toward their bed on the other side of their home. When the back of his knees hit the bed, she pushed him backward and, before he could speak, pulled the string on his trousers.

"You have taught me much in the past several moons, husband, but this is by far my favorite," she said, and lifted her dress up to her knees to straddle his thighs.

"Maggie..."

"That's two and we have not even begun," she chided. "You are terrible at your own game." Her hands reached up and she quickly pulled the faded blue curtains closed around them, enveloping them in the darkness.

"I love you, Maggie Mac Greine," he whispered into her ear. "You are the strongest woman I know."

"I love you more, Flynn Mac Greine. Now make love to me," she demanded.

How could he ever say nay to that?

* * * *

At the Beltane festival, Maggie felt love buzzing through her entire body. She watched in wonder as Flynn's family drank ale, laughed, and danced around the fire. Last Beltane, she had sat alone on a log around a fire and watched as everyone around her enjoyed themselves with family. This year, she still sat and watched, but now she was part of a family... a very large, loud and loving family. A smile slid across her face as she rubbed a hand over her flat abdomen. In just a few moons, she would give birth to yet another member of Flynn's growing family, and she felt a sense of self-satisfaction and contentment she never thought she'd feel. The best part was that Flynn was truly happy with his life as well. In the beginning, she feared that he would grow restless or resentful for having to stay tied up in Ráth Mór with a family, but she knew now that Flynn was more devoted to her and his unborn child than to anything else.

Like a caterpillar who had cocooned himself in safety and re-emerged as a butterfly, Maggie too, felt transformed. Her cocoon had been that wee hut she shared with Flynn. It had provided her the sense of calm and peace she had needed to overcome her fears, and Flynn had shown her just how wonderful and gentle a true man could be... and just how beautiful life could be.

Stars flickered overhead in the cool spring sky, and she looked up at them with a deep sigh. Her mama had been wrong. It was not a woman's place in life to accept a man's brutal treatment with submission. It had taken much too long for Maggie to realize that, but she wished she could see her mama one more time, to tell her she loved her and wished she had lived a better life. Maggie would teach her child, hopefully a wee lass, to protect herself, be strong and fearless, and that her papa would never hurt either of them. A woman need not be a warrior to be strong or fearless; she simply had to believe in herself. It may have taken Maggie too long to realize her own self-worth, but now that she did, lightness followed her wherever she went, the binds of her past having disappeared along with her fears.

Horns blasted in the distance, the sounds of men singing out of tune drifted in the air. "My wife is much too beautiful to simply sit upon a log during Beltane," she heard Flynn's voice and looked to her right, seeing his extended hand. "Care to dance with me? I admit, I am awful at it, but as long as I am holding you, I shall take the public ridicule."

With a laugh, Maggie nodded and took his hand. Flynn tugged her to her feet and twirled her in his arms as his family cheered and clapped all around.

"Last year, you did not leave that log..." Flynn mused as he looked down at her.

"How could you possibly know that?" she said with surprise.

"I watched you all that night, *mo chroí*, waiting for my chance to speak with you. I loved you even then."

"I loved you too, Flynn. I always have, and I always shall."

With a soft kiss, Maggie shrieked with laughter as Flynn swung her around, moving to the music. She knew with every part of her soul that she would never be lonely again, and in that very moment, she could swear the child within her fluttered softly, just as her heart did.

Authors Note

Thank you so much for reading the Warrior's Mission! I sure hope you enjoyed Flynn and Maggie's story. Maggie is special to me because she has suffered trauma in her life and finally had the courage to overcome those fears, especially with the help of a good-hearted man like Flynn Mac Greine.

In this story, you see more of the tension building between Tuathal Techtmar and Mal Mac Rochride who were real enemies who fought for the High Throne of Ireland in the 1st century AD. I refer to Ireland as Ériu in all my books because the words "Ireland" and "Eire" did not yet exist at the time. Those words derive from the name of the ancient goddess Ériu, who the land was named after until the word slowly developed over hundreds of years.

If this is the first of my books you have read, I encourage you to start at the very beginning with my Sisters of Danu Series. Forsworn Fate is the prequel novella that starts it all and it was awarded a perfect 5-star review from InD'Tale Magazine and received their Crowned Heart award! If you wish to stick to this series, the very first book is The Warrior's Salvation! We meet Jeoffrey in the last book of the Sisters of Danu also, but it is a standalone book! To see all my books, check out my author page on Amazon!

I know you have many authors and books to choose, so thank you for choosing mine! Book for will be available in late spring/ early summer of 2018 and is Brennain's story!

Please enjoy this excerpt from my Sisters of Danu novella, Forsworn Fate!

Forsworn Fate

Sisters of Danu Series

A Novella

By: Mia Pride

Chapter One

Ériu 55 AD

"Oh, the nerve of him!" Ceara stormed into the house, slamming the door and causing the fire to flicker with the wild gush of wind trailing in behind her. She heard her mother sigh in the corner of the house as she worked on another new dress at the loom. Her mother always sighed when Ceara and Garreth argued. For the life of her, she could not understand why her mother had arranged her marriage to the infuriating lad before either of them could have a say. It was not at all common in their village for such arrangements, and yet no amount of shouting about the lad would change Abigael's mind.

"You sigh again, Mother and yet you would have nay need to if you would just break this marriage agreement and allow me to be free of him." She crossed her arms and spun on her heels to face her mother. "Do you know what he said to me just now?"

Abigael looked up from the loom and actually gave Ceara her full attention. Ceara's hopes rose for an instant, wondering if she had finally convinced her mother to listen to her many grievances against her intended husband, but then a slow smirk spread across her mother's face and Ceara growled. "Och! It does not matter what he said, does it? The man could tell me he thinks me as hideous as a toad, and you would still encourage me to marry him, would you not?"

Abigael waved a hand dismissively in her direction and scoffed. "Ceara. Nay man in their right mind would call you a toad. And certainly not Garreth. He is quite taken with you."

A snort escaped Ceara, so loud it shook her brain. "Taken with me? Is that what you call it when a lad has a new lass on his lap every day? I just ran into him at the gathering hall. He had that lass Mary Gallagher on his lap this time. When I asked him why he even bothered with other lassies when he knew he was to marry me, he replied that he needed to sample as many lassies as he could before he became my prisoner! Prisoner! Mama, the lad does not want to marry me. He has made himself quite clear."

That seemed to get her mother's attention. Abigael stood up slowly and walked over with a sad smile on her face. "You care for the lad, do you not?" Abigael ran a finger down Ceara's face and stared her in the eyes. Ceara wanted to balk at her mother, but she was never good at hiding her emotions from anyone, least of all her mama. When Ceara was happy, which was most days, she could not contain her jovial spirit and the urge to smile at every passing villager. But when she was angry, most of the time while in Garreth's infuriating presence, she could feel the fire burning in her veins, like a force greater than herself controlling her every thought.

What she felt now was much too close to despair and she hung her head low at the tenderness of her mother's words. "How I feel about Garreth does not matter. He does not want me. And I cannot marry the lad. He will only resent me even more than he does now and take a concubine. I cannot live that way. I wish you had never arranged our marriage. I still do not understand."

"There are many things you will not understand, Ceara. But I promise you will one day. Until then, you must trust me." Her mother tucked a red tendril of Ceara's hair behind her ear and smiled. "His father, the king, and I came to the agreement together. I am afraid he wants this match for you both as much as I do, and that is that."

"So I am to just be the unwanted wife? I tell you, Mama, the man despises me!"

Abigael laughed and gripped Ceara's hand. "Nay. He despises that he has nay control over his own future, the same way you do. But it is not you who he despises. He is acting out. Perhaps because it is the only thing he can control, or perhaps tis to make you jealous. You are seven and ten summers now. Tis time the two of you married."

"You would not believe he is taken with me if you had seen him today with Mary. I barely tolerated the sight of her on his lap. When he kissed the lass, I pretended not to noticed. But when he began to drag her into a dark corner by the hand, I felt humiliated! The whole tuath knows he is what he says: a prisoner to this arrangement."

Ceara swallowed hard but could not help the tear that trickled down her cheek and under her chin. Humiliation was only the beginning of what she felt when she thought of Garreth Mac Cecht. The man had been promised to her by the time she could walk. She was just as much a prisoner to this horrible arrangement as he was. Only, where she had always honored the match and looked forward to marrying the king's son with his blonde tousled hair and bright hazel eyes, he saw her as a burden. She was no more than another responsibility for him in a world where he was born and bred to train as a warrior, and perhaps be a king one day. And who was she? Nothing. She was no more than the healer's daughter, a woman bound to a man who did not want her.

Nay. She would not disparage herself in this manner. She had much to offer a man. She would not allow Garreth to continually make her the feel at fault for their forced union, or cause her to always question her self-worth. One way or another, she would convince him to marry her or find a way to break this agreement. Ceara could stand to be stuck in the middle no longer.

***

Pulling weeds in the garden was always tedious work, but it kept Ceara's mind off a certain infuriating lad, or at least it usually did. She had seen Garreth run off with more lassies into more dark corners than she ever cared to remember, so why did the sight of him today with Mary affect her so? Perhaps it was his hurtful words or the way he looked at her with spite in his eyes before he dragged Mary away. Perhaps it was because she had never even once kissed a lad and the sting of that injustice was hard to shake. Every lad in the tuath knew she was promised to Garreth and there were few who would dare try and touch what belonged to the king's son. No lad had ever tried to kiss her. Perhaps she was, in fact, a toad.

Then there was her age. She was of an age to marry. Garreth should be done chasing the many young lassies of the tuath by now. It was time he honored the agreement their parents had made. Perhaps they need not marry right away, but could he not court her? Take a little time to know her better? He was five summers older than her and, though they had grown up together and always knew they would marry, Garreth had slowly pulled away from her over the years clearly resenting what she represented to him: responsibility, duty, and, as he described it, imprisonment.

It rankled that he should think of her in such a foul manner. Ceara yanked another weed out of the ground by the roots and felt a small wave of accomplishment at pulling the entire thing out in one piece. The rain had been heavy this spring and the weeds attacked the garden's vegetables with an unusual vengeance. She may not be able to control much of her life, but this she could, even if her mind did wander into dangerous territory as she worked.

What was it like to be Mary? To feel Garreth's lips on hers, his blonde beard scratching against her skin, his large calloused warrior hands roaming her body? Ceara closed her eyes and swallowed hard. She had to stop thinking such things. It tore her apart to watch her future husband paw another woman. He could have Ceara easily...and quite willingly if she was honest, yet he would choose any other woman instead of her. She should have more pride. But, how could she when the only man she could ever be with swatted her away as if she were a bothersome gnat?

"There you are mo stór. I have been looking all over for you." At the familiar, yet not often heard voice, Ceara gasped and dropped the weeds in her hand, spinning on her heels.

"Doran!" Ceara squealed and, standing on her tiptoes, wrapped her arms around the large shoulders of her mother's dear companion, a man who had come to be more like a father to Ceara than she could have ever expected. "What a surprise! Tis so lovely to see you!"

"Och, you as well, mo leanbh." She loved it when he referred to her as his child. She could never be so fortunate as to have a papa as kind and loving as King Doran, but for him to treat her as a daughter meant the world to her. Especially at a time in her life when she needed it most.

Doran released her from the crushing embrace he always gave her and looked down at her with pure affection in his gaze. He was a good man. Her mama had grown to love him very much over the years as he came to visit on bartering trips. He came as often as he could, which was not very often at all, being king of his own people. But even kings must journey out at times, to protect their people, or in this case, secure alliances and trade with neighboring tribes.

"Tis always good to see you, Ceara. I miss Gwynneth when I am away, but the two of you are so similar, I feel like I am close to her when I am with you."

Ceara smiled at his words. He always told her about his own daughter, Gwynneth, and how very similar they were. She hoped to meet his daughter one day but knew it was unlikely. Gwynneth had recently married a man named Baine and would likely not be traveling anytime soon. "How is Gwynneth?" Ceara asked.

There was a flicker of something in Doran's eyes. If she didn't know any better, she would have thought it was regret. Sadness pulled his mouth down at the corners. "I fear I made a mistake in marrying her to Baine. He promised to take good care of my daughter and seems to love her well. But she was in love with another and I kept them apart. I'm not certain she will ever forgive me for it."

"Oh, Doran." Ceara squeezed his arm in reassurance and gave him a sad smile. "You are a good father. I am certain you had your reasons and she will learn to love Baine." He forced a smile and nodded, but Ceara could tell her words gave him little comfort.

Ceara's heart constricted in her chest as she thought about Gwynneth's unfortunate position. Was Garreth being forced into a marriage with her when he loved another? That could explain his obvious disdain for her. Did Garreth love Mary? Unlikely. He seemed to be with a new woman quite often. But, what if he did? Perhaps this was why he resented her so. Marriage to her may be preventing him from wedding the lass he truly loved. She could never live with herself if she were the cause of pain between two lovers. The thought of Garreth in love with another woman made her feel ill, but not as ill as being the woman who kept them apart would make her.

She had grown quite fond of Garreth over the years. Knowing they were destined to wed was a strange feeling, and yet, at one point, Garreth seemed to embrace it. When Garreth was a small lad they would laugh and play together often, pretending to be husband and wife. He would defend their imaginary home with his wooden sword while she cuddled her rag doll to her chest, rocking its tightly swaddled linen body in her arms.

But time passed and, as Garreth turned into more of a man than a lad, the five years of age separating them became a gaping void of differences. He grew taller, stronger, and more handsome by the day. Lassies his age began to take notice and Garreth no longer had time to play with his childish intended wife as he trained to be a warrior. The playful days they had once spent together became lonely days of following Garreth around sadly, hoping he would turn and pay her notice. She was no more than a gangly lass, not quite a woman and not quite a child, while lassies with blooming curves started gaining his attention.

Her feelings for him had slowly become more than just curiosity and admiration over the years. She yearned for his returned affection. Even as she crossed over into womanhood and grew soft curves of her own, Garreth did not seem to take notice. By then, many years had passed and Garreth was well deserving of his reputation with the other lassies. She had somehow become nothing more than a lingering responsibility to him, a memory of a child he had once known, and nothing more.

Those years of pining for him and following in his powerful wake had worn down her patience. Ceara considered herself a spirited lass with many companions who thoroughly enjoyed dancing and laughing at nightly gatherings. But, as the other lassies began to marry and have babes of their own, Ceara became lonelier and even more aggravated as Garreth continued to push away from his responsibility to her. Too many nights of sitting alone in the hall while all other men avoided her, knowing she was already spoken for, and Garreth disappearing into the shadows with a new lass, had inflamed her anger.

Somewhere during the many embarrassingly lonely gatherings over the years, her affection for Garreth had morphed into a resentment of her own, and one he well deserved, unlike the resentment he seemed to harbor for her.

Their encounters had become increasingly hostile recently, as her pride refused to allow her to simply sit back and be disrespected. She would approach him with good intentions, but it always led to a spiteful exchange of words, shouting, and a more and more frequent agreement that neither wished to marry the other. And, after his cruel words to her this morn, calling himself a prisoner and parading Mary in front of her, Ceara had had enough.

She was done. Done with being the forlorn lass in his presence while he sent her angry glares and flirted with all the other lassies. She wanted to enjoy herself, be confident in who she was, toad or not. Garreth clearly did not want to marry her and it was weighing her down like rocks tied to her ankles. Enough, indeed. Tonight, she would speak with Garreth and tell him once and for all that she would not marry him. He could have Mary or any other lass he wanted. She was done waiting for him to choose her, and if her mother would not release her from this arrangement, she would release herself. It was time to live. She would forswear their cursed fate.

"Where is your mother?" Doran's voice pulled her out of her dark musings and her head snapped up.

"She is in the village. The ironsmith's wife just birthed a babe. She should be home soon." Ceara looked around at all the arriving warriors from Iverni as they dismounted their horses, laughing as they stretched their backs. One warrior openly rubbed his backside and she swore she heard him say something about his "sore arse". Ceara couldn't help but laugh. Men could get away with anything in public. That same warrior spotted her staring and sent her a wink.

Her eyes widened at his obvious display and she felt herself blush. No lads in Coraindt dared wink at her. She had never known if it was for fear of Garreth or because she was a hideous toad, but this warrior from Iverni with his strong jaw covered in a short black beard and his long disheveled hair floating about his face as he removed his bronze helm, looked at her with an intense lust in his blue eyes and she felt herself shiver.

Doran watched her and the warrior with a frown. "Watch it, Mac Tavish," Doran pointed at the man in warning before shifting his gaze to Ceara. "I imagine Garreth would not appreciate Aaron's attentions on you."

Ceara growled under her breath at the reminder that she belonged to a man who did not care about her at all. But tonight, all of that would change. It would hurt to break away from Garreth, but not as much as being an unwanted bride did.

About Mia

Mia is a full-time wife and mother of two rowdy boys, residing in the SF Bay Area. As a child, she often wrote stories about fantastic places or magical things, always preferring to live in a world where the line between reality and fantasy didn't exist.

In High school she entered writing contests and had some stories published in small newspapers or school magazines. As life continued, so did her love of writing. So one day, she decided to end her cake decorating business, pull out her laptop and fulfill her dream of writing and publishing novels. And she did.

When Mia isn't writing books or chasing her sweaty children around a park, she loves to drink coffee by the gallon, get lost in a good book, hike with her family and drink really big margaritas with her friends! Her happy place is the Renaissance Faire, where you can find her at the joust, rooting for the shirtless highlander in a kilt.

Connect with Mia!

Website: www.miapride.com

FB: https://www.facebook.com/miaprideauthor/

Email: miapride.author@gmail.com